# The Body in Cadiz Bay

DAVID SERAFIN

# The Body in Cadiz Bay

A Superintendent Bernal novel

St. Martin's Press
New York

The characters in this novel are entirely fictitious, but their actions, while imaginary, are set within actual events in Cadiz in April 1982.

Map by Charles Green. Reprinted by permission from *The Companion Guide to Southern Spain* by Alfonso Lowe.

Library of Congress Cataloging in Publication Data

Serafin, David.
 The body in Cadiz Bay.

 I. Title.
PR6069.E6B6   1985      823'.914      85-11734
ISBN 0-312-08742-X

First published in Great Britain by William Collins Sons & Co. Ltd.

First U.S. Edition

10 9 8 7 6 5 4 3 2 1

For Peter, who sailed these waters in his youth,
and for John, who commanded in them.

*Nobly, nobly, Cape Saint Vincent to the North-west died away;*
*Sunset ran, one glorious blood-red, reeking into Cadiz Bay;*
*Bluish 'mid the burning water, full in face Trafalgar lay;*
*In the dimmest North-east distance dawned Gibraltar grand and*
   *gray . . .*

Robert Browning, *Home Thoughts from the Sea*

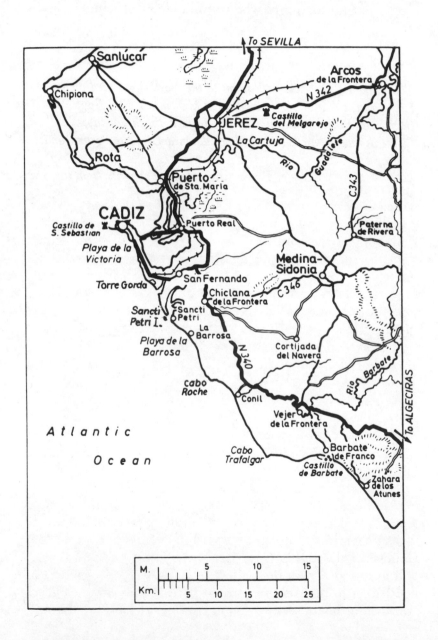

The two sailors on shore leave from La Carraca naval base stood in the lee of the old gun-emplacement at the Candelaria Battery at the northernmost point of the three-thousand-year-old city and struggled for a while to light their cheap, hand-rolled cigarettes. When one managed to get a flame to the rather mangled tube with black tobacco spilling from its uneven tip, he passed it to the other, and they returned to their desultory observation of the line of patient anglers perched some fifteen metres below them on a narrow ledge just above the spraying waves. The thick wall rising sheer from the low rocks served to protect Cadiz from the massive ebb and flow of the tides, occasioned by the meeting of the Atlantic rollers and the stiller neck of the Mediterranean waters at the north-western end of the Strait.

'It doesn't look as if they've caught a bloody thing all evening, Pepe,' said the taller of the two seamen.

'I'd be surprised if they did with the Levante blowing. It always brings a bit of dirty weather to the Bay, and can last for days on end,' muttered Pepe, in his thickly aspirated local accent.

'Let's hope the wind changes for Holy Week,' said his companion, drawing on his still ill-lit cigarette.

'There'll be no chance of a sunbathe on La Victoria beach until it veers south-west,' said the short, dark *gaditano*.

'Who cares?' replied his shipmate, who was from Corunna and therefore didn't expect to be able to lie in the sun in April. 'We'll have to make do with the disco down in the port.'

As they strolled along the top of the sea wall towards the Genovés Park and pleasure gardens, Pepe stopped again, and gestured across the wide sweep of the Bay, which was flooded with intensely red sunset light at that hour. 'Those two fishing-boats seem to be in trouble. It looks as though they've got their net stuck between those two groups of rocks.'

Pepe shielded his gaze against the angled brightness of the sun, and his seafarer's eyes adjusted to take in the scene two kilometres to the north-north-west, towards Rota.

'Those rocks are Los Cochinos and Las Puercas—the "Pigs" and "Sows"—they're a ruddy menace to shipping coming into the port. But I don't think the boats are in danger.' He noticed a darker patch in the blood-coloured water between the two notorious reefs. 'It's just that they've got a hell of a lot of fish in their net. That's why they're waving and shouting at one another.'

The anglers on the ledge far below them were also gesticulating, and watching the dark patch with sudden enthusiasm. Taking advantage of the strong breeze from the east, the boats were manœuvring to close the long seine strung out between them, without the fishermen attempting to haul it in, and were making way westwards towards Santa Catalina Point.

'I think they're going to try and beach in La Caleta inlet beyond the castle,' said Pepe. 'The wind's against them for getting to the fishing harbour. Let's amble down there and take a look-see at their catch.'

Long before the two fishing-boats rounded the point, the two shipmates had walked past the Hotel Atlántico and down the Avenida del Duque de Nájera to reach the small cove of La Caleta, with its crumbling, turn-of-the-century bathing establishment standing forlorn on rotten piers amid the high-tide flood.

By then a small crowd had gathered by the castle of Santa Catalina, pointing towards the Bay. Suddenly, just as the two sailors were getting bored by the long delay, the two boats, still kept some ten metres apart by the sweating but triumphant crews, swept into the small U-shaped inlet and ran up through the breakers, dragging the swollen and heavily thrashing seine on to the strand. At once, as the wide net opened, the beach came alive with black and silver fish, thousands upon thousands of them. The two sailors drew back in astonishment, and one of the older fishermen shouted: 'We've never had such a catch! It's a miracle the net held! It's just like the Sea of Tiberias,' and he crossed himself in wonderment at the sight.

A younger member of his crew leapt off the boat and yelled to the two sailors: 'With this catch we won't need to touch your collars for luck for a long while!'

'What fish are they, for Christ's sake?' the northerner asked Pepe.

'*Mojarras* and *herreras* mainly—the usual small hake and codling from the Bay. But I've never seen them in such numbers. There must be thousands of kilos in this pile.'

As the enormous sun was setting into the waves far beyond Cape Saint Vincent, the fishermen struggled to load the frails with their catch and carry them on their heads to the waiting lorries, while the locals from the working-class streets nearby came to assist and to help themselves in the process, for it was obviously going to prove difficult to clear the beach of fish before darkness overcame them.

'Let's go and get a hamburger before we go to the disco, Pepe,' said the sailor from Corunna, long since tired of watching the fishermen's labours.

Just then one of the townsfolk shouted: 'Look, you've brought a shark in at the bottom of the net!'

'Christ, no wonder it was so heavy!' said the youngest of the boat crew.

'It's not a shark, it's a large tunny,' said an older fisher-·man, pulling off the remaining small fish from the shining black mass, which lay lifeless near the water's edge.

'I've never seen an all-black tunny shaped like that,' commented Pepe, the local sailor, straining to get a better view over the heads of the many townspeople, who had brought every kind of receptacle in which to carry home a free fish supper.

'My God, it's not a fish at all! It's a dead man, wearing a wet-suit!' shouted the captain of one of the two fishing-boats, who had bent down to take a closer look in the fading light. 'Been in the water for some days, I'd say. The fish have had a go at his eyes.'

The youngest of the fishermen turned away to retch into the surf.

'Go and phone for the Civil Guard,' the captain said to him. 'Ask for the Comandancia de la Marina.'

When five minutes later a khaki-coloured jeep containing two Civil Guards from the Coastguard Section arrived, soon followed by a chauffeur-driven SEAT 134 bringing the Comandante, the townsfolk loaded up with their ill-gotten fish faded as if by magic into the rapidly advancing twilight and the mean and narrow streets behind El Campo del Sur, while the two sailors, the fishermen and a number of curious newcomers watched the official inspection of the corpse.

'Put a message through your jeep radio to the Comandancia,' said the Comandante to one of the Civil Guards, 'and tell them to get the police surgeon and the judge of instruction here. They can also send the mortuary van. We'll try and get the body in before nightfall.'

Superintendent Luis Bernal stood nervously by his small suitcase under the high wrought-iron vault of Atocha railway station in Madrid, near the sign that announced the departure of the *tren nocturno* to Huelva and Cadiz via Seville from platform 5 at 22.30. He looked anxiously at his watch: Consuelo was cutting it fine, but she had been adamant that he should wait for her at the station with the tickets and not go to fetch her from her house in Quevedo. 'My mother has never met you, Luchi, and doesn't know about us. I don't want to upset her at her age. She's worried enough by my secondment to the bank in Gran Canaria for six months, and has only reluctantly assented to go and stay with my brother and his wife. You know how she doesn't get on with her daughter-in-law.' And so it was that he had agreed to collect the tickets and sleeper reservations from the RENFE offices and meet her at Atocha.

He wondered for the umpteenth time if he was doing the right thing. His wife Eugenia had been appalled and totally uncomprehending when, three weeks earlier, he had broached the matter of a separation. 'You've lost your senses, Luis. We've been married for thirty-seven years and our children are grown up. Why on earth should we separate now? Anyway, it's against God's law and the Church,' she ended roundly. When he had persisted a few days later, and dared let drop the word 'divorce', she counter-attacked strongly: 'It's an old man's folly you've got, Luis. There's no fool like an old fool. If you mean it seriously, why don't you come with me to Father Anselmo our confessor and talk it over? It's all this new democracy and politicking that have put these insane ideas into your head!'

Then, with a sudden rare insight, Eugenia asked, 'You don't mean you want to go off with some chit of a girl, at your age, do you? She'll skin you alive.'

He hadn't dared tell his wife about his five-year-long affair with Consuelo Lozano, or about the secret apartment they shared at stolen moments in the Calle de Barceló. Now that Consuelo was more than five months' pregnant with his child, the testing time had arrived.

'And our children, Luis? What will they think of us?' was Eugenia's parting shot. Bernal cared little what his elder son Santiago might think; he had always been a priggish child, a slave to his mother's sanctimonious behaviour, and in any case he was married with a son of his own and another child on the way. As far as his younger son Diego was concerned, he had scattered the remnants of two incomplete university courses in medicine and geology behind him, and had become at thirty the perpetual student. In January Bernal had shipped him off to a less demanding course at Santiago de Compostela, where he would find himself in a city with fewer nightclubs than Madrid, at any rate. With his record, he would have least to criticize in his parents' matrimonial affairs.

Even to an impartial outsider it might not seem altogether odd for a sixty-one-year-old *superpolicía* (as the newspapers called him) to divorce his church-ridden wife with whom he had not had marital relations for over twenty years, and with whom he could never have been said to enjoy them in the seventeen years prior to those. The outsider might understand better if he learned of the complete accord— both mental and physical—that Bernal had developed with

11

the girl bank employee who was almost thirty years his junior, and who now was overjoyed at the prospect of providing him with further offspring.

Bernal nervously lit another Kaiser, and again consulted his watch. Consuelo was going to miss the train for sure. They'd never get the luggage aboard in time. And that would mean she'd lose her sailing tomorrow in the Compañía Transatlántica's ferry from Cadiz to Las Palmas. Why couldn't she go on a regular Iberia flight, like most people? 'I don't want to take any risks with our baby, Luchi,' she had explained, 'and I hate flying, as you know.' Privately he considered that the ten-hour train journey plus a thirty-six-hour sea-voyage might do the unborn child even more harm, but he didn't voice his trepidation. He had learned not to argue with the strong-willed Consuelo about minor things.

There was one advantage in it, he reflected: he could settle two matters in one weekend, or so he hoped: accompany Consuelo to the ferry, and visit Eugenia to make one final attempt to get an agreed separation. With her usual uncanny prescience, she had gone into religious retreat in Cadiz at a house recommended to her by the arch-conservative Father Anselmo, where she was doubtless praying for her husband's return to sanity and the paths of marital observance.

Bernal's impatience and concern at the prospect of losing the night express to Cadiz increased, because at least the RENFE liked to get their services to leave on time, even if they tended to arrive late. Just then he spotted a beaming Consuelo marching through the thinning crowds under the large four-faced station clock that showed the time as 10.26. She was followed by a perspiring porter, who staggered under the weight of a two-wheeled trolley bearing five large pigskin suitcases.

'It's just as well I sent the trunk on in advance to the ship, Luchi,' she said, giving him a hug. He noticed for the first time that the curve of her shoulders and the heavy way she walked were beginning to betray her clandestine pregnancy.

'There won't be time to check the cases into the luggage-van, Chelo. I'll have to put them on the floor of your compartment.'

He had managed to obtain a first-class wagon-lit for her, in coach no. 051, which he was amused to see she would be sharing with three nuns, while he would have to take his chance in a *litera* in a six-berth compartment. When all her baggage was stowed safely away, much to the astonishment of the religious sisters, who naturally travelled very light, Bernal took Consuelo to the dining-car for a late supper, just as the engine gave three piercing hoots and the night train to Cadiz pulled out of Atocha.

'It'll be a *recena* for me, Luchi. My brother and his wife insisted on feeding me before I left their apartment. My mother's grumbling already, but seems to be settling in with them. She says she cannot imagine why I agreed to be seconded to the Las Palmas branch of the bank for six months.'

As they shared a bottle of Marqués de Murrieta over large prawn cocktails in the almost empty dining-car, Bernal reminded her how they couldn't be seen travelling together in the old pre-democratic days.

'Do you think Eugenia will ever agree to a divorce, Luchi?' she asked. 'You know it doesn't matter if she won't.'

'I'm not sure, Chelo. She was adamantly opposed to it when she left Madrid, but I'll try again in Cadiz, now she's had time to think things over. In any case, I can sue for a decree even if she objects. It takes so much longer, that's all, and I would like our child to come into the world legitimately, even if he has to be a Great Canary-islander.'

'What makes you think you'll have a third son?' she joked. 'Why not a *grancanarita*?'

The next morning a tired-looking Bernal and a brighter Consuelo Lozano sat on the terrace of the Bar Los Patricios taking a late breakfast.

'It's just as well we got the luggage checked in at the agents, Luchi; I don't think I could have borne to have it around me after the sleepless night those nuns gave me,

13

clinking their rosary beads and muttering innumerable Ave Marias and Pater Nosters, at least as far as Seville, where the train was divided. After that, the eldest of them, who was above me, spent the rest of the journey farting in her sleep.'

'I had a worse time, love, with four soldiers playing *tute* all night in the corridor on a makeshift cardtable of kitbags and getting drunker and noisier on cheap Chinchón. What time does the *JJ Sister* sail?'

'At seven-thirty. It gets into Las Palmas at nine on Monday morning.'

Bernal glanced at the headlines in the Saturday issue of the *Diario de Cádiz*, and his attention was at once drawn to the dramatic account of the unprecedented fishing catch at La Caleta the previous evening, and the discovery of the frogman's body at the bottom of the net.

'Thank goodness I'm here on private business, Chelo, or they'd rope me into this.' He pointed to the news item.

'It's just what you need to take your mind off personal things, Luchi, and to make sure you don't get up to any mischief when I'm away.'

'It looks like a case for the Comandancia de la Marina,' he commented. 'The chap was probably a spy from an alien submarine.'

'You may be right. After all, Rota, the American base, is just across the Bay,' remarked Consuelo. 'He could have floated over from there.'

In the early evening Bernal accompanied Consuelo to her first-class cabin where she installed herself as comfortably as possible, and they said their last goodbyes. He stood on the quay as the large white-painted ferry slipped her moorings and waved to his mistress with his handkerchief as the gulls screamed overhead and the distance between ship and shore increased.

After the *JJ Sister* had slipped out of harbour and out of his sight, Bernal took a taxi from the port up through the narrow streets to his hotel in the Plaza de Calvo Sotelo. As the driver took the circuitous route up the hill to the old centre of the city, Bernal noticed a few surviving signs depicting a victoria and a horse put up in the last century to indicate the direction the traffic was to take: Cadiz had then been ahead of Europe, not only in writing and promulgating the Liberal Constitution of 1812, but also in the invention of one-way streets.

The Hotel de Francia y París in the highest, northern quarter, was a white and bottle-green-tiled Art Nouveau construction, with bright orange sunshades over all its windows, which enhanced the glow of the fruit on the orange-trees lining the pavements of the irregular triangle that formed the Plaza de Calvo Sotelo. It was all of twenty years since he had spent a few days in this old hotel, Bernal reflected, when he had come to accompany an arrested suspect back to Madrid. He was now pleasantly surprised at how skilfully it had been modernized.

After unpacking, he lit a Kaiser, and re-read the scrappy note Eugenia had left for him in their Madrid apartment: '*Luis: I'll be performing spiritual exercises and spending Holy Week at the Convento de la Palma, c/ Concepción, s.n., Cadiz. Think things over as I recommended. Eugenia.*' Reluctantly, he decided he'd better call on her before the processions started in earnest.

Bernal went out into the small square, narrowing his eyes against the intense sunset light, and tried to follow the folded plan of the old city which the pleasant girl at the reception desk had provided. He soon got entirely lost, and found himself in the Plaza del Tío de la Tiza, which was lined with potted geraniums and redolent of the local fish being grilled over wood fires. He managed to attract the attention of a busy waiter, who gave him the vaguest of directions, and he soon lost himself once more in the maze of narrow streets. This lower part of the city was quiet, almost menacing; socially, it seemed to hover uneasily between the affluence of the northern quarter and the relative poverty of the Campo del Sur to the south.

At last he spotted the Calle de Sacramento, and soon found the narrow turning into Concepción. He glanced

15

about him with some disquiet in the deserted, darkening street, and stopped under a dim lantern hanging on an iron wall-bracket to look at Eugenia's note again: *Convent of the Palm, Calle Concepción, no number.* He could see no sign of a religious house, but then spotted a large iron bell-handle set in the wall at the side of a high, spike-topped gate. This must be it, he thought, there's no other building in the street that could possibly be a convent. He pulled on the handle and, after a prolonged mechanical clanking, heard a bell tolling far inside the building. Nothing else happened.

Bernal stood for some five minutes in the street and wondered whether all the inmates of the Convent were at their devotions. He pulled on the heavy bell-handle once more, and listened again to the distant clanging. After two or three minutes of silence, bolts were drawn and a small postern in the tall gate was opened. He was quite surprised to see a tonsured cleric, dressed in bishop's garb, looking crossly out.

'What do you want?' he asked. 'We're still extremely busy. You've come before the appointed hour.'

Bernal was taken aback. There was no way they could have been expecting him. 'The appointed hour?' he echoed in puzzlement.

'Yes, of course. No one was supposed to come until Compline. That's when it will be ready. And where are your sanbenito and your hood? You know you must come properly attired to the vigil.'

'I'm afraid there's a misunderstanding,' said Bernal in increasing confusion. 'This is the Convent of the Palm?'

'Yes, yes,' said the cleric crossly. 'Of course it is. Aren't you a penitent?'

'I thought there would be nuns here,' said Bernal in some embarrassment.

'So there are. But why would you be wanting the holy sisters?' inquired the cleric with growing suspicion.

'It's not them I want to see, but my wife.'

'A nun can't be your wife,' said the apparent bishop in disbelief, making as if to close the door and shut this obviously insane person out.

'Señora Bernal, Eugenia Carrero de Bernal, that's who my wife is,' said Bernal in desperation.

'Why, Comisario, you should have said so at once! Do come inside,' said the cleric in a sudden change of tone. 'I am Bishop Nicasio. I will take you to the Señora, who is in the main patio, I believe, helping to decorate the float for tomorrow, which is our great day, you know.'

Bernal didn't know, but embarrassed by the initial confusion he thought he'd reserve his questions about this strange mixed house for his wife.

As they went through the cool vestibule decorated with blue tiles, they passed a cloister edged with large earthen pots planted with waxy white madonna lilies and enormous scarlet blooms of amaryllis. Bernal was surprised to see three more clerics in episcopal attire strolling under tall palm trees. They were accompanied by an admiral in white uniform.

'Is there a convention of bishops, Father?' he could not resist asking his guide.

'No, no, Comisario, they all belong to the Order. The admiral is one of our lay members.'

Bernal was more mystified than ever. What sort of Order was it that could contain bishops? In the wide corridor connecting the cloister to the church, he was further astonished to see three quarter-life-size statues set in niches in the wall, with candles lit beneath them and small vases of spring flowers. As they walked past, with the priest hurrying Bernal along, he thought that one of the images looked remarkably like José Antonio, founder of the Falange Party in the Thirties, but he didn't get the opportunity to check the other two closely.

A blaze of arc lamps marked their sudden emergence into a large courtyard, surrounded by tall date-palms. In the central paved area stood five *pasos* or religious floats, consisting of larger than lifesize statues of the Virgin and Our Lord and scenes from the Passion. On the float nearest the double gate, which was clearly meant to be the first to leave during the Holy Week celebrations, Bernal could see three nuns threading hundreds of yellow and purple flower-heads on

17

to a net that formed the floor of the scene of the Entry into Jerusalem, and behind the large figure of Christ mounted on the ass was Eugenia, dressed in a loose brown habit, and placing fresh palms around the upper edges of the float.

'Doña Eugenia, here's your husband,' said the bishop or surrogate who had acted as his guide.

'Luis, what good timing!' exclaimed Eugenia. 'Start handing me up those freshly cut palms from that pile, will you? We must get this float finished before Compline, when the penitents will come for the vigil.'

'But I want to talk to you in private, Geñita.'

'Later on, when we've got this finished. Many hands make light work. Come on now! Take your jacket off and roll up your shirtsleeves.'

By nine p.m. Bernal was perspiring heavily, very red in the face from the exertions Eugenia had enforced upon him.

'You'd better take a rest in that basket chair, Luis. The float is ready at last,' she said with much satisfaction. 'Isn't it splendid? The figures were carved out of five different valuable woods by a local artist from San Fernando especially for the Order of the Palm. Aren't they beautifully done and so tastefully painted?'

Bernal mopped his brow and asked if he could smoke.

'That's not a very nice thing to do in a convent, Luis,' said Eugenia sharply.

But the oldest of the nuns said, 'Let him have a quick one, Doña Eugenia. Men must have their little weaknesses.' The other nuns giggled. 'I'll get him some chilled lemon water.'

Luis looked beatifically up at Sister Encarnación. 'How kind and charitable you are, Sister. A lemon juice would be splendid. Have you nothing stronger to lace it with?'

'Luis, behave yourself,' rebuked Eugenia. 'We're still in Lent, remember.'

But when the nun brought the cool tall glass and he took the first delicious sip, Bernal could have sworn that it had a faint taste of liquor, although he wasn't sure of what kind, and Sister Encarnación winked at him from behind a palm-tree.

'Now, Luis, we've just got time for the chat you want before Compline. You'll be attending the service, of course. After all, you're on holiday, I take it.'

Luis gulped the pleasant drink down faster than he'd intended. 'But I should look in at the Comisaría, Geñita, as a matter of courtesy. Perhaps we could have our talk tomorrow?'

'As you wish, Luis, but remember I'll be in the procession all the morning from eleven o'clock onwards. It's Palm Sunday tomorrow, don't forget, and you really ought to confess this evening so as to be in a state of grace.'

In the Hospital de Mora, the old police surgeon and the young hospital pathologist looked hard at the cadaver that had been fished ashore at La Caleta and now reposed on their mortuary slab.

'How long has he been in the water, do you think?' asked the younger man, turning the mangled hands of the corpse to examine the palms. 'The fish have made a hell of a mess of the exposed parts.'

'Let's get the wet-suit off him first. Help me pull the boots off.'

'Phew, let's get some formalin on him. Decomposition's quite advanced.'

'Not yet,' said the older man. 'Not till we've removed the organs.' He stopped to wipe his brow on the sleeve of his white gown. 'This is always the worst part.'

When they came to the upper part of the black rubber suit, they found it resisted over the left breast.

'Hullo, there's a wound or something here,' said the younger pathologist. 'There's an indentation in the rubber, and it's stuck fast.'

'Let's have a look,' said the surgeon. 'Yes, the rubber's frayed, or melted into the flesh in an irregular star shape, just above the heart.'

'A bullet wound?'

'I'm not sure. We'll have to probe it and look for a

possible exit wound. Let's cut around the obstruction for the moment.'

When they had removed the black wet-suit, a helmet of the same material, boots, and rubber belt with special pockets and fittings, all of which were empty, they placed each object in a transparent plastic bag and carefully labelled it for later forensic examination.

'Let's turn him over now and look for marks or wounds on the back,' ordered the older doctor. 'Ah, there are patches of lividity. That's odd: he must have floated on his back for some time after death. There are no other marks that I can see.'

'Nor can I,' agreed the younger man. 'The greenness of the abdomen shows that internal putrefaction has well set in, and marbling has spread into the larger veins, look. Been dead six to seven days, do you think?'

'Much longer, I'd say. I've seen a fair number of bodies taken from the sea over the years, and a body decomposes in air twice as fast as in water and eight times as quickly as in dry earth. At this time of year the mean sea-temperature can only be between ten and twelve degrees Centigrade, and the wet-suit has protected most of the body surfaces from attack by marine creatures. My first guess would be eleven or twelve days.'

'As much as that? But wouldn't detachment of the cutis on the hands have occurred?'

'And it has,' said the more experienced man. 'Only the dermis remains and the fish have had a go at that. Identification of this cadaver is going to be very difficult without even dermal prints in complete form.'

'There's a blue tattoo on the left upper arm, but it's hard to make out because of the hypostasis.'

'We'll have it photographed under the ultraviolet lamp. That should bring it up.'

'What nationality do you think he was, apart from being fairly short, dark-haired and white-skinned?'

'I'm not sure about the white skin,' said the police surgeon. 'It's very sallow, even in the protected parts. I'd say he had some coloured ancestry. Or he might have been Slav;

look at the heavy brow. We'll take shots of the head from various angles.'

'And the age?'

'Quite young, I'd say; early twenties or even younger. We'll examine the state of the thymus, and take X-rays of the skull plates. We can calculate the age best from the amount of fusion of the brow plates. Now, let's get the photographer in, and then we'll open the cadaver and find out the cause of death.'

'But he drowned, surely?' asked the young doctor in some surprise.

'I don't take anything for granted when the Navy or the military might be involved; you should have been here in the Second World War to see some pretty odd cases. For a start, we'll have to dissect that wound in the chest. It's quite easy to miss a bullet when decomposition is so advanced.'

The pathologists finished labelling the various organs of the dead frogman ready for sending to the path. lab for expert examination. Before stitching up the cadaver, they looked again at the wound above the heart under a powerful magnifying glass.

'There's no deep penetration into the flesh, you know,' said the younger doctor. 'It could be a light stabbing-wound from a small pointed object.'

'It doesn't look like a stab wound to me, more like a bullet entry,' said the more experienced man. 'Yet there's no bullet and no real orifice. I've never seen anything quite like it. There are no vital signs around this small wound, so we must assume it occurred at the time of death or after it, but not before death. Yet it can't have been the cause of death, because there's no visible damage to the heart or any other organ.'

'The most puzzling thing is that he didn't drown,' said the younger man. 'Although there's sea-water in the windpipe, little reached the bronchiæ and none got to the lungs. Nor are there any petechiæ on the pulmonary surfaces. We can't check the eyes, of course, since they've been destroyed.'

'Definitely not drowning,' pronounced the police surgeon,

'but we'll get confirmation from the lab technician and he'll check for diatoms in the bloodstream. You know how useful those little algæ can be in cases of immersion.'

'But what cause of death do we put in the report? Cardiac arrest?'

'That would be a last resort. Let's tell the truth, and say that "the cause of death cannot be established until results of laboratory tests are available; but deceased did not die by drowning".'

Comandante Juárez, who had supervised the lifting of the corpse from the beach at La Caleta on the Friday evening, read the pathologists' brief preliminary report with some surprise. If the frogman hadn't drowned, how had he died? He would have to wait for the lab reports. More important to him was the question: who was the deceased and what had he been up to? Juárez checked the list of clothing found on the cadaver: there were no markings of any kind. He found that curious. If the man had been a holiday-maker addicted to sub-aqua diving or fishing, then it seemed almost inevitable that some part of the equipment would bear a commercial label or an indication of origin. Yet there was none. And what had happened to the goggles he must have been wearing, and the air-cylinder and mask? It was odd too that the pockets of the belt had been quite empty.

Then there was the question of provenance: the body could have floated to the rocks two kilometres east of the port from almost any direction. It could have come with the prevailing Levante wind north-westwards from the Spanish Navy headquarters at La Carraca, or westwards from the harbour at Puerto de Santa María, since the outflow of the River Guadalete caused a westerly current there. But the surgeon thought the corpse had been in the water for eleven or twelve days; he'd have to check the wind directions during all that time. It wasn't impossible that the frogman had floated south-south-eastwards from the American base at Rota. On the whole the Comandante thought it unlikely that the cadaver would have come all the way across the Strait from Tangiers, let alone been swept back from the

Pillars of Hercules and the British base at Gibraltar, or the Spanish port of Ceuta.

He decided to send an urgent report to Naval Intelligence at San Fernando, and to the Ministry of Marine in Madrid. There was more to this case than met the eye, and the authorities would surely send someone of higher rank to investigate.

Bernal thought he had better stick to his word and pay a courtesy call on the inspector-in-charge at the city police station. Inspector Fragela was delighted to meet the famous superintendent from the Directorate of State Security in Madrid, and immediately invited him to dine.

'We'll go to the best sea-food restaurant in the city, Comisario—El Faro. It's near a small bay called La Caleta in the suburb of the Vine.'

'Isn't that where the extraordinary catch was brought in yesterday evening?'

'I see you're well up with our local news, Superintendent. Would you like to hear more about the case? I've just had a copy of the Marine commandant's initial report.'

'No, not at all!' exclaimed Bernal, despite his curiosity. 'I'm on a private visit to see my wife, and thought I'd got away from work for the weekend.'

In the smart restaurant, done out in an Andalusian tiled décor, Bernal and Fragela pored over the large menu.

'You'll have to tell me what these fish are, Fragela. These local names are double-Dutch to me.'

'Let me recommend one or two local dishes, Comisario. There's the sea-pike cooked in salt, and served from a wooden box: the scales come away with the salt, and one has it with mayonnaise or vinaigrette. Or there's the *parrillada "Costa de la Luz"*—a platter of grilled fish and shellfish, which is a speciality of the house.'

Bernal looked doubtful at these suggestions. 'I think my stomach would find them too "aggressive", as my doctor puts it. I've got to be careful with the scar of an old gastric ulcer, you know.'

'Well, try the *lenguado al Tío Pepe*; it's filleted sole with a bland sherry sauce, decorated with a few sea-hedgehogs.'

Bernal gulped at this last piece of information, but decided to risk the dish, and to swallow it down with a dry white Rioja.

When they got to the dessert of oranges prepared in kirsch, Inspector Fragela finally came to the point. 'There's a real mystery about the cause of death of this unknown frogman, Comisario, and our local forensic chaps can't solve it.'

'I'm sure our Dr Peláez would be interested in the case, Fragela. He's the most outstanding forensic scientist in the country. But you'd have to put in an official request to Madrid, and that would cause delay.'

'Even so, I think I'll make the request and see if we can bring him down here as soon as possible.'

'Make sure the cadaver is kept refrigerated under optimum conditions, or Peláez will be cross.'

'I'll see to that. Have you any advice about how to identify the body, Superintendent?'

'You've tried all the usual things, I take it? Missing Persons? The dentition, and the fingerprints?'

Fragela nodded. 'No luck so far. The dentition's no use. He had no natural teeth, and the false teeth are missing.'

'But that's very significant,' commented Bernal. 'Why would anyone go skin-diving and not put his teeth in? If you can get Peláez, I expect he'll do X-rays of the buccal cavity and sinuses. Occasionally some prior illness or operation is revealed which can help to make an identification from medical records.'

'The fingerprints have been completely destroyed by marine creatures, so not even dermal prints can be taken.'

'As a last resort you might be able to identify him from a blood-print, or from occupational deformations and scars. Are you sure he was a Spanish national?'

'No, we simply can't tell. He could be Latin or Slav, to judge by the shape of the head, the build and the complexion.'

'You'd better let Peláez decide; he's very good on heads.'

★

When Superintendent Bernal returned to the Calle de Concepción the next morning to keep the appointment with his wife, he was surprised to see a very long queue of young and middle-aged women outside the Convent of the Palm, most of whom were dressed in penitential purple, with scapularies in silver frames around their necks; each of them clutched an empty glass bottle. As he approached the head of the queue with some apprehension, he noted that he was the object of increasing curiosity and comment. He was staggered by the wide racial variety of the faces turned towards him: Tartessian, Phœnician, Carthaginian, Roman, Berber and Slav were all represented. The most strikingly beautiful were the descendants of the *puellæ Gaditanæ*, so prized in ancient Rome: the black hair framing a complaisantly open, pear-shaped face, wide-set amygdalous eyes with highly arched brows, a flattened, broadly snub nose with flaring nostrils, thick, generously bowed lips and small sparkling teeth. What really gave them the ancient Tartessian effect were the immense amounts of personal adornment: one dusky beauty was wearing long earrings of gold filigree, two silver necklaces of shark's teeth, five gold bangles on the right wrist and seven of silver and coral on the left, with a variety of rings—two or three on each finger. Her body swayed slowly to the rhythm of an ancient *tanguillo* that she was humming as she waited patiently to be admitted to the sanctuary.

The woman at the head of the queue was a tall, large-boned blonde with hazel eyes that shone behind her butterfly-framed spectacles. She looked Bernal up and down with wry amusement.

'Yer've come to the wrong place, mister,' she said boldly. 'This queue's only for the Sisters of the Diurnal Adoration.'

The women behind her cackled at his growing discomfiture.

'I'm expected here, señora; my wife is a temporary resident.'

'Expected!' She laughed uproariously. 'Well, join the crowd of us who wish they were expecting!'

The other women in the queue laughed and waved their glass bottles at him.

'Do you mind if I ring the bell?' Bernal asked the tall woman, who spoke with a pronounced Catalan accent.

'Go ahead! But they won't let anyone in until high tide, when the water comes out of the rock, we hope. Just yer make it clear who's rung, OK? Otherwise Sister Serena will pin the blame on me for being impatient.'

More puzzled than ever by the conversation, Bernal agreed to own up when the door was opened, and he pulled on the large metal handle. The other women craned forward to listen to the distant clanging.

'Yer'll be lucky if they let you in,' said the *catalana*. 'I've never seen a man allowed in here for the Diurnal Adoration.'

The small postern-gate set in the large door was opened, and a nun looked out.

'Who's being impatient, then?' she asked crossly. 'The flow hasn't begun yet.'

Then she recognized Bernal from his visit the night before.

'Oh, Comisario, do come in. Your wife is still busy with the arrangements for the procession, but I expect she'll spare you a few moments.'

In the large cloister, Bernal saw two bishops chatting to an army officer, who appeared to ignore his passage through the archway that led to the rear yard. There he could see that the float of The Entry into Jerusalem was now ready for the day's ceremonies, though he could see no *costaleros* or bearers as yet.

As they passed the illuminated niches of suspect saints, Bernal took the opportunity of asking Sister Serena about the queue of women outside the main gate.

'They come here most days for the Diurnal Adoration in the Holy Cave below the high altar. Quite often, at high tide, the holy spring begins to flow with fresh water, though on some days it's only a trickle.'

'But does the water have special properties, Sister?'

'Of course! That's why so many of them come here. If

they have faith, the water helps them conceive; even women who've been barren for many years.'

Bernal began to understand the comments of the women waiting in the street. 'I've never heard of this spring before, and wasn't aware there was any fresh water in Cadiz. Have its properties been known for a long time?'

'You'd have to ask Bishop Sanandrés. Before the Order acquired this house, he did a lot of historical research, and it was at his orders that the excavation was done and the Holy Cave discovered. Perhaps you'd like to see it before you leave?'

'I would indeed. It's a fascinating business.'

'More than fascinating, Comisario,' said Sister Serena in a tone of disapproval, 'it's miraculous. You know that Bishop Sanandrés has the stigmata?' She crossed herself on uttering the last word.

'No, I didn't,' said Bernal, wondering what sort of convent his wife had got herself mixed up in. 'Is the diocesan bishop aware of all this?'

'He never visits us, Comisario. But there's no doubt that Bishop Sanandrés will be beatified, perhaps canonized one day. He's a wonderful man, with tremendous powers.'

The nun showed him into the parlour and said she would go in search of his wife. Bernal sat miserably in a most uncomfortable upright chair and gazed unhappily at the luridly coloured nineteenth-century prints of the fourteen Stations of the Cross that adorned the whitewashed walls. He reflected how wonderful it was that Eugenia, whenever a matrimonial dispute was impending, always managed to gain the better ground. How could he pursue the divorce proposal with her in this setting? He wished he had the courage to light up a Kaiser, put his feet across the table and tell Bishop Sanandrés and Sister Serena to go hang.

When he saw Eugenia enter the parlour still dressed in the brown habit of a novice, he had a sudden flash of inspiration.

'Geñita, I'm sorry to interrupt again when you're obviously still busy with the preparations.'

'I can spare you a quarter of an hour, Luis,' she said

somewhat suspiciously. 'The spring hasn't started to flow yet. The bishop tells me that it takes at least an hour from high tide for the sacred water to emerge, and even then it doesn't happen every time. He sometimes has to assist it with special prayers.'

Bernal wondered, with his customary suspicion of clerics, what other assistance was required.

'And it's so beneficial for those poor women, Luis, and helps them to conceive. All these cases for which modern medicine can do nothing! The barren woman, if she has sufficient faith, comes here to the Diurnal Adoration and partakes of the sacred water. Then with a little every day for a month, the miracle works in her and she conceives.'

'Without any help from her husband?' asked Luis incredulously.

'Don't be crude, Luis. Of course they must assist, but without the water from the Cave it would be of no avail. Now,' she said sharply, 'what do you want to say to me before you return to Madrid?'

Bernal summoned up all the courage he could muster. 'It has struck me in the last year or two, Geñita, that you are much happier here, or in a setting like this, than at home, now that our sons have grown up and gone away. It must be extremely dull for you alone in the Madrid flat while I work such long hours. Have you considered the possibility of becoming a novice and entering an Order? Not necessarily this one, of course.'

Eugenia looked at him coldly. 'That's clearly impossible for a married woman with two sons, Luis. You must be out of your mind.'

'But we could ask for an annulment through the Church, Geñita, and that would make it possible.'

'It's no good your going on, Luis. I will admit that if I were ever to be widowed, which God forbid—' Luis looked at her suspiciously—'then I might consider it. But as things are there's no possible ground for an annulment, and a legal separation just won't do for the Church, as you well know. What would my status be in the eyes of God? What can't be remedied must be borne. You'll have to get used to the idea that you've got me for the rest of our natural days. Now, let me get on with the preparations,' she ended briskly. 'You'll be going back to Madrid soon?'

'I'm not sure. Perhaps tomorrow, if I can get a seat on the TALGO.'

As Sister Serena accompanied him once more through the yard, Bernal asked her to show him the Holy Cave.

'Of course, Comisario, but if you want to see the spring itself, you'll have to go down the ladder on your own. It's too steep for me.'

Bernal was impressed by the size of the basilica constructed over the Holy Cave, and by the richness of the gold and silver pseudo-baroque décor. The nun showed him a door at the side of the altar, and he descended the wrought-iron ladder with considerable caution. At its foot he found himself in a natural cave, the ceiling of which was covered with fossilized oyster shells that ran in strata between limestone pebbles. He was surprised to see large wet footprints shaped like duck's feet leading to and from the opening of a well in the middle of the cave; he looked over its edge but could see nothing in the gloom of the natural funnel, as he supposed it to be. He followed the footprints back to a steel door at the far corner of the cavern, and opened it quietly. Inside he found what appeared to be a small changing room, and hanging from the wall was a dripping black wetsuit.

'Are you all right, Comisario?' Sister Serena called from the top of the iron stairs.

'Yes, I'm coming up now.'

'Has the water level risen in the well yet?' she asked.

'No, I couldn't see anything.'

'Ah,' she said, 'perhaps the miracle won't work today. It doesn't always, you know.'

He said nothing about his small discovery as he said goodbye to her at the gate.

Back in the Hotel de Francia y París, Bernal asked for a pot of coffee and the morning newspaper to be brought to his room, and decided to take a *canóniga*—that small siesta taken by Spanish clerics before lunch. He glanced at the headlines in the *Diario de Cádiz*: NO MORE LIGHT SHED ON FROGMAN MYSTERY: POLICE BAFFLED, screamed the main black-letter leader. THREE PALM SUNDAY '*PASOS*' WILL BE BORNE THROUGH THE STREETS OF CADIZ TODAY BY THE FOLLOWING BROTHERHOODS . . . There followed a list of the churches involved, and details of the routes to be taken. On an inner page of *sucesos locales* there was a series of brief reports of attacks and robberies in the streets of the provincial capital the day before, and a list of cars broken into or driven away without the owners' consent. Bernal never ceased to be amazed at the large amounts of money and valuables drivers left locked in their car boots, or which passers-by always seemed to be carrying on their persons when assaulted.

There followed a long account of the fishing-ground dispute between the Spanish fishermen and the Moroccan authorities, and a report of the detention of three boats from El Puerto de Santa María at Tangiers. As a protest, the fishermen of El Puerto were to keep their boats in harbour and refuse to fish.

Just as he was dozing off, the telephone at his bedside rang.

'Comisario Bernal?' a girl's voice said, 'this is the *centralita* of the hotel. A Navy messenger has arrived with an envelope for you. Shall I send him up? He says he must deliver it into your hands.'

'I suppose you'd better,' said Bernal, whose intuition warned him that something was up.

A peremptory knock at the door brought him to his feet, and the naval motorcyclist saluted and demanded to see his official DSE badge.

'Thank you, Comisario. Please sign for this message.' Then he saluted again smartly and marched off down the corridor.

Bernal took the large white envelope to the table by the window and examined the red wax seal, which bore the impression of the Armada; below it was the blue epigraph of the Capitanía General de la Marina, San Fernando. He cut open the flap with a pen-knife and saw that the message was headed *Secret*:

MINISTERIO DE LA MARINA: SECCIÓN SEGUNDA BIS

Coded message received 0600 hours 4 April from
Sub-Secretary,
Ministry of the Interior, Madrid. Decode reads:
Comisario Luis Bernal. Kindly remain in Cadiz to take
charge of investigation into decease of unidentified subaqua
diver, in full cooperation with Inspector Fragela, Cadiz
Judicial Police, and in consultation with Naval Security and
Sección Segunda Bis, Captaincy General of the Marine,
San Fernando. This order emanates from the President of
Ministers and the CESID, Ministry of Defence. All person-
nel and facilities you may require will be made available.
Written personal authority follows.
Message ends.

Bernal pondered the missive for a long time, with feelings
of excitement and dismay. Excitement at being asked to
take on what promised to be a fascinating case; dismay at
having to operate outside the territory he knew best: Madrid.
Born and bred a *madrileño*, he knew the capital backwards.
Here in Cadiz he would have to work in a provincial port
of 130,000 inhabitants, with their own peculiar Andalusian
ethos he neither shared nor fully understood. The terrain
was complex: an old fortress-type city of whitewashed narrow streets built on a limestone promontory, connected
to a larger modern section comprising high-rise buildings
constructed on the isthmus and the land reclaimed from the
Bay beyond the Puerta de Tierra—the Land Gate that once
marked the southern limit of the old port. Further to the
south-east, across the Suazo Bridge, lay the headquarters of
the Spanish Navy at San Fernando, with 85,000 inhabitants
who were known to the *gaditanos* as *cañaíllas* after the sea-
snails that abounded there on the Isle of Lyons. Thence to
the east and north-east was the mainland, with the small
ports around Cadiz Bay: Puerto Real, El Puerto de Santa
María (connected to Cadiz since the early Seventies by a

modern swing-bridge), and the joint US–Spanish military base at Rota.

This case of the dead frogman might have connections with naval espionage, of which Bernal had no experience. On the other hand, unidentified corpses with cause of death unknown attracted his outstanding detective abilities—that firm desire to find out the truth and enable justice to be done, if possible. He could never resist such a temptation, which in any case presently arose from a direct order from the Government: 'Kindly remain . . .' A very polite imperative, if ever he had read one, but an imperative nevertheless. The other side of the coin was the full authority and all facilities he was being offered. At least he'd start with that: he would demand an operations room in the Cadiz Comisaría, with direct communications with the DSE and the Ministry of the Marine in Madrid, and with the Captaincy-General of the Navy at San Fernando. He would also need a car and driver for himself and transport for his subordinates.

How many of his regular team would he need, assuming they could be rounded up from their holiday destinations? Inspector Navarro first of all, the king-pin of his system, who would organize the operations room and control the gathering of data. Navarro would probably still be in Madrid: with a wife and ten children he wouldn't have gone off anywhere for Holy Week, and his conscientiousness would take him into the office on most days to keep an eye on the night reports and the mail.

Bernal suspected that the other members of his team would be out of town: Inspectora Elena Fernández would have accompanied her parents to some elegant resort; Inspector Ángel Gallardo was probably living it up with one of his many girlfriends at a more popular watering-place noted for sun, fun and sin, such as Torremolinos, Benidorm, Palma de Majorca or Ibiza. His two older inspectors, Miranda and Lista, might still be in Madrid taking their respective families on day trips.

He decided to ring Navarro without delay and caught him just as he was packing his children into the station-wagon.

'Navarro? It's Bernal. We've got an urgent job to do. Tell your wife I'm sorry to spoil her holidays. Try to get as many of the Group to Cadiz as you can.'

'Don't worry, *jefe*. It's cold and just starting to rain here, so we shan't be sorry to call off our day trip. I'll start ringing around.'

'What about Varga? Is he in town?' asked Bernal, realizing he would need the best technician he could get from the Brigada Criminal.

'Yes, chief, he's finishing a job for the Drugs Group.'

'Remember we have overriding authority, Navarro, and we'll use it to get everyone we need. Ask him to assemble his equipment and drive down here as soon as he can.'

'OK, chief. The biggest problem will be to get in touch with Elena and Ángel, but I'll see what I can do.'

'It's more important for you to reach Peláez. I want a second autopsy done on this cadaver they fished out of the sea on Friday. The local pathologists can't establish the cause of death. I'll reserve hotel accommodation for everyone here. The local inspector is very cooperative. We'll be working with him, and the naval authorities. His name's Fragela.'

Inspector Fragela, who had just received his orders from the Ministry of the Interior, greeted Bernal warmly and showed alacrity in making all arrangements for an operations room and a temporary technical laboratory. Bernal realized that his younger colleague was doing his utmost to hide his chagrin at having the case taken out of his hands, and went out of his way to be conciliatory.

'The powers that be think there's more to this case than meets the eye, Fragela, and they've obviously taken advantage of my presence here on a private visit to put me in charge. There's nothing you or I can do about it, so we'll do our best together. How do you get on with the naval security people at San Fernando?'

'Very well, Comisario. Rear Admiral Soto and I are old friends; we went to the same school in fact, and did our military service together in the Navy.'

33

'That's a great advantage to us, Fragela. I didn't realize you were a naval man.'

'It's in our blood, Comisario; most of us *isleños* opt to go to sea. Can I say how pleased I am to be under your command?'

'I'm sure we'll get on splendidly. I'll be relying on you for all the local knowledge.'

'Soto will see us right away if you'd like to come with me to San Fernando. It might be better for you to see the whole naval set-up of the Bay at the Capitanía.'

'Let's go at once. I'll read your detailed report on the dead frogman on the way.'

As the Super Mirafiori 124 threaded its way through the traffic on the N-VI that ran between the main Madrid-Cadiz railway line and the sand dunes of the Cortadura beach, now bathed in the intensely white light filtered through the clouds borne westward by the Levante wind, Bernal scanned the report on the discovery of the corpse of the frogman thirty-six hours earlier at La Caleta inlet, and then perused the autopsy report with some care. His attention was caught by the chest wound over the heart that had at first been mistaken for a bullet-hole, and by the opinion of the local pathologists that it had not been serious enough to have been the cause of death. He would have to ask Peláez to take a close look at that.

Then he looked at the list of clothing and noted the paucity of the equipment found on the diver. Bernal took out his packet of Kaiser and offered one to Fragela, who politely declined and said he preferred Virginia; Bernal saw that the packet of Winston the local inspector produced had a blue seal rather than the official brown seal of Hacienda—*de comiso*, contraband, from one of the naval vessels probably.

'Did anything strike you as odd about this list, Fragela?'

'I wondered why there was none of the usual equipment of an aqua-diver on the corpse.'

'Exactly. It's as though it had been stripped clean deliberately, to prevent identification. So we must treat it as murder from the outset. Once Peláez has done the second autopsy, we may find out much more about the cause of death, and that may lead us to the perpetrators.' Bernal closed the file of reports and turned once more to Fragela. 'What do you know about the Convent of the Palm, in the Calle de la Concepción, Fragela?'

Fragela looked surprised. 'Very little, except that it's a fairly new religious house, founded on the site of a much earlier building in the old part of the city. The man who runs it, Father Sanandrés, was a novice in a different order, but got involved with one of the Cofradías or brotherhoods that organize the Holy Week processions, and gradually acquired the funds for this new set-up. I get the impression that the suffragan bishop doesn't approve of the goings-on there; it's entirely unreformed, with all the offices in Latin.'

'And it's a mixed house,' commented Bernal, 'and there can't have been many of them since the Middle Ages.' Noting Fragela's puzzlement, he continued: 'I'd better explain that my wife, who's fanatically religious, is doing spiritual exercises there this week on the recommendation of the parish priest who's her confessor in Madrid. He, too, is very right-wing in all matters. But it isn't that which concerns me. When I was there this morning, I saw an army officer talking to the group of clerics in the cloister, and yesterday evening there was an admiral in full dress uniform visiting there.' Bernal paused. 'When you have the opportunity, perhaps you could make very discreet inquiries as to who that admiral is and about his relations with the Convent.'

'Do you think there's any connection with the case we're investigating?' asked Fragela, in considerable surprise.

'Oh, almost certainly not,' said Bernal, 'but I saw a recently used wet-suit hanging on a hook in the cave below the high altar. Now why on earth should they want one in a convent?'

They finally drew up outside the imposing colonnade of the Captaincy-General of the Marine, and Fragela and

Bernal were conducted by a smartly turned out junior officer to the headquarters of Naval Security.

Rear Admiral Soto turned out to be a stockily built man, with short legs that seemed designed to stride up and down a quarter-deck rather than dangle from an office chair. He had dark hair and an olive complexion, and Bernal judged him to be in his mid-forties. He greeted them gruffly but in a friendly manner, speaking in short, almost unintelligible bursts with a marked San Fernando accent.

'We're honoured to have you here, Comisario,' he said. 'Our Ministry has instructed us to cooperate with you fully in this matter.'

'I'm grateful, Contraalmirante. I'm afraid a good deal of the work will fall on you and Fragela and your men, at least until my team gets here. Could you show me on your wall map exactly where the frogman's body was netted in by the fishermen on Friday evening?'

Soto took up a wooden pointer and walked over to the large operations map of the Cadiz Bay area and indicated the two small groups of rocks east of the promontory on which the city stood.

'These rocks, known as the "Pigs" and the "Sows", are usually covered at high tide, Comisario, but there are marker-posts which remain some three or four metres above high water, and to the east there are red buoys, lit at night, which mark the main shipping channel into the inner harbour. The channel passes some two hundred and fifty metres to the east of the rocks. They can be approached with caution by small fishing craft, and the locals know them well, because they act as a refuge for fish. It's a dangerous spot, because of the cross-currents, and the jagged fossil-limestone will break a wooden boat to pieces very quickly. The main channel is dredged periodically to ensure there is sufficient draught for ocean-going liners and large naval vessels at high tide.'

Bernal asked about the amount of shipping.

'It's much reduced nowadays, Comisario, but four or five commercial vessels enter the commercial port each day, and our light cruisers and frigates have to round those rocks to

dock at Los·Puntales near the city, or to enter the inner
harbour under the new bridge to cross to Bazán and La
Carraca near here.'
'If the cadaver was fished up there, between the rocks,
where do you consider it might have floated from?' asked
Bernal.
'That's a knotty one, Comisario. We can't be sure if the
corpse was free-floating or whether it had got trapped on
the rocks. At the time it was found it was only two hours to
high water, which means that the rocks were nearly covered.
If the rising tide had freed the corpse from some wedged
position, there's no knowing which currents brought it there
or how long it was there before its discovery. The main
current proceeds from the east-north-east, from the mouth
of the River Guadalete, but there are minor currents from
the east occasioned by the three smaller streams that flow
into the inner Bay, and towards high water the currents
swirl and are temporarily reversed as the Atlantic surges
from the north-west. There are dangerous undertows around
the two groups of rocks which the fishermen understand
much better than we do. There's also the problem of the
change in wind direction.'
Bernal examined the wall-chart closely, noting the depths
shown in metres, the safe channels and the marker buoys.
'Let's assume, Admiral, that the cadaver was not trapped
by the rocks. The examination of the wet-suit showed that
there was no damage from underwater obstructions. How
long would the body have taken to float to where it was
found from any point around the Bay?'
'Hard to say,' said the rear admiral. 'The wind changed
from west to east on Thursday, and so much depends on
the weight of the cadaver.'
Bernal remembered the local pathologists' view that the
corpse had been in the water for eleven or twelve days, but
wondered whether Peláez would confirm that. 'Let's assume
the body entered the water about eleven days before it was
found last Friday, let's say the twenty-first of March, in the
evening, after dark.'
The rear admiral consulted tide-tables and a meteoro-

logical record book, and did some calculations on a notepad.

'Very well, Comisario, let's start by assuming it set out from La Carraca, our naval arsenal, on the south-east side of the inner harbour. High water was at twenty-two twelve on the twenty-first. The ebbing tide would have carried the free-floating body north-westward, towards the new bridge and the exit to the outer bay, but there was a westerly wind of about fifteen knots, which would have retarded its progress. Let's say it floated half a kilometre to the north.'

'Then the morning tide would have brought it back again, wouldn't it?' asked Bernal, 'especially if the wind was still westerly.'

'That would depend on the exact time of immersion of the corpse the night before. And we must take account of the small streams entering the inner bay near La Carraca, which provide some north-westerly current.'

'By the night of the twenty-second, after another evening tide and still with a westerly breeze, where would you place it?'

Rear Admiral Soto did some calculation and measured the wall-chart with a large wooden rule. 'I'd guess about here, some seven hundred metres to the north-west. That's allowing for the surface currents only.'

'Fair enough,' said Bernal. 'The corpse must have been floating face down, of course, with the lungs providing some buoyancy, since the pathologists found no water in them. Drowning wasn't the cause of death. It wouldn't have offered much purchase to the wind, would it? But against that it would have lain too shallow to have been affected by much of the undertow.'

'I think that's right, Comisario, and the wind was westerly all that week. It was only sixteen hours before the discovery of the cadaver that the wind veered to a strong Levante of thirty-five knots, which would have tended to push it north-westwards into the outer bay.'

'But the direction you've indicated for the first two days would have beached it on the western shore of the inner bay, surely,' objected Bernal. 'There's no way it could have cleared the José León de Carranza Bridge and drifted ten kilometres towards Rota.'

'I agree,' said Soto. 'And there's another thing. Why wasn't it spotted? The inner harbour is crossed and recrossed every day by a lot of vessels, large and small. It's almost certain a ship's lookout would have sighted it.'

'Then let's try a second theory,' said Bernal, looking at the wall-chart. 'What if it started out from the city of Cadiz itself?'

'That's what I wondered first of all, Superintendent. I've often noticed amateur scuba-divers fishing below the sea walls, under the Batería de Candelaria in the summer months. But it's early in the season for that. The sea is very cold still.' He riffled through the reports and found the one he was looking for. 'The sea temperature on the twenty-first was six degrees Centigrade at six hundred hours. It would be a hardy man who would have gone out on such a cold day wearing only a thin rubber suit.'

'What ships were in the commercial port that evening?' asked Bernal.

'Only two. A Russian cruise liner, which had a party of tourists ashore, and the *JJ Sister*, which sailed at eight-thirty for Tenerife on its twice-weekly crossing.'

'I too doubt whether our unknown diver was fishing,' said Bernal. 'After all, there was no equipment found on him. But he may have been interested in the Russian ship. Let's try and work out if he could have set out from there and ended up two and a half kilometres to the north-east.'

Soto shook his head. 'It's very unlikely. The tides would have moved him on a north-east–south-west axis, assuming that he had managed to float out of the port. It's very difficult for a corpse to float out of a commercial dock, because of the many obstructions, and the rocky breakwater to the north-west in this case, that runs out to the Punta de San Felipe. I should have thought it was bound to have been washed up along there and spotted by the numerous anglers.'

'And if by chance it did manage to be swept out into the outer bay, Admiral?'

'Then the combination of wind and current would have tended to take it north-westwards, towards the Atlantic, especially after the wind changed.'

'Well, then,' said Bernal, with no sign of impatience, 'we can be reasonably sure that the body of the frogman did not set out from the places we have already considered. That leaves us with El Puerto de Santa María, north-east of where it was discovered, or Rota to the north.'

Inspector Fragela intervened. 'It's unlikely anyone would have gone diving at El Puerto, Comisario,' he said in a very polite Andalusian manner. 'There are long sandy beaches there, and a lot of river silt which pours into the bay from the Guadalete. Nor is there any shipping worth mentioning nowadays. The sherry and manzanilla is all transported by road.'

The rear admiral nodded his agreement. 'It's much more likely to have been the American–Spanish naval and air base at Rota, especially if espionage was involved.'

'Let's try plotting its movements from Rota, then,' said Bernal. 'You'd better explain the currents to me.'

The rear admiral took up the long wooden pointer and indicated the mouth of the River Guadalquivir at Chipiona to the north.

'The outflow of the Guadalquivir is far greater than that of the Guadalete at El Puerto, Comisario. It's navigable all the way up to Seville, of course, by medium-sized vessels.' He then pointed to a curve round the coast to Punta Candor, just west of Rota. 'The outflow of the Guadalquivir runs powerfully southward here to Candor Point, and turns at Rota Light into Cadiz Bay. It's very noticeable at low water.'

'So if the body left Rota at high tide on the twenty-first, which way would you expect it to float?' asked Bernal.

'Probably south-eastwards at first,' said Soto, 'towards El Puerto.'

'Then at low tide during the early hours of the twenty-second?'

'South-west, towards the open sea, or even slowly in a southerly direction, because of the light breeze from the west.

Then the next high tide, combined with the Guadalquivir outflow would take it north-eastwards again.'

'Carry on,' said Bernal, 'let's plot it from tide to tide up to the point it was found.'

Fragela and Bernal watched in fascination as Soto moved a circular red marker across the transparent plastic cover of the map, writing in the dates and times with a black crayon. Gradually an irregular zigzag was drawn, starting from the naval base at Rota and crossing the outer Bay of Cadiz.

'By last Thursday evening it might have got to here, Superintendent,' said Soto, 'but remember that we can't be at all sure how far it would have floated with each tide. I've taken four hundred metres as a mean distance.' He pointed to a spot well to the north-west of the two groups of rocks where the body was actually found.

'How high was Thursday night's tide?' asked Bernal.

'That's just the point,' said the rear admiral. 'It was a high spring tide. I think it would have borne your corpse well to the north-west of the rocks.'

'But what about the outflow of the Guadalete?' asked Bernal. 'Wouldn't that start to come into play just there?'

'It's possible,' admitted Soto. 'If we allow for that, it would have tended to bring the cadaver somewhat to the south-west.' He still appeared doubtful.

'And the veering of the wind on the Friday morning,' recalled Bernal. 'I think you said it blew some thirty five knots from the east.'

'That is the most important factor,' the rear admiral agreed, 'if we assume that the body was still offering some resistance to the wind and wasn't floating just under the surface.'

'Ah, but that's just it!' exclaimed Bernal. 'The pathologists noted that putrefaction was quite advanced, and the gases in the body would have raised it further out of the water.'

'In that case I'm in agreement,' said the naval chief. 'The strong Levante wind would have blown it towards the rocks where it was found.'

Bernal lit another Kaiser and Soto went to a cupboard and brought out a bottle of Johnnie Walker Black Label, and three large glasses. *De comiso*, like the Winston cigarettes, thought Bernal, cheaply obtained from the Navy stores. He reflected on how much better the military lived than the Madrid judicial police, even though the generals and admirals complained about their low salaries.

As they drank the generous slugs of whisky the rear admiral had poured out, Bernal asked him to explain the set-up at Rota.

'I've got official permission to explain the military defences of the Bay to you and Fragela, Superintendent, but I don't know whether you've got it in mind to pass it on to your team when its members get here.'

'I'll pass on only what is strictly necessary for the investigation. They're all perfectly reliable, and I'll clear it with the Minister if appropriate.'

'Very well, then. I take it you're most interested in the naval base at Rota. It was built by the US Navy consequent upon the 1953 bilateral agreement, by which the Americans would have three air bases—at Zaragoza, Torrejón and Seville—and a submarine base at Rota, as well as a number of radar posts on our territory. As an aftermath of the nuclear accident at Palomares in 1963 and the political changes after Franco's death, it was agreed in the 1976 renegotiation of the pact that all the US bases would be denuclearized by 1979, and now it has just been agreed in this year's renewal that all the bases will be jointly operated by the US and our military forces. As a result, we're in the process of integrating the command at Rota, and the flags of both countries now fly over the base.' The rear admiral was obviously pleased with this development.

'If Rota has been denuclearized,' asked Bernal, 'I don't see that it's of much use to the Americans. I take it we have the right of inspection?'

'Oh, we shall have, don't worry about that. It's nuclear weapons that the ban refers to, not nuclear-powered submarines. And you must recall that we've recently taken our seat on the North Atlantic Council, although we haven't integrated our forces with the NATO countries yet. Even so, we form part of the early warning system of SACEUR, the NATO southern command, with its headquarters at Naples, and the Rota base is the most important link in the chain between the Canaries and the Balearics. It's also the starting-point of the old pipeline the Americans built that runs across the Peninsula to Zaragoza.'

'And what defences does the Rota base have?' asked Bernal, looking critically at the wall-chart. 'It seems easy to approach from the Bay.'

'After 1963 the land area of the base was much enlarged, necessitating diversion of the local road that ran from El Puerto to Chipiona. The land perimeter has two fences, the inner one of which is electrified, and there is a constant helicopter patrol along it.'

'And the sea defences?' asked Bernal.

'This is classified information, as you'll appreciate, Comisario. The Americans installed two lines of passive sonar on the sea-bed across the harbour mouth, and we've cooperated in putting in hydrophones at intervals across the outer Bay, from Punta Candor to San Sebastián castle at Cadiz.' The rear admiral unrolled another wall map. 'Here's a plan of their positions. You can see that these systems can detect intruding submarines and surface craft crossing these lines at any time and under any weather conditions. The Americans have also placed anti-submarine nets, which are raised into position at Yellow Alert, across the harbour entrance at Rota.'

'But what about the long coastline to the west of the harbour?' queried Bernal. 'It stretches for more than five kilometres.'

'There are coastal defences and regular patrols, both on and off shore.'

'If our frogman had tried to penetrate those defences, to get among the US submarines and supply vessels, how would we have fared?'

'Ah, we'd have to ask our US colleagues about that. I'd say he'd have needed some kind of craft to get there, and the passive sonar should have picked it up.'

'What if he used a small fishing-boat?' asked Bernal. 'There are so many in the Bay, and some of them are no larger than rowing-boats. The coastal patrols at the base would be used to seeing them.'

'If he used a small wooden boat without a motor, he might have slipped through,' admitted Soto.

'I think we ought to talk to your opposite number at Rota as soon as possible,' Bernal concluded. 'Could you arrange that?'

'I'll get on to him straightaway, Comisario, but I'd better warn you that he's a Yankee who speaks very little Spanish, and he only has the rank of commander. They don't have as many admirals as we do,' he joked.

'I always suspected that we have more admirals than ships,' Bernal said, smiling.

After a lengthy telephone call to Rota, it transpired that Commander Weintraub, the head of US Security there, was at a baseball game, but was expected back at his office at 5.30.

'Good,' said Bernal, 'say we'll be there at five forty-five; if that suits you, Admiral.'

Bernal submitted, with such grace as he could muster, to the minor indignities of having a Navy security pass made for him, knowing that the coloured photograph of his broad features would show him to be hopelessly unphotogenic; he nearly always came out looking like General Franco in the Fifties, with his dark moustache starting to go grey and an almost totally receded hairline above the high forehead. He put on his sternest look as the young able-seaman adjusted the lights and advanced to the tripod camera.

The small fishing town of Rota, with its sweeping beaches of white sand overlooked by a few small hotels, had once had aspirations to become a seaside resort like El Puerto de Santa María twelve kilometres to the east, but the arrival of the American troops in the Fifties had brought a commercial decline, apart from the gains made by those property-owners able to exploit the presence of the military. The fishing harbour was still animated, Bernal noted, as the official Seat Super Mirafiori 124 conducted them to the entrance to the base, where the Stars and Stripes flew on the left flagpole and the *bandera rojigualda*—the red-gold-red stripes of Spain—was now hoisted proudly on the right, with guards of each country on duty under their respective standards.

Their passes were duly inspected by the guards of each power, a phone call was made to Central Security, and soon they were waved through and directed to naval head-quarters.

Commander Weintraub met them still dressed in his baseball cap, though it never became clear to Bernal whether he had been playing or merely supporting the Navy team. Weintraub bit off the end of a large cigar and shook hands very firmly with the three Spaniards, while a young US Navy interpreter hovered nervously at his shoulder. Soto explained the purpose of their mission and left the questions to Bernal.

'Has there been any recent suspicious activity in or near the Rota naval base, Commander?' He waited for the in-terpreter to perform his task, and then wished he could understand the nasalized utterances of the American Secur-ity chief, who spoke through the left corner of his mouth, past the cigar.

The reply was unequivocal. 'There has been no activity, except for occasional Russian spy trawlers, which carry more radio interception devices than fishing-nets and try to listen in to the base's local communications.'

'When was the last such incident, Commander?'

Weintraub consulted a log-book on his desk. 'On Monday last from twenty-one hundred hours to twenty-four hundred, and on Thursday from one hundred thirty to four hundred hours.'

'The Russian trawlers sail in as regular as clockwork, Comisario,' interposed Rear Admiral Soto, and the Ameri-can nodded his agreement.

'How far inshore do they come, Commander?' asked Bernal.

'They usually stay outside the old three-mile international limit; otherwise we send out a corvette to chase them off.'

'Are there men trained in underwater combat here at the base?'

'Yes, of course. We have combined Spanish and US training teams, and they inspect our vessels in port regularly, in case of sabotage or surreptitious enemy action.'

'Can all the members of your teams be accounted for?'

'We've had no report of anyone getting lost.'

'Could you arrange for us to see one of the wet-suits and the normal equipment used by your men in these underwater teams, Commander?'

'Right away,' said the commander. 'I'll arrange for one of our guys to put on his outfit.' Weintraub picked up the phone and issued rapid instructions, still retaining the rather wet cigar between his lips. 'In ten minutes we can go down.'

'I've only one more question for the moment,' said Bernal, somewhat intimidated by the American's façade of whizzkid efficiency: 'If your electronic defences outside the military harbour alerted you to the presence of intruders, say unidentified frogmen who were approaching the base under cover of darkness, how would you combat them?'

'We'd use Plan 221, Superintendent. There would be a Red Alert, each ship's crew would be on emergency watch, the anti-submarine nets would be raised and our patrol vessels would search the port, using sonar and infra-red detection. When we'd located the intruders, we'd send in one of the underwater teams.'

'What weapons would they be armed with?'

'The usual anti-personnel underwater guns and harpoons.'

'Could I see those too?'

The commander paused. 'Yeh, I guess so,' but Bernal gained the impression that the American was less forthcoming about this request. He was at pains to repeat that there had been no such deployment except for training purposes during the three years he had been at the base.

In the submarine sheds at the port, Bernal inspected the black wet-suit worn by the US Marine with interest, noting that it was of a more sophisticated design than the suit found on the frogman's corpse. He also observed the rubber shoes with long flippers, which had not been worn by the dead man. The Marine's belt was connected to cross-pieces at back and front which supported two air-cylinders, and a considerable amount of special equipment was carried round the waist. He examined too the harpoon gun, the powerful lamp with batteries at the diver's belt, the knife and the small row of hand-grenades.

'These grenades, Commander,' he asked the Security Chief, 'how are they fired underwater?'

'From this pressure-gun, Superintendent.' He indicated a very wide bore, stubby pistol in a flap on the diver's belt. 'They will stun the target, and have a range of ten to twelve metres. Their main disadvantage is that they are cumbersome to load.'

'Could we borrow a complete set of the wet-clothing and the weapons for a few days to do some tests? I'd like my pathologist to check it out.'

The commander readily agreed, and as they took their leave, Bernal got the faint but definite impression that Weintraub was relieved; perhaps he hadn't been asked all the right questions.

Just as Soto was telling Bernal that he would stay on for a while at Rota to do some routine business, the driver of their Super Mirafiori came up to tell them that there was a message for Bernal on the car radio.

The girl at police headquarters at Cadiz read the text over to Bernal: '*Aviaco Flight AO 223 from Madrid–Barajas lands at Jerez airport at 2145 with Inspector Navarro and Dr Peláez on board. Could they be met?*'

Bernal was delighted and confirmed that he would go in person to meet the first members of his support team to arrive.

'We'll have time for a snack before the plane lands, Fragela. Where do you suggest?'

'There are a number of good restaurants in El Puerto, Comisario, and it will be on our way.'

★

47

Opposite the new bottling plant of the Terry wine-cellars, Inspector Fragela ordered the driver to pull in at the Venta de Sanmillán, where he informed Bernal they could have an early meal. The very large inn provided them with a comfortable place to talk over Larios *gin-tónics* and a portion of *ostiones*, large oysters which were the speciality of the Bay.

'What was your impression of our interview with Weintraub?' Bernal asked.

'It was difficult to gain a clear one because of the language problem. It's strange the Americans haven't appointed a security chief with some smattering of our language.'

'But we don't seem to have anybody at San Fernando who speaks English well.'

'Even so, they have large bilingual areas, which must produce some naval officers,' Fragela objected.

'I felt that the Americans were keeping something back. They answered all our questions, but didn't volunteer anything, did you notice?'

'Perhaps they'll tell Contraalmirante Soto more when he's on his own with them. After all, they've only just begun this bilateral control, and they must be feeling their way at the moment.'

Bernal turned to the menu with some dismay: a gourmet's delight, no doubt, but was there anything acceptable to his ulcer?

The SEAT Mirafiori 124 sped quietly along the old N-VI until they came to the outskirts of Jerez. There they took the ring road to the north-west, and soon came to the small military airport, which had only been opened for civil flights in the early Seventies, virtually coinciding with the opening of the José León de Carranza Bridge across the Bay. This meant that Cadiz now had access to an airport only thirty kilometres to the north, though there were very few flights, and all of them were domestic.

As they sat waiting in the small, recently refurbished waiting hall, Bernal pointed to the four Mirage jets outside the military hangar some distance away from the civil terminal.

'Are those the latest type of Mirage III, Fragela?'

'I think so. We've just taken delivery of a new batch. Our pilots train on them here.'

Bernal noticed a number of small private aircraft parked to the north side of the field.

'Are they for sport, Fragela, or business?'

'The larger ones belong to the sherry companies for their directors' use. There are a couple of foreign ones there, with Algerian or Moroccan markings. A lot of their business is in textiles, which they ship in to Málaga or Cadiz.'

As the sun set with subtropical rapidity, leaving hardly any time for dusk, the rows of blue and red runway lights were switched on and the loudspeakers crackled into life. *'Aviaco announce that their Flight AO 223 from Madrid–Barajas is expected at 2155.'*

'Ten minutes late,' sighed Bernal, 'but that's not too bad. I expect Navarro and Peláez will want some food. We'll drive straight back to Cadiz and they can take pot luck there.'

Soon the DC8 roared into sight, used the whole of the short runway to make its landing, then turned and taxied back along it to the small control tower. As the passengers came down the gangway, Bernal thought that the flight had been pretty full, probably with holiday-makers coming in for Holy Week, although only a dozen or so were waiting for the return flight to Madrid. He soon spotted the tall figure of Navarro crossing the tarmac, and behind him the gleaming bald pate and thick pebble lenses of Peláez.

The two Civil Guards at the entrance recognized Fragela and saluted. Bernal introduced his Cadiz colleague to the newcomers.

'Just like you to ruin Holy Week for me, Bernal,' complained Peláez.

'Where were you planning to go? Up to the sierra?'

'No, not at all. I'd hoped to finish my handbook on post mortems for the publishers and check all the photographs that will accompany the text. Do you realize that our pathology students have had to rely on foreign handbooks? My *magnum opus* should put me in the international class, especially with the extraordinary cases you bring me. Now, tell me about this dead frogman.'

49

'You can read the local pathologists' report in the car, Peláez. You'll see that they haven't been able to establish the cause of death.'

'I hope you've kept the *fiambre* in good condition for me, Bernal. I expect the locals have hacked it about, though.'

'It's on ice for you at the Hospital Mora.'

As the official driver took them back to Cadiz via the new motorway, which was virtually deserted, no doubt because of the toll charges, Bernal put Navarro in the picture about the investigation so far. Soon they were crossing the new bridge over the harbour and turned into the long avenue that led to the Puerta de Tierra. Almost at once they ran into a candlelit religious procession, but the *gaditano* driver managed to avoid the narrow streets, and with great skill got them at last into the Plaza de Calvo Sotelo, recently renamed San Francisco.

After Navarro and Peláez had checked into the Hotel Francia y París and left their luggage, Fragela took his leave, after recommending one or two restaurants to them.

'I'm still recovering from the giant oysters I ate at El Puerto,' Bernal explained to his Madrid colleagues, 'but I'll accompany you.'

Just as they were leaving the elegant foyer, the polite, dapper hotel receptionist came over to Bernal. 'There's a call for you from Admiral Soto, Superintendent. Will you take it in the cabin along the corridor?'

As he picked up the phone in the mahogany cabinet, Bernal at once warned Soto that this was an open line.

'Just to tell you that there's some activity along the coast, Comisario. My chaps and the Civil Guard Marine Division are investigating. May just be smugglers from across the Strait. I'll keep you informed.'

'Very well, Soto. Can you tell me what kind of activity?'

'Flashing lights off Cape Roche signalling the shore. I've sent out a fast launch and the coastal radar operators are watching for any suspicious movements.'

At 8.30 the next morning, which was Monday of Holy Week, Bernal sat reading the provincial *Hoja del Lunes* as he finished his breakfast. Dr Peláez had gone off at eight to the Hospital Mora to perform the second autopsy on the dead frogman, in the presence and with the assistance of the local pathologists who had earlier been unable to determine the cause of death. Navarro had accompanied Fragela to set up the temporary operations room in the local Comisaría, while Bernal had volunteered to await Lista and Miranda, his two other inspectors, who would soon arrive on the *expreso nocturno* from Madrid. There was still no sign of the youngest male member of his team, Ángel Gallardo, to whom Navarro had sent a telegram at the hotel in Benidorm where he was spending Semana Santa, nor had the only female member of his group, Elena Fernández, reported in: she was believed to be with her parents at their luxurious holiday chalet at Sotogrande. Unfortunately there was no telephone there, so the local Algeciras police had undertaken to pass on the message from the DSE in Madrid.

Bernal noted from the newspaper that there were to be four processions of *pasos* that day in Cadiz alone, which would set out from different churches and follow different routes, though they would all pass through the Palillero in the centre of the old city, where a competition of *saeteros* was to be held on the balcony of the *Cine Municipal*. These professional singers only came into their own during Holy Week, when they would be inspired by the statue of Christ or the Virgin Mary on a passing float to launch into an unaccompanied throat-catching *saeta* that combined Christian fervour with an ancient, definitely pagan, melodic line.

He began to doubt the wisdom of having his operations room in the old city during Holy Week: at frequent intervals the narrow streets were blocked by *pasos*, each consisting of a group of twenty or thirty barefoot penitents, robed in the colour of their brotherhood, with very tall, Inquisitorial-type *capirotes* that hid their heads and shoulders completely, leaving only two menacing slits for their eyes; they were led in each case by a master of ceremonies bearing a large crook, with which he beat the ground to mark the slow,

51

deliberate pace, and they were followed by an assistant who carried a small mace or hammer to tap on the float from time to time, thus giving coded instructions to the bearers hidden beneath as to when they should lift their enormous burden and shuffle forward, or turn to the right or left. When there was no actual procession in sight, the alleys were still packed with sightseers, some of whom sat on rows of folding chairs placed there by each neighbourhood. The normal life of the city had come to a halt for eight days, Bernal realized, and this hiatus would only end on Easter Sunday after the recently restored Grand Procession of at least sixteen *pasos*.

Through the window of the hotel, Bernal saw a taxi depositing Lista and Miranda under the orange-coloured canopy, and he went out to greet them.

'I'm sorry to have had to bring you here and spoil your plans for Semana Santa,' he said, after shaking hands with his two colleagues.

'The weather's bad in Madrid, *jefe*,' replied Lista cheerfully. 'It'll be a delight to get away and see something of the processions here.'

'It's exactly that that concerns me, Lista,' said Bernal. 'They're making it almost impossible to get about. After you've checked in, we'll go over to Fragela, the local inspector, and see if he can fix us up in a better office, close to the main highway.'

When the official car took them to the local headquarters of the Judicial Police in the Avenida de Andalucía, just outside the Puerta de Tierra, they at once realized that there was no traffic problem there: the difficulty consisted only in getting to and from the hotel.

'Lista and I could move to the RENFE Hotel near the station, chief; we'd be nearer the office and it would be cheaper for the Brigade's accounts.'

'It's not the expenses I'm worried about, Miranda; I'm expecting the Presidency or the Ministry of Defence to pick up the tab for this investigation in any case. But it'll be difficult to obtain alternative accommodation in Holy Week.

We'll see if Fragela can bring some pressure to bear.'

In the suite of offices that had been placed at their disposal, they found Rear Admiral Soto awaiting them.

'I thought I'd better report on the night's activities, Comisario.' The rear admiral turned to a large wall map that had been installed in the main office, and picked up some yellow circular markers. 'Our coastguards spotted some signalling by lights from the sea. The first report came in at twenty-three forty-two from the Marine Division of the Civil Guard at Cape Roche. There's an old fort there above a small harbour that's being turned into a yachting marina. In the pine trees along the littoral between Chiclana and Cabo Roche an elegant estate of private chalets has been constructed and some important politicians have bought properties there. The Civil Guard patrol the site regularly, and they have a small cabin at the edge of the cliff over Roche cove.'

'How far off the shore were the signals made, Admiral?' asked Bernal.

'The Civil Guards estimated them at just over two sea-miles to the south between their observation post and Cape Trafalgar. They thought the Trafalgar light had gone wrong at first, but then they realized that the fainter intervening signals were being emitted from a vessel. They radioed to their control point at San Fernando, so that the coastguard cutter could be sent out to investigate.'

'Didn't the lighthouse-keeper at Cape Trafalgar see anything?'

'The light there is unmanned, Superintendent. It's checked daily, of course, but it is operated automatically.' Contraalmirante Soto placed the first yellow marker, on which he first wrote the date and time of the sighting, to the north-west of Trafalgar Point. 'The second report came at just after twenty-four hundred hours from Torre Bermeja; that's near the popular beach called La Barrosa, south-west of Chiclana. The Civil Guards on the headland there reported a light signalling to the shore from a distance of about one sea-mile to the south of them. Neither of them could make sense of the signals, although they have some training in reading Morse. They observed the shore carefully, but could see no answering signals. But of course they wouldn't have, if the shore contact was hidden between cliffs or in a small bay. There's even the possibility of the use of infra-red signalling lamps. I've ordered the issue of the special infra-red binoculars to the coastguards from today, and instructed them to watch carefully tonight.'

'And the coastguards at Roche?' asked Bernal. 'Did they see any response from the shore?'

'No, nothing, Superintendent.'

'What about the coastguard cutter? From the sea they should have had a better chance of seeing an answering signal.'

'But they took some time to get to the spot from Torre Gorda, where their base is, Comisario,' said the rear admiral. 'The last report came at zero-one-twelve, from a retired sergeant of the Marine Branch of the Civil Guard. He looks after the old quay at the village of Sancti Petri, near the entrance to the Sancti Petri Canal, to the south-west of San Fernando. He wasn't on duty, but he says that something disturbed him and he got up and went to the window of his cabin. To the south-west, beyond the island of Sancti Petri which lies astride the mouth of the canal, he saw a series of flashes, which he recognized as a Morse signal, but he could make no sense of it.'

'Did he make out any letters at all?' queried Bernal.

'Just an M, an L, a K and a T, followed by a further rapid series of letters he couldn't decipher. I've asked our Ciphers Department to look into it.'

'So the mystery ship was sailing from the south-east a mile or two off the coast towards Cadiz,' commented Bernal, who was studying closely the position of the yellow markers on the wall map. 'Was it picked up on shore radar?'

'Yes, our men plotted it soon after the first report until it was west of the island of Sancti Petri, then it disappeared from our screens.'

'Disappeared?' echoed Bernal. 'Was it a submarine, then?'

'That's what puzzles us, Comisario. The blip seemed to be too small to be a surfaced submarine of the type we or

NATO operate, and we have no official information that any was in the vicinity at the time. The radar operator thought it was a yacht or large launch, and he's very experienced at interpreting the signals.'

'Then how could it disappear?' asked Bernal. 'I think we'd better go and talk to the retired marine sergeant at Sancti Petri. He sounds like an intelligent fellow. You'd better come with us, Lista, while Miranda helps Navarro set up the ops room here.'

They left the modern part of the city of Cadiz without difficulty, and sped along the Vía Augusta Julia to San Fernando, where the driver took them around the back roads to avoid the processions. As they left the salt-pans, which looked stark under the intense white light filtered by the thin cloud cover, they joined the usual crawl on the N 340 that led to Chiclana. Bernal handed round his packet of Kaiser, while they watched with impatience their driver negotiating the tortuous streets of the prosperous-looking town, and took the local road that led west to El Molino de Almaza and Sancti Petri.

'I did part of my military service here, *jefe*,' commented Lista. 'At the Sancti Petri camp.'

'Did you really?' asked Bernal in surprise. 'Your local knowledge may come in useful.'

'The camp is closed now,' commented the rear admiral, 'and the huts are in ruins. The retired Civil Guard is kept there to keep an eye on the site, and on the locals who fish from the quay.'

'Is the tunny-fishery still there upstream on the west bank of the canal, Admiral?' asked Lista.

'No, that's closed too. It's amazing, isn't it, how those old industries that must have gone on for hundreds, perhaps thousands of years, have all gone during the past twenty years, presumably because of the industrial boom and the new affluence. Yet they had survived in the seventeenth and eighteenth centuries, when Cadiz was receiving millions of tons of silver a year from the New World. It was the richest port in Europe then.'

'*La tacita de plata*—the little silver cup—isn't that what you call your city?' asked Bernal.

'It's more like *la tasita de surrapa* nowadays, more's the pity,' sighed the rear admiral, in his sibilant Andalusian accent.

Soto would have been outraged if an outsider had called his city 'the little cup of muck', but perhaps the jewel of the west wasn't as pristine as it once had been.

At El Molino de Almaza they took the right turn across the old salt-flats to the deserted village of Sancti Petri, and soon reached the empty military barracks, where the broken shutters flapped forlornly in the keen sea breeze and the last graffiti drawn by the long-departed conscripts were barely legible on the cracked walls.

They drew up at the rickety wooden landing-stage and looked about for the retired Civil Guard. The Levante wind blew unpleasantly across the channel from Chiclana, and under the lowering clouds Bernal could see the ruined castle of Sancti Petri on the long ladle-shaped island half a sea-mile to the west of where they were standing.

The rear admiral banged on the door of the civil guard's cabin, but there was no response. Among the fishing-boats and nets stretched out to dry on the wooden pier, they saw a boy of eight or nine years carving a whistle with a penknife.

'Have you seen the coastguard, sonny?' Soto asked him.

'Not this morning, sir. I thought Don Pedro was still asleep, but he may have gone into Chiclana for supplies. I didn't see him when I got here at ten o'clock.'

'Where do you come from, lad?' asked Bernal in a kindly manner.

The boy pointed towards El Molino de Almaza. 'My father has a smallholding there, but he lets me come here to talk to Don Pedro when there's no school. He teaches me how to make seaman's knots and carve things out of wood.' He held out proudly the whistle he had nearly finished carving.

'Thank you, sonny,' said the rear admiral. 'We'll wait for him to come back.'

*

56

After they had waited for more than half an hour for the return of the retired coastguard at the quayside in Sancti Petri, Bernal suggested to Inspector Fragela that he contact the Guardia Civil at Chiclana over the car radio to see if they could help to locate him.

Bernal looked thoughtfully at the mouth of the Sancti Petri Canal, which was over a hundred metres wide at that point, and asked the rear admiral about the depth of the channel.

'It's not really navigable for modern vessels, Superintendent. Here at its widest point there's only two and a half metres' draught in the centre of the stream, but it's much silted up as one goes further inland towards San Fernando. There's also a fossil-shell reef at the entrance, in line with the island of Sancti Petri. Only craft that draw very little water could come up here. Mostly small fishing-ketches and pleasure craft, as you can see.'

'Are there any passive sonar devices installed across the mouth of this canal, Admiral?' asked Bernal.

'Good Lord, no; it's far too shallow for submarines. They'd get stuck in the river silt.'

'But the canal runs right around San Fernando, doesn't it, up to the naval repair yards and the arsenal at La Carraca?'

'Yes, and it emerges into the Bay there. It's not a man-made canal, you realize, but a natural *caño* or inlet of the sea which makes the Isla de León into an island. It was widened at various points in the seventeenth century and was used extensively by the Navy in the days of sailing ships, since it meant that they could sail out via this channel towards Trafalgar for tactical reasons or because of the wind direction. The existence of the channel made it possible to surprise an enemy fleet by our caravels' suddenly emerging from behind the island of Sancti Petri instead of Cadiz Bay where they would have been expected. But they'd have to have sailed at high tide, in order to get over the bar.'

'And your modern ships couldn't do that?'

'Not a hope. They'd run aground in the silt or fall foul of one of the modern road bridges long before they got down here. We dredge the short section of the canal from Bazán and La Carraca into the Bay, of course, where even a large assault-ship such as the *Velasco* can dock. It's there now, actually, having an overhaul.'

'What other ships are in port?' asked Bernal.

'There are three frigates moored at Los Puntales, just outside the new bridge across the Bay, and a light cruiser in the inner harbour.'

As Bernal pondered this information, a jeep with two Civil Guards drove up to them, and one of them with the rank of captain jumped out and saluted them.

'Rear Admiral Soto?' he inquired. 'Capitán Barba, *a sus órdenes*. I have to report that the retired guard from the Marine Section, Pedro Ramos, hasn't been seen in Chiclana today. We've made inquiries in all the places he usually calls, and there's no sign of his motorbike parked in the town.'

'Do you know where Ramos kept his motorbike here, Captain?' asked Bernal.

'Here in the open, near his cabin, sir.'

Fragela and the Civil Guards began to search the quayside but could see no sign of the cycle.

Bernal peered through the windows of the locked cabin with growing unease. 'I think we'd better break into his cabin and see what's in there,' he said to Inspector Fragela. 'Do you think we can get this padlock opened? It's a pity Varga isn't here yet.'

Lista produced a skeleton key and offered to have a go at opening the lock. The small boy who had talked to them earlier suddenly called out to them from the far end of the wooden pier, where he sat with his legs dangling over the edge. '*¡Señores, vengan a ver!*—Come and see!'

Bernal and Fragela hurried across to where the boy was sitting and looked down at the water following the direction of his urgently pointing arm.

'The tide's gone down and there's Don Pedro's motorbike in the water!'

The Civil Guards obtained a dinghy from the mooring-place and paddled it around the quay to the place the boy had indicated. With the assistance of a grappling-hook, they managed to free the motorcycle from the river silt and drag it slowly towards the small beach of grey sand beyond the mole.

'It's definitely Don Pedro's bike,' said the boy excitedly. 'He gives me rides home on it sometimes.'

Bernal consulted with Fragela and the rear admiral out of earshot of the others. 'You'd better institute a search of the whole area, Fragela. Lista will help you.'

'Shall I call for reinforcements?'

'It would be best to send for Miranda. Three expert searchers are better than an army of half-trained guards trampling all over the evidence. I fear something has happened to Ramos,' Bernal said with growing concern. 'How would he have reported the light signals he saw last night, Fragela? By radio or telephone?'

'He has a small transponder which is picked up by the Civil Guard radio control centre at Chiclana, Comisario. There's been no telephone here since the army camp was closed down. The village is deserted, as you can see.'

'All those empty buildings will have to be searched,' said Bernal. 'I wonder if last night's signallers intercepted his radio message? They might have been listening in on the coastguard frequency.'

Dr Peláez was conducting the second autopsy on the frogman in his usual brisk fashion, talking into a small microphone held under his chin so that a rough draft of his report could be typed up by an audiotypist soon afterwards. He had always hated the paper work that was an occupational hazard of pathologists. The two local doctors watched him in admiration.

'Initial incision very skilfully made, and organs properly removed,' Peláez reported to his microphone, while the younger of the two local pathologists blushed behind his mask. 'Hello, what's happened here?' Peláez took a magnifying glass to examine the area over the heart more carefully.

'We had to dissect out a small wound,' said the older of the two local men. 'I made a slide of the cross-section. We thought at first that it was a bullet entry-wound.'

'H'm, strange injury,' commented Peláez gruffly. 'I've never seen anything quite like it. Electrocution, do you think? An electrode that cut into the flesh?'

'But there'd be vital signs, wouldn't there, if such an injury had been inflicted when he was still alive?' objected the younger doctor very politely.

'Did you find anything corresponding to this injury on the heart, behind the wound?' asked Peláez.

'No, no sign of electrocution, Doctor, although that's what I thought it was at first. The heart seemed perfectly normal.'

'But it stopped, didn't it?' said Peláez. 'What made it stop? A vagal inhibition, perhaps? We'll have to find out.' He dissected the whole area of the sternum widely, and took cross-sections at regular intervals to make new slides. 'There are signs of intense burning here, at the outer edges of the wound. What the hell can it have been?' he asked, temporarily forgetting the microphone and the later reactions of the audiotypist. 'And was it the fatal injury?'

'There's no sign that the wound penetrated to the heart, is there?' commented the senior local pathologist.

'No, but if you're right and there's no other apparent cause of death, then there must be a connection here. What does it take to cause cardiac arrest? Asphyxia? But in this case there's no sign of drowning, suffocation, strangulation or embolism, nor is there any indication of cardiac or arterial disease, or of renal or hepatic failure, or of drug or alcoholic abuse. I see that you've checked all those possibilities and ruled them out. In short we have to consider the likelihood of vagal inhibition or electrocution. Now you've carefully dissected the heart and found no sign of electrocution, or did you?' asked Peláez penetratingly.

'No, we didn't,' said the senior pathologist.

'Then we must consider inhibition of the vagal nerve in the neck,' said Peláez.

'We thought of it as a last resort,' said the younger pathologist, 'but we couldn't see any sign of constriction.'

Peláez pondered the question further. 'I'd like to run further tests on the heart tissue, and examine the damage to the chest area of the wet-suit. Can I use your lab facilities?'

'Of course, Dr Peláez. It's a great honour to have you working here.'

'Thank you,' said Peláez, with the natural assumption of greatness of a leader in his profession. 'Bernal wants information also about the chief characteristics of the deceased—race, approximate age, occupation, etcetera. Have you good radiographical facilities here? I've made a study of skull-types, you know.'

'We've read your articles on the topic in the journals, Dr Peláez. Yes, we've got quite up-to-date equipment in this hospital. But anything lacking would probably be available in the Naval Hospital.'

'Did you send the sea-water samples from the trachea to the lab for the diatoms to be examined? They may show provenance of the corpse when they are compared with samples of the sea-water from the various points around the Bay.'

'Yes, we did, Doctor, and we should get the results later today.'


After an hour, Dr Peláez stood up from the work-bench in the hospital path. lab where he had been using the high-powered microscope, and beamed with satisfaction. He went to seek out the two local pathologists.

'I've got it! I'm pretty sure I know how that frogman was killed. The main valve of the heart was cooked!'

'Cooked?' echoed the older pathologist. 'We didn't heat it in any way, you know.'

Peláez waved his disclaimer aside with impatience. 'The tissues of the heart were subjected to sudden, very intense heat, such as that emitted by microwave or an extremely high frequency beam, which was sufficient to stop the valve.'

'A beam?' queried the younger pathologist. 'What sort of beam could do that?'

'I'm not really sure, but a type of laser-beam might be capable of doing it. I've not seen a death caused by it before,

61

though I've seen one or two cases of laser-burns from the engineering lab at the University City in Madrid. No wonder you were mystified! It's probably the first case of a laser-beam fatality in Spain, at least as far as I know. Definitely a case to add to my memoirs!'

'But how could it have been applied?' asked the young local doctor. 'And why didn't the rubber of the wet-suit melt away completely at that point?'

'Lasers are extremely precise and directional,' said Peláez. 'Only the smallest area is affected. My guess is that the frogman was partly submerged when the laser-gun was directed at his chest. Thus it was able to penetrate to the heart along a very narrow beam, while the sea-water rapidly cooled the edges of the entrance-hole. Death must have been very quick, because there are no vital signs around the orifice itself.'

'Who would have such a gun?' asked the older pathologist.

'That's for Bernal to find out.'

Just then a female lab assistant entered with a large buff envelope which the older local doctor tore open.

'Here's the lab report on the diatoms in the sea-water found in the trachea of the deceased,' he said to Peláez. He turned to the last page of the document. 'They've compared the sample with sea-water samples taken at various points around the Bay. They conclude that there is most similarity with the sample taken from the sea at Punta Candor, just outside the outflow from the River Guadalete.'

'Where is that exactly?' asked Peláez.

'Just west of Rota.'

'Ah, that will help Bernal a lot. Now let's have a look at the X-rays of the skull. Bernal wants to know about the racial characteristics of the deceased. I see that you checked the skull-plates. Age about twenty-five to twenty-eight, would you say?'

'That's what we thought.'

'I agree. Now let's compare the profile of the skull shape with my standard set of racial types.' He drew out a number of X-ray plates from a large attaché case and pegged them on to an illuminated observation screen.

The local pathologists looked on with keen interest.

'It's vital, of course, to get actual X-rays,' said Peláez. 'You'll note that I have twelve examples of each main type of skull: various European ones, Asian, Negro, North African and so on; three men and three women of different age-groups within each type, with profile and frontal views of each specimen.'

He pinned up the X-ray plate of the dead frogman and asked his Cadiz colleagues to start making comparisons. 'While you're getting a visual impression, I'll do some measurements of our man's skull. It's important to calculate the proportions of the length, breadth and height of the cranium, and the angles of the occipital and frontal planes.'

After spending some minutes doing calculations on a pad, Peláez looked up. 'Well?' Have you come to any conclusion?'

'It's certainly not European or Negro,' said the older man. 'But it could be Slav or North African.'

'I think the latter,' said the younger pathologist. 'Although it's similar to the second Asian skull you have here, the nostrils are wider.'

'Ah, you've got it, I think,' said Peláez. 'My calculations suggest that it's North African, so let's get out some sub-types from this folder.'

He produced another large brown envelope from the attaché case. 'Here I've got examples from Egyptian and Sudanese to Arab and Berber.'

'How did you come by all these?' asked the older local doctor. 'You can't have obtained them all from your Institute in Madrid.'

'Most of them came from my good friend at the Cobalt Therapy department at the Gran Hospital. He specializes in brain tumours, and of course takes many cranial X-rays with his new scanner. Others have come from my pupils now practising in Ceuta, Melilla, El Aaiún and Cairo. I've got an enormous collection in Madrid, but I've only brought the standard sets for initial identification.'

Peláez now removed the first series of plates and pinned up the second series of North African sub-types.

The Cadiz pathologists eagerly compared the new series

with the cranial X-rays of their unidentified corpse. 'It seems to be a Berber type,' said the older man.

'I agree,' said the young doctor. 'I'm very impressed with your system.'

'The calculating tables are useful,' commented Peláez, 'but you can't beat a comparison with actual specimens for real accuracy. At least we can report pretty definitely that our man was a Berber from North Africa. It's a pity there's no dentition at all. You can see that all the teeth had been extracted, except for one unerupted third molar and the remains of the roots of two second molars. It's odd he had no dentures in place when he was found. He certainly wore false teeth because I've noted signs of rubbing on the flattened gums. Why would anyone go to the bother of removing the false teeth after he was dead? To avoid possible identification, perhaps?'

'What about his occupation?' asked the younger pathologist. 'Can we say anything about that?'

'Let's have a look at the X-ray of the shinbones,' said Peláez, putting up another two plates on the illuminated screen. 'You see those marks of pressure on the lower end of each? That means he'd been in the habit of squatting, which is the usual method of resting in North Africa. I don't think we can deduce much else, except that he was in excellent physical condition, with well developed musculature. An active, outdoor type—you observe the weathering of the skin over the shoulders?'

'A military type?' asked the older local pathologist.

'Could well be,' answered Peláez. 'Did you notice the flattening of the feet? Probably from marching or sentry duty. Very short hair-cut too, which helps to confirm it.'

'What about the tattoo on the upper left arm?' asked the younger pathologist. 'We couldn't make anything of it. The effect of the immersion and the putrefaction have obscured it.'

'Ah, we'll try to get it now,' said Peláez. 'Can you call your photographer back? I take it he can do ultra-violet shots, and infra-red? I'll insert some glycerin under the skin with a hypodermic needle to bring up the design.'

\*

At 11.45 a.m. Peláez and the two local pathologists sat looking in great puzzlement at the infra-red photographs that had just been developed.

'It's not a recognizable design, is it?' commented the younger doctor, staring at the picture of the tattoo found on the dead frogman's left arm.

'No, and it's not a word or a phrase; just a series of fine squiggles,' said the older local man.

Peláez turned the photograph around. 'I think we've been looking at it upside down. Let's check its position against the cadaver itself.' He pulled out the refrigerated drawer and removed the sheet from the upper portion of the corpse. 'There, you see that hypostatic staining under the elbow? The photo should be this way up.'

'The tattoo is still meaningless to me,' said the younger pathologist.

'It's in Arabic, I think,' exclaimed Peláez. 'There seem to be five characters. I've never studied that language myself, but I've seen depictions of the script often enough. We'll need to obtain the services of an Arabist. Is there one in the city?'

'I'm sure there will be at the University,' said the older local man. 'At least this confirms your view about the deceased's being a Berber.'

'I'll take these photos round to Bernal as soon as the audiotypist finishes the report,' said Peláez. 'He can take up the business of the tattoo with the local expert. We've done all we can.'

By midday the Levante wind blew more strongly across the wooden jetty at Sancti Petri, raising unpleasant swirls of dust from the narrow streets and enveloping the deserted village in a shimmering, caliginous haze.

Bernal returned from his somewhat desultory search of the quayside to confer with Rear Admiral Soto, who sat disconsolately in the back seat of the official car.

'As soon as Miranda gets here, Admiral, I'll put him in

charge of the search and drop you off at San Fernando on my way back to Cadiz. I need to find out about the time of Varga's arrival, because we require an expert technician and a fingerprint man to check out this cabin.'

'I could send you some of my men from Segunda Bis at San Carlos if necessary, Comisario.'

'That's very good of you. I hope they won't be needed; but I can't understand what's holding up the technical team. They left Madrid by road yesterday.'

As he spoke they saw a large brown van, preceded by a black SEAT 134 saloon, approaching along the dusty road from El Molino de Almaza. 'This looks like them now,' exclaimed Bernal excitedly. 'And Miranda's with them. On receiving the radio message we sent, he must have decided we needed the technical team at once.'

Varga tumbled out of the van as it stopped near the landing-stage, and approached Bernal. 'The van broke down outside Jaén, chief, but with the help of a local garage we managed to do some running repairs. What's up here?'

'We're looking for a missing retired sergeant of the Marine Division of the Civil Guard called Pedro Ramos. That's his cabin over there. Fragela, the local inspector, Lista and I with the help of Captain Barba have made an initial search of these deserted barracks. That's the missing man's motor-cycle, which we've fished out of the channel, off the eastern end of the jetty. But there's no trace of him. This wretched wind is raising a lot of dust and making it impossible to spot any tracks.'

'Have you looked under the piers of the mole, *jefe*?'

'Not yet, Varga. The tide's still too high. The rear admiral says that low tide won't be for another four and a half hours yet. The bike was caught on the silt at the water's edge.'

'Do you want my assistant to fingerprint the cabin, chief?'

'Yes, please, and then make a thorough search of it. The Civil Guard will surely have Ramos's prints in their personnel files at Chiclana.'

Miranda now came over from the official SEAT, where he had been giving instructions to the driver. 'Now we've got an extra car, chief, you could return to Cadiz in it and leave us with this one and the van. Navarro says to tell you that he is expecting Elena Fernández and Ángel Gallardo to report in shortly.'

'That's excellent, Miranda. I've got interesting plans for them both. Will you conduct the search here in cooperation with Inspector Fragela and Captain Barba? In the meantime I'll go back and organize things with Navarro. We'll arrange to send you food and drink. It doesn't get dark until about seven-thirty.'

'Don't worry about provisions, *jefe*. The Cadiz Comisaría stocked us up with all sorts of stuff, mostly fried seafood, and two crates of the local Cruzcampo beer.'

'Rather you than I, Miranda. I'm still queasy from yesterday's giant oysters. Anyway, I'd better be off in time to catch the suffragan bishop.'

'The bishop?' asked Miranda in some astonishment. 'Is the Church involved in this case?'

'I hope not, but one never knows.'

Back in the modern headquarters of the Judicial Police outside the Puerta de Tierra, Bernal found that Navarro had organized the office space most admirably, and had set up an operations table and filing system on the dead frogman.

'You may have to set up a separate system for the retired sergeant of the Marine Division of the Civil Guard, Paco. I fear something unpleasant has happened to him. We found his motorbike tipped into the Sancti Petri channel.'

'I've already asked the Civil Guard at Chiclana to send us a copy of his personal file, chief. Have Miranda and Varga begun the search?'

'Yes, but the Levante's raising a hell of a lot of dust and making things pretty difficult down there. Has Peláez brought in his autopsy report on the deceased frogman yet?'

'Not yet, chief, but he promises it for later this afternoon.'

Just then Ángel Gallardo breezed in, most informally dressed in safari jacket, T-shirt and blue jeans, carrying a travel bag. The youngest of Bernal's male inspectors, he had all the ebullience of the typical *madrileño*.

'I'm not sorry you called me back to duty, chief. Those two chicks I took with me to Benidorm on a Holy Week package holiday started quarrelling before the coach reached Albacete, and then the Benidorm hotel turned out to be only half constructed, on a muddy site at the farthest end of the bay a good three kilometres from the night spots. It was no picnic, I can tell you.'

'Whatever possessed you to take *two* girlfriends, Ángel?' asked Paco Navarro in astonishment. Being a naturally shy person, he himself had taken two years of courting to summon up enough courage to ask Remedios to marry him, and he never ceased to be amazed at the boldness of the generation after his.

'It's worked out OK before,' replied Ángel cheerily. 'It keeps each of them on her toes when there's a bit of competition.'

'I've got an undercover mission to keep you on tiptoe, Ángel,' said Bernal severely, 'and I want you to get cracking right away, once Navarro has briefed you on this case of the unidentified frogman.'

'Shall I book into an hotel here?' asked Ángel.

'No, that's just the point,' said Bernal. 'I want you to stay in those clothes and look like a tourist with little money, and go to Rota across the Bay. Take the ordinary bus service, and book into a cheap *pensión*. Then you can chat in the waterfront bars with the local fishermen and with the servicemen from the military base, and keep your ear to the ground. Try to find out about any suspicious naval operations or strange vessels or light signals they may have spotted, especially at night. And don't get involved with any of the *roteñas*, however enticing their charms.' Bernal was well aware that Ángel Gallardo's entire success in the Brigada Criminal had been due to his ability to mix in the middle and lower strata of the social scene and gain information without raising suspicion.

'OK, chief, will do. How do I report in?'

'Ring Navarro at this number once a day, say at noon, or at once if you discover anything of interest. And don't exceed the usual daily expenses allowance that you'd be allotted in Madrid. It should prove more than enough for a fishing port like Rota.'

While Navarro was briefing Ángel about the frogman and the missing Marine sergeant from Sancti Petri, Bernal sought out the Madrid telephone directory arranged by streets and was soon looking up the Calle de Lagasca. He spotted the number he wanted and was shortly speaking to Father Anselmo, his wife's confessor, who promised to send him what he wanted by express post that afternoon.

The other two inspectors in Bernal's team, Miranda and Lista, sat with Inspector Fragela and Barba the Captain of the Civil Guard at the back of Varga's van eating *bocatas* of prawn omelette and fried squids' tentacles, which they washed down with generous draughts of local wine from a leather *bota*. The dust-raising Levante had removed any possibility of finding tracks in the rutted streets of the deserted army camp, and there was no trace of the missing retired sergeant. Low tide wouldn't be reached until 7.34 p.m., when they planned to make a search under the wooden jetty; Captain Barba had sent to Chiclana for five pairs of gum-boots.

In the meantime Varga was finishing his technical examination of the Marine sergeant's cabin, and his assistant had photographed the latent fingerprints they had found on the sparse furniture, which was now covered with the fine grey dust they had applied from a small pair of bellows.

Miranda looked out at the ruined castle on the island of Sancti Petri, and asked Fragela about the tower he could see at the southern end.

'It's a lighthouse, Inspector, one of the many along this coast from Cape Saint Vincent to Tarifa. It emits a white light at sixteen-second intervals which is visible for up to twelve sea-miles. It's checked periodically by the Marine Division, who send men out there by launch.'

'Does anyone live on the island?' asked Miranda.

'No, not nowadays. The castle was constructed in the late sixteenth century to protect the entrance to this channel. The local tradition has it that it was built on the site of the Temple of Tyrian Hercules, where one of the two great pillars stood. The old official history of Cadiz claims that the other pillar stood on the west side of Cadiz, near La Caleta, where the Santa Catalina fort is now. The pillar here was described by the Roman and Arab historians as being surmounted by a large golden statue of Hercules holding a club in one hand and a bunch of keys in the other, with the words *Non plus ultra* inscribed beneath. That island was then called Heracleum.'

'Why was it later called Sancti Petri?' asked Miranda.

'They say it's because of the keys in Hercules's hand on the statue. When a Christian religious house was founded in the ruins of the pagan temple, the figure was identified with St Peter.'

'And when were the pillars demolished?' asked Lista.

'It's said that they were pulled down during the Viking raids along the coast. The pillars had acted as landmarks for their longships to navigate by.'

'You're a student of local history, I see, Fragela,' commented Miranda.

'My wife dragged me along to a series of lectures at the University last winter,' Fragela said, smiling.

Varga now joined them and politely declined the offer of the remaining *bocadillo*, which consisted of a large hunk of omelette pressed between a quarter of a *pistola* or long Vienna loaf.

'I think the tide's low enough for us to make a start,' he commented to Miranda. 'The mud's clear of water at the edge of the mole.'

The group of police officers and Civil Guards donned the gum-boots, which reached to their upper thighs, and walked to the small beach of grey sand east of the wooden jetty in order to gain access to the piers beneath. The sun appeared to be setting behind the racing dirty-white clouds, and Varga led the way with a powerful torch, which he shone along the first row of piers nearest to the muddy water of the channel.

'There's nothing along this first row,' shouted Varga to the others as he proceeded to enter the second row of piers, where much less natural light penetrated.

Again the careful search proved fruitless, but as the small party turned into the third and final row of rotting wooden posts, which were festooned with seaweed and encrusted with limpets and periwinkles, a macabre sight confronted them. From one of the high cross-beams a corpse was suspended, its heavy boots bent backwards more than a metre from the sandy floor, with sea-water dripping slowly from its clothing. The rope extended upwards from the neck to a high beam over which it rested to descend to the dead man's ankles where it was firmly tied, so that the body swung forward at an acute angle. The head was twisted grotesquely to the left, half-concealing the knot in the heavy noose that encircled the neck, and the staring eyes extruded from the sockets in a deathly grimace.

Varga reached up to feel for a pulse at the right wrist as the small group of policemen looked on aghast.

'He's been dead for many hours,' said Varga. 'Would you call my assistant to bring down the tripod camera, Inspector? I suggest we follow the usual procedure and leave him as he is until the chief and Dr Peláez can be sent for.'

'Can you identify him?' Miranda asked Captain Barba, who was obviously much shaken by the sight.

'Yes, that's Ramos all right. He was an excellent sergeant, Inspector. My father used to serve with him at Conil back in the Thirties. I hope we get to find the bastards who did this to him.'

'You don't think it could be a case of suicide, then?' Lista asked him.

'Suicide? Ramos? Never! He was too tough an old bird to succumb to that.'

'It must have been a lonely life for him, though, out here at Sancti Petri,' commented Lista.

'But that's what he liked about it,' said Barba. 'After his wife's death he asked to be transferred here. He ⚬sed to study the movements of the migratory birds that stop over in these salt-pans on their way to and from North Africa.'

'I noticed some ornithological books on the shelf in his cabin,' said Varga.

'He said this place was the perfect hide from which to

observe the sea-birds,' added Barba. 'He was the last person to get depressed at being on his own most of the time. He was completely self-sufficient, and he used to come into Chiclana three evenings a week to play *tute* with his cronies in the back room of the Bar Alameda. Shouldn't we cut him down before the tide comes in again?'

'We will, but not yet,' said Miranda. 'Lista has gone to send a message over the car radio to Comisario Bernal, and he'll want to see everything exactly as we've found it. How long have we got before high water?' he asked Fragela.

'At least four hours before the water reaches this part, and the Superintendent should get here in about half an hour.'

Bernal returned from his interview with the suffragan bishop feeling somewhat better informed about the House of the Palm and its strange activities, but the bishop had not been able to throw any light on the hidden well in the Holy Cave under the convent church nor on the curious properties of the water that periodically issued from it. The prelate had suggested to him the name of a local archæologist whom Bernal might care to consult about the matter.

In the ops room he found that Inspectora Elena Fernández had arrived, as usual dressed with exquisite taste in a Courrèges pastel-toned woollen creation.

'My father drove me over from Sotogrande, chief,' she said as she greeted him. 'It's nice to get back to work. The weather's cold and dull there and my mother does nothing but go to bingo with her rich friends in the luxury hotel down the road from our chalet. It's much too boring for me.'

'Navarro will brief you about this case, Elena, but I've got a little job for you to do. How would you like to enter a convent for a few days, just for Holy Week, and find out what's going on there?'

Elena looked astounded, but said she looked forward to this new experience.

'Has my wife ever met you, or talked to you on the phone?'

'We've never met, *jefe*, but we talked once on the phone

some months ago. We didn't have much of a conversation.' She was obviously puzzled by the question.

'I'd better fill you in: my wife is doing spiritual exercises in a weird convent called the House of the Palm in the Calle de la Concepción up in the old city here, and there have been some strange goings-on. I think we can risk your going there under your own name, together with a letter of introduction from Father Anselmo in Madrid. The letter should get here by tomorrow morning. Don't reveal your profession to anyone in the convent, but you'd be free to talk about your parents and family background. You could confide in my wife in an emergency, but I'm hoping to arrange a communications contact for you with one of the women who visits the convent every evening for the vigil.'

'All right, chief, I'll do it. Will I need different clothes?'

'No, you'll be perfectly in character as you are. They'll expect you to be well dressed. I'll brief you more fully in the morning before you present yourself there.'

Dr Peláez now arrived from the Hospital Mora with his autopsy report on the dead frogman and the infra-red photographs of the tattooed mark found on the right forearm of the deceased.

'The man was definitely a Berber, Luis, and the tattoo on his arm is in Arabic. I don't know what it means. The most unusual feature is the cause of death.' Bernal pricked up his ears. 'His heart was stopped by some kind of high-frequency beam, probably a laser beam. I've read an article about injuries from lasers in laboratories, which were thought to be mainly of overheating, but now it's appreciated that three other biological changes may occur: photo-chemical, thermo-acoustic and electrical. The injury in this case resembles the thermo-acoustic type of injury caused by shock waves from an intense pinpoint of light which can rupture tissue. I'll leave you and Varga to inquire into where such a weapon might be available.'

'I suspect the Americans at Rota,' said Bernal. 'The Commander at the base there was definitely holding something back when we interviewed him.'

Navarro rushed in from the outer office. 'We've had a

radio message from Lista, *jefe*. They've found the retired Marine sergeant hanged beneath the wooden jetty at Sancti Petri.'

'We'll leave at once,' said Bernal. 'Fetch your bag of tricks, Peláez.'

Varga and the local Civil Guards had fixed up arc-lamps powered by a small generator in the technicians' van, so that by the time Bernal and Peláez reached the scene in the rapidly gathering dusk the piers and cross-beams beneath the jetty at Sancti Petri were illuminated by a stark white light. After making a thorough inspection, Bernal called the others up to the shelter of the dead sergeant's cabin to allow the pathologist and the technician a clear field to work in.

'They'll call us if they need assistance,' Bernal said to Miranda. 'We'll have to recover the body soon, before the tide starts coming in.'

Bernal questioned Captain Barba in detail about the deceased's known habits and his likely state of mind. 'From what you say, Barba, it seems most unlikely that he killed himself, despite the fact that most cases of this nature turn out to be suicide. You saw that there was a lower beam on which he could have balanced while throwing the rope over the upper cross-beam and before tying it to his ankles?'

'But that seems a very rare and complicated way of hanging oneself, Superintendent,' objected Barba. 'Admittedly I've only seen some local cases here, but none were carried out like this one.'

'You may be right,' allowed Bernal, 'but the upper beam across which the rope was slung would have been too high for him to reach without a ladder. And there's no sign of one here. There would have been no alternative to slinging the rope up and over the beam and catching it the other side. Then where could he have secured the end of the rope away from the noose except to his ankles?'

'He could have tied it round the lower beam, on which he was standing,' said Lista. 'But then he would have risked leaving too much slack, perhaps.'

'That's just it,' objected Miranda. 'Either there would be

too small a drop and he wouldn't achieve the desired result, or it would be too great and his feet would touch the floor.'

'Much will depend on whether he died by strangulation, which could have taken some hours,' said Bernal, quickly noting Captain Barba's distress at his words, 'or whether he died by a rapid fracture of the cervical vertebræ and the spinal cord.' He turned to Barba and suggested he go out and call Chiclana, to see whether the judge of instruction was on his way.

'We'll have to cut him down soon, chief,' said Miranda.

'I'll be interested to see what Varga finds out about the rope fibres,' said Bernal. 'At least he'll be able to tell how much of the rope ran over the edge of the beam as the deceased dropped. How heavy would you say he was?'

'Very stockily built, with quite a paunch,' said Lista. 'I'd guess his weight at around ninety kilos.'

'And what would be a rough estimate of the drop?'

'Just over two metres, chief.'

Bernal took out a small gold-plated ballpoint pen and did a mathematical calculation in his notebook. After a while he looked up in puzzlement.

'If you're right about Ramos's weight and the falling distance, Lista, then his head should have been wrenched off. I make it a striking force of almost one thousand eight hundred kilos. Varga and Peláez will check the weight and distance accurately later, of course, and they'll check with the standard Table of Drops. Peláez will also tell us if there's a fracture dislocation of the vertebræ, which I'd certainly expect in this case.'

Varga now returned from the scene of the hanging and asked Bernal whether they could take down the body from the beam before the tide rose again. 'I've put markers on the rope at various positions, *jefe*, and we've photographed the knots, which we'll leave in place. It's a particularly thick weave of hemp and nylon, so I'll have to get the large cutters from the van.'

'We'll give the judge ten more minutes to get here, Varga. If he isn't here by then, I'll authorize the recovery of the corpse.'

Bernal stood in the doorway of the small cabin, and

shivered in the strong evening breeze from the east, glad he'd brought his camel-hair coat. He lit a Kaiser between cupped hands and pondered on the two cases. He felt sure they must be connected. The North African frogman's disastrous incursion into Rota harbour on or about 21 March couldn't have been an unsupported operation. He must have had a back-up team who assisted him to get into the military base if he approached from the sea, which seemed the most likely way. The land defences on each side of the harbour made it improbable that he had swum out from the public beaches at the Playa de la Vieja to the west of the port or from the fishing port itself, because the distance involved was too great. According to Rear Admiral Soto, any surface craft or submarine of metallic construction would have been detected by the passive sonar at the harbour mouth, and only a wooden or fibreglass boat would have a chance of getting through the electronic defences. But perhaps Soto was reasoning badly: if the frogman had been a specially trained member of a North African navy underwater team, he would surely have been brought into Cadiz Bay as near as possible to Rota by a naval craft—a small submarine would have been the thing, thought Bernal—which would have awaited his return or arranged to pick him up at a fixed time. But he had not returned, and that might mean that the undercover operation had been detected by the Americans, who had taken appropriate defensive measures.

Which of the three countries of the Maghreb would have the capability to mount such an operation and why? He recalled reading in the press that Morocco, Algeria and Tunisia had recently held a summit meeting and had pledged themselves to a future federation of the Maghreb, which the newspaper commentators had considered designed to annoy their neighbours, particularly Libya to the east and Mauritania to the south. When Franco was on his deathbed in November 1975, the Spanish Council of Regency, faced with the threat of the 'Green March', had ceded the Spanish Sahara in great haste to Morocco, and since then relations with that country had been reasonably cordial, despite the periodic demands for the cession of the remaining Spanish enclaves of Ceuta and Melilla. It was noticeable how the timing of these demands seemed to coincide with internal problems in Morocco, just as the Caudillo had used the bugbear of Gibraltar to distract public attention whenever the political scene required it.

Now, Bernal asked himself, what possible interest could the Moroccans have in the Rota base? The USSR and the Warsaw Pact countries had an intense interest in it, of course, and the American Commander had commented to him on the frequent spying activities there by those powers. But Morocco had recently agreed a very favourable bilateral defence treaty with the USA: what possible reason could she have for spying on her new ally's joint base across the Strait? He would have to have a full discussion with Soto and the naval political advisers at San Fernando. Yet he was convinced that the meaning of the dead frogman was that the Rota defences had been penetrated, but unsuccessfully; somehow the incursor had been neutralized. Did the Spanish Defence Ministry really want him to find out how?

Then there was the hanged Marine sergeant now swaying grotesquely beneath where Bernal stood. He had reported by radio to his HQ certain mysterious light signals off the island of Sancti Petri, had recognized some of the Morse letters used, and had passed the information on. By the next day he had disappeared and by the evening had been found hanged. Once Peláez had completed the autopsy and Varga had examined the forensic evidence, they should be able to tell him the cause of death and the approximate time at which it had occurred. The *terminus a quo* was 1.12 a.m. when Ramos had last reported in. Bernal was inclined to think that this was not a case of suicide. There was too much of a coincidence in the timing between his observation of the clandestine signalling and his demise. His radio message could have been intercepted and immediate action taken to silence him.

Bernal wondered grimly what had occurred on this rickety wooden mole in the strong wind and lonely darkness of the night. Miranda and his searchers had found no sign of a struggle in the cabin or outside it. What else had Ramos seen which he hadn't had a chance to report and which necessitated, perhaps, his elimination? Surely the intruders wouldn't think that the post would be left unmanned after Ramos's disappearance or apparent suicide was discovered? Or did they? If so, then their activities must involve Sancti Petri, which was the back door, as it were, to the arsenal at La Carraca. But the rear admiral had said that the Sancti Petri channel wasn't navigable by any naval craft except a small launch. Such a craft would have been at risk of being spotted further up the channel at the road bridges and by the marines guarding the Bazán dockyard and La Carraca itself. And why should the North African intruders want to enter the Spanish bases clandestinely? To test their defences? It seemed unimaginable that any of the countries of the Maghreb could have either the resources or the desire to attack the Spanish mainland bases.

Bernal's musings were soon interrupted by the arrival of an official car bringing the judge of instruction from Chiclana, and of the mortuary van. Captain Barba of the Civil Guard introduced Bernal to the keen-eyed local magistrate, who listened to a rapid summary of the circumstances and read Bernal's official orders from the Ministry with solemn gravity. He at once authorized the cutting down of the body and its removal to the Cadiz hospital mortuary for an official autopsy to be performed.

The Civil Guards assisted Bernal's team to lift the body on to a stretcher, and it was then enclosed, with the noose still around the neck and the rope tied to his ankles, in a fibreglass tube, which Peláez sealed. Before they left for Cadiz, Bernal spoke to Captain Barba. 'Could you arrange for some of your men to guard the cabin and keep watch by night and day? They'd better be well armed.'

'Of course, Superintendent. I'll arrange them in shifts of four. These men can complete the first turn of duty, and I'll send a relief team at eleven p.m.'

'Tell them to watch out for any craft in the channel or in the approaches to Sancti Petri island, and issue them with infra-red binoculars if they're available. I want them to watch for signalling from the sea and any answering signals from the land. Would it be possible to fix up a land-line to Chiclana? It would be preferable if they didn't report in by radio, in case the messages are intercepted.'

'I'll see what can be done, Superintendent. The Navy people may be able to help us.'

Early on the Tuesday morning of Holy Week, in their temporary operations room Bernal and Navarro were examining the photographs of the frogman's tattooed arm while awaiting the arrival of the Arabist from the University.

'What time did he say he'd be here, Fragela?' Bernal asked the local inspector.

'At nine o'clock, Superintendent.'

'While we're waiting, perhaps you could get in touch with the harbour master and the chief customs officer in the port here and inquire about the movements of North African vessels and traders. You could try Jerez airport as well, Fragela; I recall seeing a couple of light planes there with Moroccan markings.'

'The Immigration Department will have the cards filled in by passengers entering the port, Comisario,' commented Fragela. 'Shall I ask them to dig out those relating to all North African visitors?'

'Can they do that easily?'

'We're computerized now, Comisario, and I believe they will have been put into the data bank here. Then the computer could cross-check them with the central records in Madrid. That would turn up those with a record of illegal activity.'

'It would be useful if you could run a check on those entering and leaving the country within the last fifteen days, say. I suppose you should include all Moroccan, Algerian and Tunisian nationals.'

'Jerez airport should be easy to check, Comisario. It's all computerized there.'

'What an amazing advance Records have made in a few years,' commented Bernal. 'When I was younger, we used

79

to have to plough through all those cards filled in at the ports, which weren't kept for more than six months. But this brings a completely new approach to detective work, and we'll need men with a different training from my generation's. It really involves rethinking the way one goes about an investigation, especially because of the speed with which thousands of record cards and report sheets can be cross-checked. Perhaps I should apply for early retirement.'

'Don't say that, chief,' protested Navarro. 'All the computers in the world would be useless unless someone is capable of formulating the right questions and interpreting the replies intelligently.'

'That's all very well, but I still think I need to be trained in the capabilities of computerized police investigation if I'm going to carry on in the profession.'

'It can certainly save a lot of leg-work, Superintendent,' commented Fragela. 'I've seen that in a number of recent cases here.'

'Yet surely there's no substitute for examining the scene of crime, and wandering about the streets of a city or the countryside to get the feel of a case,' said Bernal. 'That's how I've always worked. People may call it intuition, but in reality it's passive observation at work. You don't consciously record every tiny detail your eyes take in, every face you scan, every grouping of objects you peruse, but later that passive memory can react with some newly acquired, urgent piece of information, and lead you to a solution.'

The phone rang and Navarro picked it up. 'It's Dr Peláez for you, chief, from the mortuary.'

'How goes it, Peláez?' asked Bernal. He listened gravely for a time. 'I see. I expected something of the sort. It was too much of a coincidence. I look forward to seeing the full report.'

He put the phone down and turned to his colleagues, with signs of growing excitement. 'It's a murder case, as I suspected. Peláez says that the retired Marine sergeant Ramos was strangled with a fine cord by an assailant attacking from behind and was then strung up with a thick rope tied into a noose to simulate a self-suspension. He expects

Varga and the technical team will be able to verify his conclusions from the state of the rope. The sea-water has complicated matters for him, because when the tide rose yesterday morning the hanging corpse became waterlogged. That fact is making it more difficult to calculate the approximate time of death, but he says that the deceased's wristwatch had stopped at five thirty-seven. What time was high water at Sancti Petri yesterday morning, Fragela?'

The local inspector consulted a tide-table. 'At seven fifty-six a.m., Comisario.'

'H'm. Varga will have to measure the heights of tide relative to the position of the hanging body and the right wrist of the deceased, but I think we can work on the hypothesis that Ramos was killed within four hours of his last radio report at one-twelve a.m.'

'That suggests that the vessel he saw signalling put in at Sancti Petri quay,' said Navarro, 'since it disappeared from the radar screens soon after the time of his report.'

'But in that case why wasn't it observed again later on, after Ramos had been disposed of?' objected Bernal. 'It could mean that the mysterious vessel intercepted Ramos's radio message to his Control Centre at Chiclana, and then sent a message to their accomplices on land to go to Sancti Petri and deal with Ramos. Then the craft makes off to the open sea, or even, perhaps, submerges, if it was a submarine. After all, the people on it were signalling to someone on shore for some purpose still unknown to us.'

Just as coffee was brought in, the Arabic expert arrived from the Faculty and introductions were made by Fragela.

'Dr de Castro is well known for his lectures on the history of Cadiz, Comisario. He is a great-grandson of the famous historian of the city.'

'I understand you know Arabic, Doctor,' Bernal said politely.

'Mainly Classical, I'm afraid, Superintendent. I took my degree in Oriental Studies at the University of Granada.'

'Will the script have changed in Modern Arabic?' asked Bernal.

'No, but there may be words I'm not familiar with.'

'It's only a question of a few letters. Perhaps you'd care to look at this photograph. It's not very clear, but it's the best our photographer could do.'

Dr de Castro looked carefully at the enlargement of the tattoo on the dead frogman's forearm. 'They are certainly Arabic characters but they are rather blurred. From the bluish tint they look like part of a tattoo.' He looked up at Bernal questioningly.

'Very observant of you, Doctor,' said Bernal. 'Now what do they mean?'

'Nothing that strikes me immediately, Superintendent. There are five consonants, and no diacritic points, so we'd have to guess at the missing vowels. The first would be transliterated into Roman script as an M, then there's an L, then a guttural KH or Q.' He puzzled further over the blurred photograph. 'I can't think of any obvious or common Arabic root composed of those characters,' he said slowly. 'The last two seem to be an R and a T.' He looked up again. 'Could it be someone's name, perhaps? That's the sort of thing people have tattooed on their arms. But nothing occurs to me for the moment. May I take a copy away and look up some dictionaries of Modern Arabic?'

'Of course, Doctor. I'd be very glad if you could throw some light on this mystery for us. It may help to identify the person concerned. You will keep the inquiry secret, won't you? In particular it would be unwise to discuss the matter with any native speakers of Arabic.'

'Of course not. I'm happy to be of some assistance.'

After the slightly stooped, scholarly figure of Dr de Castro had departed, Bernal sat looking quietly pleased, and lit up a Kaiser. After a while he turned to Navarro and Fragela: 'I think we're getting somewhere.'

'Really, chief?' asked Navarro in some surprise.

'At least we've got a definite link between the two deaths, don't you see? That little fact, although we don't yet know what it signifies, will shape the whole inquiry.'

Inspectora Elena Fernández sat on the uncomfortable edge of her truckle-bed in the small cell on the upper floor of the

House of the Palm, wondering at the odd places her police work was taking her to. At least the small barred window overlooked the street at the front of the convent; she had gathered from the kindly Sister Encarnación who had shown her up to her cell that this floor was reserved for the female lay visitors. Elena looked at the simple brown woollen habit hanging from the wardrobe door and made a grimace: it wouldn't be very becoming for someone with her ideas of fashion, but Father Sanandrés, in the brief interview she had had with him on arrival, had suggested that it would be appropriate for the lay persons living in to adopt the humble dress of a novice while carrying out their spiritual exercises. He had accepted her letter of introduction without demur, and inquired in kindly terms about her father's health, though she was sure that they weren't acquainted; it was merely that the reference Bernal had obtained for her mentioned her father's importance as one of the heads of the construction industry—perhaps Father Sanandrés harboured hopes of a large donation to his peculiar Order.

This self-appointed prior, curiously dressed as a bishop, had struck her as a weird fanatic; he had railed against Vatican II and the new reforms within the Church, and had uttered extreme strictures about the dangers of the modern secular state. In religion she concluded that he was a follower of Cardinal Lefèbvre and in politics she placed him well to the right of the late General Franco. When she asked him about the Order of the Palm, he claimed it was merely a refounding of an older religious house that had once existed on the same site, and that its rule was based on that of the Premonstratensians.

In the quietude of the cell, she settled down to study the pamphlet of guidelines for lay visitors, and noted that she would be expected to attend the celebration of the canonical hours seven times a day with the religious brethren and sisters in the chapel. Meals would be served in the refectory after Prime, Sext and Compline, and no meat would be served in Holy Week until Easter Saturday evening. She could take part in the penitential processions each day if she wished and felt in a proper state of contrition: Father

83

Sanandrés would himself confess her if she desired. The rest of her time would be free for contemplation, but she might wish to assist the sisters in their domestic chores and other duties from time to time.

Elena got up and looked through the small barred window down to the narrow Calle de la Concepción and wondered how she could establish a secure means of communication with the police operations room in the Avenida de Andalucía. Superintendent Bernal had told her to be sure to be on hand when the women arrived each afternoon for the Diurnal Adoration: he would try to arrange a contact through one of them. The only alternative would be for her to take part as a barefoot penitent in one of the processions when a *paso* left the convent, and then when she was out try to get to a telephone.

Elena took off her expensive Courrèges outfit and hung it up in the tiny wardrobe with feelings of regret. The brown habit felt rough and unpleasant to the touch—more like sackcloth than merino wool, she thought—but she quickly donned it and tied the hempen girdle round her waist, then slipped her feet into a pair of blue *alpargatas* or rope-soled sandals. She saw she had half an hour to spare before Terce, and stepped quietly out into the corridor, the windows of which overlooked the larger of the two quadrangles. Far below her she could glimpse Father Sanandrés, attired in bishop's garb just as she had seen him earlier, engaged in earnest conversation with two army officers—a colonel and a captain, as far as she could judge from the insignia on their khaki caps. She was too high up to overhear them, though their voices resonated in the quiet of the palm-filled cloister. She decided to descend to the ground floor in order to get closer to them.

Inspector Ángel Gallardo, having installed himself in a clean *pensión* near the fishing port of Rota, was in his favourite ambience, a smoke-filled bar on the waterfront. The long glass-topped counter displayed an enormous variety of local seafood, as well as a selection of meat and vegetable *tapas*. The floor was nearly ankle-deep in prawn shells, olive stones, wet cigar- and cigarette-butts, crumpled and stained paper napkins and torn, unsuccessful tote-tickets; the noise of the harsh voices of the fishermen was deafening.

Ángel beamed with contentment as he bought a round of *copitas* of the local *manzanilla* for a group of five fishermen, who were glad to accept the hospitality of the talkative *madrileño* tourist and pour out their discontent with the Moroccan authorities and their scorn at the Calvo Sotelo Government's gutless attempts to get them a better agreement to fish off the African coast. They had refused to fish for four days because one of their friends' boats was being held captive at Tangiers.

Ángel encouraged their chatter, ordered a portion of oysters fried in batter and slowly began to turn the conversation to the Russian trawlers. One of the older, more weatherbeaten fishermen, dressed in a tight blue-and-white striped T-shirt which heightened the pronounced musculature of his torso, laughed loudly at Ángel's query.

'We see them nearly every night, usually two of them together, and they'd don't do any trawling, I can tell you. They're no competition to us. They're fishing for other catches, with that mass of aerials they mount in the rigging. Their crews are quite cheerful when we get in close, and they've thrown us a bottle of vodka now and then—the best Russian kind. The Americans send out a corvette to chase them off if they come in too close.'

'What about the sub that nearly capsized the *Estrella del Mar*, Eusebio? You remember that?' asked one of the younger men. Ángel pricked up his ears.

'A funny business, that. A few weeks back, on a Saturday night, it was. We'd been fishing with the *Estrella* off Cape Spartel, west of Tangiers, and we both took on good catches. We left the Moroccan coast before their fishery protection vessel spotted us and made like the clappers for home. We put our lights on as we left African waters, and as we entered the outer Bay here, the *Estrella*, which was three hundred metres abaft us, was suddenly lifted out of the water by what they thought was a whale. It was a damned good job they didn't have nets out or there would have been a hell of a tangle.'

'And what was it?' asked the youngest of the seamen. 'The sub, I mean.'

'We never found out. It was a small black job, not much more that four metres long and a metre and a half wide, and it surfaced right under the *Estrella*, nearly turning her arse over tip. It sped off out to sea at a hell of a lick, at about thirty knots, Joselito estimated. It was so small that it couldn't have had a crew of more than four or five. But the power of the thing was fantastic. The Americans must have been trying it out in the Bay, but I've never seen one like it surfaced in the daytime.'

The conversation naturally turned to the American base and to how life had changed in Rota since the Yanks arrived in 1953.

'It's brought a lot of money to the town, you must admit,' said one of the younger men.

'But the fishing's never been the same,' objected Eusebio, the older man. 'The best times here were in the Forties and Fifties when food was scarce and we got good prices for our catches. Now all these underwater sonar devices and antisubmarine nets frighten the fish and make it hard for us to get in and out of the harbour, not to speak of the bloody Africans when we do get out.'

This brought them back to their current preoccupations, but Ángel thought he had got something of great interest to Bernal.

Elena Fernández had gained the shelter of a large date-palm in the northern walk of the main cloister of the House of the Palm, and sat on a marble bench fingering a rosary and pretending to read a small book of hours bound in white parchment. She was getting used to the roughness of the sackcloth, and was indeed glad of the protection it afforded from the coldness of the seat. She was well screened by some large terracotta pots filled with madonna lilies and scarlet amaryllis, the intense scent of which made her feel faint.

The silence was broken only by a silvery tinkling from a

fountain shaped like an angel holding a trumpet to its mouth from which the thin, intermittent stream issued forth; beneath its light echo she could just catch the lowered voices of Father Sanandrés and the two army officers, who were holding a peripatetic conversation, and she hoped they would stroll in her direction. She had a clear view of the archway at either end of the north walk, which did not seem to be as much frequented by the religious members of the house as the southern one that connected the main vestibule with the chapel.

As the masculine voices drew nearer, she huddled into the corner of the marble bench, trying to look even more intent on her devotions. At last she was able to make out a few words: '. . . castle of Santa Catalina . . . night operation . . . safe place . . .', and then whole sentences, which she thought were uttered by the older of the two officers, who was a colonel:

'The whole thing's been a scandal, of course. The head of the JUJEM shouldn't have interfered. And the attitude of the police was nothing short of treasonable.'

Elena could catch Father Sanandrés making deprecating murmurs.

'Well, Father, Saturday evening after dark would seem to be the best time, just when the garrison will be least defended because of the holiday weekend.'

'Won't they put up road-blocks at once?' Elena heard the younger officer ask.

'Of course, that's why we must fox them by not leaving the city for another week at least. How about it, Father?'

'You mean here? But that would be very dangerous!' The prior sounded very alarmed, Elena judged. 'There are frequent visitors and some lay people living in, at least until next Monday. One of them's the wife of a Comisario from Madrid.'

'But our chaps would appear to be just two more lay visitors, Father,' said the colonel wheedlingly. 'There'd be no problem.'

'Their faces are well known since the trial,' objected Father Sanandrés. 'They've been seen on television and the

87

newspapers have published photographs of them.'

'They could just stay in their cells for a week, and then we'll get them out by sea.'

This secret conversation, so fascinating to Elena's ears, began to fade as the three speakers turned their backs on the spot where she was half-crouching, and much to her disappointment they soon left the cloister in the direction of the prior's room. She looked at her watch and decided she just had time to go back up to her cell and write a brief but urgent report for Superintendent Bernal before she would be called to the chapel for Nones.

Apparently observed by no one, Elena reached her small room and shut the door and bolted it behind her. When she opened the wardrobe door to get her suitcase out, she had the faint impression that the clothes she had hung there had been moved slightly. She went to the drawers of the dressing-table and examined the underclothes she had placed there earlier. Again there were signs of disturbance. Had her things been gone over while she was downstairs? She went back anxiously to the wardrobe and took out the suitcase and placed it on the truckle-bed. She unlocked the case which was ostensibly empty, and looked carefully at the lining. Inserting a second key into the underside of the handle, she pulled at the silk lining-straps and the inner part of the base snapped open. She sighed with relief: the searcher had not found this false compartment in the suitcase Bernal had provided, where there was a supply of writing paper and envelopes, a small Derringer pistol, a powerful electric torch, an electronic device for listening through walls, a pair of night-glasses, a micro cassette-recorder and a miniature Rolleiflex camera so small, it fitted into her hand.

After taking out a sheet of paper and an envelope, Elena closed the secret compartment, relocked it, and returned the case to the wardrobe. She sat down at the small table under the barred window, feeling cheered by the street noises which increased as the shops began to reopen at 5.30 after the siesta. She soon became engrossed in writing her report, and failed to hear the well-oiled *mirilla* or judas-hole being opened softly from the corridor, nor did she notice the cold eye observing her.

Superintendent Bernal and Inspector Lista sat in an unmarked green Renault 4 which they had parked in the wider, upper section of the Calle de Jesús Nazareno, whence they could keep observation on the Convent of the Palm. Bernal sighed with impatience. 'They're sure to start turning up soon, Lista. This was the time I saw them here on Saturday. It's essential that we arrange a contact for Elena as soon as possible. If I can spot the woman I have in mind before she reaches the convent door, it won't attract anyone's attention.'

'Do you think she will be trustworthy, *jefe?*'

'I hope so. I chatted to her for a while the other day, and she seemed a level-headed sort, especially if we offer to pay her for her services.'

Just then a tall, large-boned figure came into sight, walking towards them from the lower, poorer part of the town.

'That's her, Lista. Get out and talk to her now. Show her your badge and bring her to the car. She'll recognize me, I'm sure.'

Bernal could see Lista having an animated interchange with the tall woman, who was waving her empty bottle at him. She approached the car with obvious suspicion and distrust, and looked at Bernal through the wound-down window.

'Hey, mister! What's all this about?' The lower-class Barcelona accent was strongly marked. 'I ain't done nothing. You're a copper, aren't yer? I got to find out from Sister Serena. She tells us who those lay visitors are. The old dame who orders us around in there is your missus, ain't she?'

'Yes, all that's perfectly correct. Now as far as I know you haven't done anything wrong. It's just that I've got a little job for you, which is completely legal, and will be well paid.'

The Catalan woman's interest increased and her attitude

changed immediately. 'Well, why didn't yer say so? What do I have to do?'

'First of all, keep your mouth shut about it. Say nothing to anyone, you understand?'

'OK, I promise. What do I do?'

'Bring out a letter as required from the convent without anyone seeing you.'

'Is that all? How much do I get?'

Bernal calculated an amount not too high to arouse her suspicions and not too low for her to betray him. 'A thousand pesetas each time.'

She narrowed her eyes, obviously wondering whether to haggle for more. 'How far do I have to take it? Shoe-leather's expensive, y'know.'

'Where do you live?' asked Bernal.

'Down in La Viña, in the Calle de San Félix.'

'Do you have a telephone at home?'

'Yer must be joking,' she cackled. 'How could a poor fisherman's wife afford the rental on a phone?'

'The Calle de San Félix, you say?' mused Bernal. 'Isn't the Restaurant El Faro there?'

'Yeah, it's just down the street.'

'That's splendid. Whenever you are given a letter to bring to me, go to your street as usual when you leave the convent, and call this number from a 'phone-box or a neighbourhood bar.' He wrote out the 'phone number for her. 'Ask for Inspector Navarro. He'll tell you at what time to go into the bar of El Faro and hand the letter over to Inspector Lista here. He'll then pay you the thousand pesetas.'

'OK, it's a deal. Your wife will give me the letter, I suppose?'

'No, I don't expect so. It will be a young lady, Señorita Fernández.' He showed her a photograph of Elena. 'Make sure no one sees you talking to her or taking the note from her.'

'What are they up to in there, eh?' She nudged Bernal suggestively. 'Not keeping a disorderly house, are they? Always thought it odd with nuns, monks and bishops all mixed up in there. But my husband says, "Let's give it a go. You always wanted kiddies." My sister conceived after drinking the water from that old spring before the convent was reopened. So what 'ave I got to lose?' She shrugged her shoulders in a gesture of resignation. 'Mind, can't say it's done me any good so far, but with 'im at sea every night, it isn't likely to, eh?' She nudged Bernal again, and cackled loudly. 'Still, if it'll bring in a thousand pesetas now and then, I'll keep taking the monks' holy water, whatever's in it.

'Now how will this señorita know I'm to be the postman?' she asked.

'I've told her to look out for you this afternoon,' said Bernal.

'Hey, you knew I'd take it on, didn't yer? I should've asked yer for double.'

As she strode up the street with mannish gait, Lista watched her with some misgiving. 'Are you certain she won't mess it up, chief, by talking to the other women or to the nuns?'

Not she!' said Bernal confidently. 'Not unless Father Sanandrés offers her more, and with luck he won't find out what she's up to. The Catalans are like clams where money's concerned. It'll work like a charm, you'll see.'

When leaving the fisherman's bar facing the harbour at Rota, Inspector Ángel Gallardo made his way to a 'phone-box to report in to his colleague Paco Navarro. While still talking to Navarro, he noticed through the window of the kiosk a large Cadillac with Arabic number-plates draw up outside the elegant hotel across the square, and four burnoused figures emerge from it and make for the red-carpeted steps leading to the foyer.

'Didn't the chief want the movements of all Arab nationals checked, Paco?' he inquired. 'Well, a posh car has just driven up and deposited four of them in the four-star hotel in the main square here.'

'No harm in your finding out who they are, Ángel, and what they're up to.'

'It's a pity I haven't got an unmarked K-car here, Paco. They may go off somewhere else.'

'If you need back-up, give me another ring. I'll talk to the local inspector, Fragela, and see what K-car facilities they possess in Cadiz.'

Ángel walked nonchalantly into the hotel lounge and made his way to the almost deserted cocktail-bar to the right of the reception desk. He ordered a San Francisco, thinking he'd better keep a clear head, and began to chat to the young barman. There was no sign of the four Arabs, who had presumably gone up to their rooms.

After exchanging some pleasantries, particularly concerning the two young girls at Reception, Ángel asked casually about the number of guests during Holy Week.

'It's not like it used to be,' said the barman, 'but some American officers come here with their wives when they're over on a visit. They give terrific tips. I don't think they understand our money half the time. Mostly they just use dollars.'

'What about the Arabs?' asked Ángel casually. 'Do they give good tips?'

'Not on your life. They never come into the bar. It's said they don't drink alcohol in public, but they bring in their own duty-free stuff from the ferry,' the waiter said with some feeling. 'I never get anything out of them, nor does the chambermaid.'

'Why do they come here?' asked Ángel. 'They don't look like holiday-makers, do they? Are they businessmen?'

'Not according to Marifé in Reception. She's the pretty one who fills out the registration cards for them and has to ask what their profession is, since she can't read the Arabic in their passports, nor the French for that matter. She says they're high-ups over there—big shots from Rabat.'

'Do the same ones come here all the time?'

'I couldn't say. They all look alike to me with their beards and those burnouses. God only knows what they do shut up in their rooms all day.'

'Don't they go out much?'

'Only to the Casino at El Puerto. They're great gamblers, their drivers say, but they don't throw their dirhams about round here.'

92

Ángel realized he wouldn't be able to examine the Arabs' passports or police registration cards in the hotel without breaking his cover, but the local police could be asked to make a routine inspection of the hotel records. He decided to ring Navarro again from the call-box in the street, in case the hotel receptionist listened in to his call.

Superintendent Bernal was reading with considerable interest Ángel Gallardo's phoned-in report on the fishermen's conversation.

'We'll have to request a further interview with the security commander at the Rota base, Paco,' he commented. 'Not only do the Americans appear to have a novel type of anti-personnel weapon which uses a high-power laser beam, but now it seems they've got a new kind of midget submarine which our Navy hasn't been informed about. You'd better ring Rear Admiral Soto at San Fernando and ask him to fix up an appointment.'

'OK, chief, I'll ring him now. What shall I do about Ángel's Arabs? He thinks he'll need back-up if they move out of that hotel in Rota.'

'See what Fragela can provide in the way of K-cars. I'm afraid it will turn out to be a wild-goose chase. The first analyses Fragela brought in show a considerable influx of North African traders through Algeciras, and a number of them come to Cadiz and Jerez on business, but they are mostly small fry. Ángel's Cadillac with the Moroccan number-plates sounds a bit more promising. We might as well let him follow them, and offer him some assistance. I didn't foresee he'd have to do any travelling. Has any message come through from Elena yet?'

'Nothing yet, *jefe*, but Lista is standing by to make contact with the Catalan woman when she rings.'

Elena Fernández had hidden her sealed message for Bernal in the sleeve of her novice's habit, and when the bell rang for Vespers she made her way to the passage that led to the chapel. She knew that Bernal had hoped to arrange a contact through one of the women who visited the convent late each afternoon and she hung back from the chapel doors with considerable impatience.

Father Sanandrés bowed gravely to her as he led the small group of monks through the cloister, and the nuns whispered to her to wait with the lay visitors and sit on the right side of the aisle behind the religious sisters. Elena spotted a stiff-backed figure in a brown habit similar to her own, who had the beaked nose and haughty expression of Doña Carmen Polo, widow of the late dictator, and realized that this must be Señora de Bernal, her chief's wife.

Sister Serena went to unlatch the wicket-gate in the main door to let in the noisy gaggle of women clutching their empty glass jars. 'Now show some respect,' the nun reprimanded them. 'We don't know if the holy water will flow today, and if you aren't careful, it probably won't.'

Elena scanned the faces of the new arrivals anxiously, wondering which of them would attempt to make contact. She was nervous in case an inexperienced amateur would do so too obviously and be spotted by Father Sanandrés or one of the nuns. However, Sister Serena shooed her into the chapel ahead of these daily visitors, and she reluctantly took up her position immediately behind the person she took to be Bernal's wife. As the office began, Elena took surreptitious glances at the women behind her, but none of them appeared to take the slightest interest in her presence.

Elena followed the Vespers office automatically, hardly glancing at her missal, and as Father Sanandrés came to the final words, she began to feel a sense of desperation, and the letter intended for Bernal seemed to burn against her arm under the sleeve of the habit. When the service ended, the women behind her suddenly got up and made for the altar. They pushed forward and craned their heads to look past Father Sanandrés at a glass panel in the floor in front of the altar. High above them loomed a larger-than-life statue of Our Lady of the Palm in majesty, with arms appealingly outstretched, but with that coldly inhuman facial expression commonly imposed by local artists on such images. The two women nearest the altar pressed forward and looked anxiously at Father Sanandrés.

'Is it working, Father? Is it flowing for us?'

The strange figure in purple episcopal vestments stood facing them, with outstretched arms as though transfixed, his head turned to one side in an attitude of prayer. He could be an El Greco portrait of a saint, thought Elena. An eerie mood, almost of being in the presence of a pagan mystery, entered her, increased by her own nervous anticipation, and the sensation was heightened by a sudden coarse cry from the tallest of the lay women, a large-boned creature with chestnut-coloured hair.

'Here it comes, girls! It's starting to flow.'

Some of the others began to utter shouts of encouragement, and finally Father Sanandrés opened his eyes and looked down.

'The miracle has worked once more!' he exclaimed in sepulchral tones. 'Here is the water of life from the living rock!'

He motioned to an acolyte, who descended the steep steps into the cave beneath the altar and soon emerged with a large silver chalice. The women pressed around eagerly and uncorked their bottles. The prior, after uttering a blessing over the cup, poured some of the crystalline liquid into each receptacle held out before him.

Elena slipped out of her pew and made for the door of the chapel while all eyes were upon the unusual ceremony, and soon the tallest of the women emerged from the throng and strolled nonchalantly down the aisle. As she passed, she whispered quite loudly: 'You Señorita Fernández, then?'

Elena nodded and quickly followed her into the passage.

'Got something for me to take, 'ave yer?'

Elena slipped her the envelope and gripped her hand gently, in a gesture of thanks, then returned as unobtrusively as she could to the rear pews of the chapel. No one seemed to have noticed her brief departure.

After telephoning Paco Navarro for the third time and warning him that the four Arabs might visit the new Casino north of El Puerto de Santa María, Ángel sat on a high stool at the counter of a modest bar opposite the four-star hotel, whence he could keep watch and await the K-car which Inspector Fragela was to provide; the vehicle was to be a small red SEAT 500.

While Ángel had been keeping watch on the hotel entrance, a plainclothes sergeant from the Rota Comisaría had gone to the reception desk and made what appeared to be a routine inspection of the registration cards of the guests who had checked in for Holy Week. The girl at Reception, who knew him and was well used to these periodic checks, showed him into the manager's office and handed him the small pile of white cards, as well as four passports.

'I haven't finished filling in the cards for these yet,' she told him. 'I always have trouble with the Arabic ones.'

The sergeant asked if he could use the photocopier, and when she had switched it on for him, she left him to his task. He at once took copies of the four passports belonging to the Moroccan guests who had arrived earlier, just as Fragela had instructed.

Angel, still perched on his stool at the window of the bar opposite, paid him no more than a casual glance when he left the hotel, unaware that through that discreet visit he would shortly be provided with the details about the North African suspects. Almost fifteen minutes later, he noticed the K-car, the small red SEAT, pulling up in the side street alongside the bar. He paid for the three coffees he had drunk, folded his copy of *El País*, which had only arrived from Madrid by the afternoon train, and strode out. He held his official DSE badge open inside the folded newspaper and showed it to the driver of the K-car through the open left-hand window. The *gaditano* greeted his Madrid colleague and opened the right passenger-door for him.

'A bit low-powered, this, isn't it, if we have to chase a Cadillac?' Ángel asked the Cadiz police driver, who like him was attired in T-shirt and jeans.

'It may look low-powered, but the small five-hundred c.c. engine has been replaced by a souped-up job. You'll have to hold on to your sunglasses when we hit the motorway.'

He handed Ángel an envelope he had been told to collect from the Rota Comisaría, and Ángel examined the photocopies of the passports belonging to the four Moroccan visitors, who still hadn't descended from their rooms. He showed the documents to his Cadiz colleague.

'The photos have come out badly, but these are the suspects. How good is your French?'

'I know a bit, because I was stationed in Ceuta for four years.'

'Then you'll know some Arabic as well,' exclaimed Ángel, 'and these passports are printed in Arabic and French.'

'I can't read the script, unfortunately,' confessed the local policeman; 'never could make out those squiggles. But I might manage the French.'

'What occupation does it give for these two? *Marchand de vins*: wouldn't that mean "wine merchant"?'

'Yes, that's it.'

'Doesn't that strike you as an odd profession for Muslims to be engaged in?'

'I don't know about that. A lot of wine was imported into Ceuta, and it wasn't all drunk by our countrymen who live there.'

'What does it say about this chap?' asked Ángel, pointing to the third photocopy. 'Isn't he a pilot officer in the Royal Moroccan Air Force?'

'Yes, that's it,' confirmed the driver. 'Perhaps he piloted the others over; you can see that the entry stamps are dated today at Jerez airport. That must mean they came in by private plane, since there are no international flights to Jerez.'

'And the fourth man is a general trader, apparently,' commented Ángel. 'Now why would an air force officer pilot in two wine merchants and a trader?'

'Perhaps he's related to one of them?' suggested the Cadiz man. 'Of course you can't tell from their names, because of the peculiar system of patronymics over there. They just call themselves "son of so and so", or even "grandson of what's-his-name". I used to think they were all related to one another.'

Just then they observed the hotel doorkeeper waving to the driver of the large Cadillac which was drawn up in the palm-shaded car park, and the four burnoused Arabs appeared at the canopied entrance.

'Here we go,' said Ángel. 'You'd better start up.'

Superintendent Luis Bernal's expression was grave as he read Elena Fernández's first brief report smuggled out of the convent.

'Call Fragela in, would you, Paco?' he asked Navarro. 'He may be able to throw some light on this affair.'

While he waited for the arrival of the local inspector, Bernal studied the large wall plan of the city and noted that the castle of Santa Catalina jutted out in the shape of three points of a pentacle from a small rocky promontory to the west of the old city, alongside the deserted bathing-establishment at La Caleta, not more than half a kilometre or seven or eight streets away from the Convent of the Palm.

When Fragela came in, Bernal invited him and Navarro into his small inner office and shut the door.

'Now, Fragela, tell us what you know about the garrison at Santa Catalina point. Is it large?'

'Not at all. Ten officers and thirty-five men at most. Most of the army garrison is housed up in the old barracks in Dr Gómez Ulla, facing the Parque Genovés. He indicated the group of buildings on the wall map.

'And who is kept prisoner there, at the castle of Santa Catalina, I mean?' inquired Bernal.

'Two of the junior officers convicted at the court-martial in Madrid after the abortive military coup last year, but it's not public knowledge, you understand. The Ministry has scattered those sentenced throughout all the military regions, and it moves them about from time to time.'

'To prevent further plotting, I suppose,' commented Bernal. 'You'd better read this report, Fragela, which has come in from our agent at the Convent of the Palm. You'll see that she overheard two army officers, a colonel and a captain, apparently planning an assault on the Santa Catalina garrison which is to take place on Saturday evening. The conspirators are intending to free the prisoners and were proposing to Father Sanandrés that the convent be used as a safe house.'

Inspector Fragela read the report slowly. 'It wouldn't be easy to bring off,' he commented sceptically. 'There's only one gate into the fort, and the battlements are guarded by armed sentries day and night. The plotters couldn't possibly approach from the sea: any vessel they used would be driven on to the shell-limestone rocks and torn to pieces.'

'But they are counting on the garrison being lightly defended on Easter Saturday evening, when the celebrations begin, and in any case they may have accomplices inside. If they got the prisoners out, how could they best make a getaway from there?' Bernal went back to the wall plan, where he was joined by Fragela and Navarro.

'If the alarm wasn't raised immediately, they'd have a good chance of driving along the Campo del Sur to the Puerta de Tierra, and from there along this wide avenue to the Vía Augusta Julia, or to the José León de Carranza Bridge and across the Bay. If we received immediate warning, we could activate our normal plan of a road-block just this side of the Puerta de Tierra, which effectively seals off the old city, with a further block this side of La Cortadura, which would seal off Cadiz-2 from the Bay. But it would take five or ten minutes to set up, probably.'

Knowing the rate at which Andalusians usually moved, Bernal wondered whether Fragela's estimate was not perhaps over-optimistic.

'Then their proposal to take the freed prisoners to a nearby safe house isn't such a bad one?' he asked. 'Especially if they keep the escapees there for a week or so, until the excitement has died down?'

Fragela admitted that the plan would work. 'The only risk would be that they'd be spotted entering the convent.'

'But the people who live in that street are used to seeing army officers going in and out. And the town would be having a fiesta that night.' Bernal pondered for a while. 'I want you to make discreet inquiries into the identity of the colonel and the captain who visit Father Sanandrés.

Meanwhile I'll talk to the Ministry of Defence on the scrambler phone.'

The sun was setting, casting a blood-red light over the waters of the Bay of Cadiz as Ángel Gallardo and the plainclothes driver in their red SEAT 500 followed the large Cadillac with the Moroccan number-plates at a discreet distance along the local road that led eastwards from the fishing-port of Rota. They were held up temporarily in the narrow streets of El Puerto de Santa María: the result of a procession of the Brotherhood of María Santísima del Desconsuelo—the Inconsolable One—whose waxen features gleamed above a float carpeted thickly with white and red carnations, and whose inhuman eyes, gazing into infinity, glistened in the deep yellow light thrown up by the fat tallow candles bobbing in their engraved glass shades as the penitent *costaleros* bore their heavy burden through the rapidly darkening streets.

When the Cadillac managed to escape through the side-roads and emerge on to the wider N-VI edged with the famous *bodegas* of Terry and other wine-shippers, the Arab driver put his foot down and the gleaming saloon almost shot out of sight.

'You'll have to use some of that hidden power you boasted about,' Ángel said to the Cadiz policeman, 'or we'll lose them.'

The little SEAT soon began to gain on the Cadillac when the Carretera Nacional VI entered a series of narrow bends in the low hills to the east of El Puerto, and in five kilometres they reached the well-signposted left turn to the Casino, which had been opened there in the wake of the post-Franco liberalization. They noted that the Cadillac driver was indicating to take the difficult left turning.

'Hang back a bit,' said Ángel, 'we don't want to reach the Casino car park directly on his tail.'

The minor road wound for a short distance through the hills overlooking the now darkened Bay, and suddenly they saw the floodlit, whitewashed two-storey building, nestling in a hollow and looking for all the world like a Tetuan *dar*. Its outline certainly recalled that of an imposing Arabian house, with its series of simple arches filled in with green lattice-work along the upper and lower floors, without genuine windows.

The two policemen parked their K-car and entered the main reception hall, where the arch motif was repeated throughout the décor, which otherwise was painted in bold primary colours, with a central spiral stairwell adorned with what appeared to be a dead olive-tree.

'Do you think they'll let us in dressed like this?' Ángel asked the local man.

'Oh yes. It's not a gala night and the tourists and holiday-makers are admitted without ties or jackets. But hadn't you better talk to the Head of Security here? He's an ex-policeman.'

Ángel cast his eye over the queue of visitors waiting to be issued with entrance tickets, but there was no sign of the four Arabs. He noticed the prices of admission: 400 pesetas for a daily ticket, 2000 for a weekly, 4000 for a monthly, and 10,000 for an annual one. Ángel wondered how the four Arabs had managed to enter so quickly; he supposed they must have season tickets.

The desk clerk looked at the two plainclothes policemen in a most supercilious way, obviously disapproving of their appearance. 'The Head of Security will be here shortly. Would you step this way?'

The desk clerk took the two policemen into a small room to the right of the main entrance to the gaming rooms. Ángel sat on the table in the middle of the room, and lit a Marlboro. Soon the security chief arrived, dressed in black coat and pin-striped trousers.

'Inspector Gallardo?' he said, somewhat uncertainly.

'That's me,' replied Ángel, showing him the official DSE badge with its heavily embossed silver star inside a leather case. 'This is Sergeant Pérez from Cadiz.'

'How can I help you, Inspector?'

'We're keeping four Moroccan visitors under discreet

surveillance and they have just entered the gaming rooms. Here are copies of their passports. Could you check them in your records and tell us how often they have visited the Casino?'

'Of course, Inspector. Our computer records should provide the information in a few minutes. Will you wait here?'

'While you get us the gen, I'd prefer it if we could go into the gaming rooms and see what they are up to.'

'Just come this way. I'll bring the records in to you in a few minutes.'

'Better meet us at the bar in ten minutes,' said Ángel.

He was surprised at the size and elegance of the main Sala de Juegos, with its rows of French and American roulette tables and the smaller horseshoes for blackjack at the extremities. The prevailing architectural theme of simple arches and sweeps of contrasting primary colours was sustained in the heart of the establishment. Only four roulette wheels were in operation at that early hour, though Ángel's keen eyes took in a number of well-preserved and presumably rich ladies of a certain age standing near the walls, each playing one or two Bally fruit-machines simultaneously without ever glancing at the moving reels or deigning to look down at their winnings as they gazed fixedly at all the likely young men in the room. His and the plainclothes sergeant's entrance had caused something of a flutter among these bored denizens of the gaming room.

For appearance's sake, Ángel approached the nearest roulette table and changed a five-thousand-peseta note with the croupier. He could see two Arabs in white burnouses at the end of the room where the tables with the highest minimum stakes were placed, but he felt that he shouldn't get too close to his prey. He and Sergeant Pérez began to bet, the latter placing only a hundred-peseta chip on *rouge* or *noir*, while Ángel more typically scattered his chips on single numbers all over the board. When nearly ten minutes had passed and the sergeant had squandered all his chips, Ángel signalled to him, picked up his considerable winnings and threw some chips to the croupier, who dexterously caught them with his rake and swept them into the shoe reserved for gratuities in the edge of the table.

As they made for the bar, the two Arabs could still be seen at the boule table.

'Are you sure those Arabs are two of ours?' asked Ángel. 'They all look alike to me.'

'I think so,' said the sergeant, 'but I can't see their two companions anywhere. They can't be in the loo all this time.'

'Have a look in the upper restaurant,' said Ángel. 'I'll wait here for the security chap.'

He ordered a Skol lager and paid for it with a couple of poker chips from his winnings. The head of security appeared at a door at the side of the bar and beckoned to Ángel, who strolled casually over carrying his drink.

'Here is the record of visits of two of your four Moroccans, who have annual tickets. You'll see that they are much valued clients. The third man and the pilot have not been here before. The director usually invites the two regular clients to a Sala Privada, with a few other chosen guests, where there is no limit on the stakes or winnings, and where they can play chemin de fer, which is their favourite game. We've withdrawn it recently from the public room, where it's more trouble than it's worth.'

'Is that where they are now, in the private rooms?' asked Ángel.

'The two regulars are already installed there and their companions will join them when they've had a look round here. We don't consider these two are serious gamesters.'

'Is there any way we could keep observation on the Sala Privada without being seen?'

'I'll have to consult the director,' said the security chief doubtfully.

'Get me in there somehow,' said Ángel. 'I'll wait in the bar.'

There Ángel found Sergeant Pérez and told him of developments. After five minutes had passed, they were beckoned back through the private door and confronted by the imposing figure of the director attired in tails and white tie.

'I take it this is a very important matter, Inspector?'

'A matter of state security,' said Ángel firmly.

'Then I shall conduct you to an observation point, but I hope you will not reveal its existence to anyone.'

'Only to my superior officer, Comisario Bernal.'

'Very well. Come this way.'

Ángel and the sergeant were led up a narrow flight of stairs and through a very low-ceilinged corridor where the hum of the air-conditioning was most noticeable. The director ushered them into a small room and held his finger to his lips. 'No noise, now.'

He pressed a button and a panel slid back in the floor to reveal a view of the *salle privée* where the players and croupiers could be observed from above. Ángel saw that, in addition to the two Moroccans there were three other players, dressed in white American naval uniform.

'Who are the other players?' he whispered to the Director.

'From the Rota base,' he murmured. 'I'll have copies of their registration documents sent up to you.'

'Can we hear what they are saying?'

'Just press this control-button and you'll get the sound from microphones hidden under the gaming table. My head of security will assist you to record any part of the conversation you require.'

'Is all the Casino wired up in this way?' asked Ángel curiously.

'All that's necessary for the security of ourselves and our clients.'

Superintendent Bernal slept only fitfully in his comfortable bed in the Hotel de Francia y París. His mind kept going over the Ministry of Defence's decision not to intervene to circumvent the plot to free the military prisoners from the castle of Santa Catalina, apart from ordering an increase of the guard on Saturday afternoon and keeping a close watch on the conspirators once their identity had been established. Bernal thought this a risky decision, but he saw the point of letting the plotters incriminate themselves before pouncing on them. What concerned him and kept him uneasily awake was the relationship if any between this internal political plot and the cases of the dead frogman and the hanged Marine guard at Sancti Petri; he could see no obvious connection. On the other hand, what real link had he established between the two murders, not to mention the mysterious light signals, a miniature submarine spotted in the Bay and other vessels disappearing off the radar screens? Just one word: MELKART, or MELQART, or even MELKHART, which had occurred in the dead frogman's tattoo and in the Morse code message reported by the Marine guard shortly before his death. He really must find out what it meant, for he had nothing else to go on.

Just as he was dozing off again, the phone at his bedside rang harshly. He sat up, switched on the light over the bed and lit a Kaiser as he put the receiver to his ear.

'Yes, this is Bernal. Soto? What time is it? One-forty? What's up?' He listened for a while with growing attention. 'Then it disappeared off the radar screen just like last time? What was the radio message?' He took up a notepad and wrote down the words Rear Admiral Soto dictated to him: '*Melkart to Erythrea: Rendezvous Whale Bay 2330 hours on tenth. Confirm by light signal prior to landing.*' Bernal looked at his diary. 'The tenth of April is this coming Saturday, Soto. Where is Whale Bay? There's no such place on the map? You'd better get your Intelligence chaps to pore over their gazetteers. Very well, Soto. I'll see you in the morning, say at eight-thirty before we go to see the American commander again. *Hasta mañana.*'

Bernal sat up in bed and puzzled over the latest intercept. He took out a folding map of the Costa de la Luz: numerous bays and coves were marked, but none to do with whales. He looked again at his diary: the tenth was Easter Saturday, just when the local military plotters were planning to spring the two prisoners from Santa Catalina fort. Was there after all a connection that escaped him? His mind worked furiously over the problem, and he despaired of getting any sleep. Only one thing for it: he'd read a boring technical book until his mind sank under the heaviness of the text. He'd always found such books, packed with useless information, better than any sleeping pill. His own collection of works on the early history of Madrid had commonly served to cure his insomnia. Now he took up Adolfo de Castro's *Historia de Cádiz y su provincia*, published in 1858, and balanced the weighty tome on his distended and queasy stomach. Soon he became bogged down in the complex discussion about the Classical authors' various names for the three main islands that Cadiz and San Fernando had once comprised, and the somewhat unclear attempts by Don Adolfo to relate the ancient references to present-day geographical reality.

Just as he was dozing off, his eye was caught by the word 'Erythrea', an ancient name for Cadiz. Hadn't he recently heard that word? His tired brain gave up and he yielded to sleep at last.

At 2 a.m. Ángel Gallardo left the Casino well pleased: in his pocket he carried a cassette-recording of the brief but earnest conversation conducted in English between the Moroccan visitors and the three American naval officers. At the gaming-table in the *salle privée* little had been said: he noticed that they had all drunk liberal quantities of ten-year-old Glenmorangie malt whisky, but had spoken no more than the game required. The stakes had seemed enormous, judging by the wads of US dollars the players took out to change into chips from time to time. When the lavish buffet had been brought in, the game was suspended, and it was then that the private conversation had taken place. How fortunate that the Casino's surveillance system was so very efficient. When the Casino servants had served the gamblers with plates piled with lobster, crab and other seafood, the small group had sat alone round a large glass-topped table decorated with a bunch of dead hazel-twigs surrounding a modernistic table-lamp which was wired for sound, and Ángel had got the whole conversation on tape. The only thing was, neither he nor his plainclothes sergeant had a sufficient grasp of English to follow what was said, though he had caught the mention of a number of place-names: Alhucemas, Ceuta, Melilla, and, possibly, 'Melkart'.

106

Hadn't Bernal warned him to listen out for that mysterious word or codename?

When the players had returned to the green baize-topped table, he and his colleague had been brought excellent sandwiches and bottles of beer by the head of security, and they had settled down for another boring wait.

It was well past 1.30 a.m., long after the strangely high-pitched voice of 'La Perica' had finished the last *schottis* in the cabaret below, that the private gamblers picked up their chips and left the Sala Privada. Ángel and his driver waited in the small SEAT near the exit to the car park and observed the impeccably waxed Cadillac being driven up to the main steps of the Casino. They also noticed an American Navy car with its driver parked under a palm tree and Ángel noted down its registration number: no doubt it was the US naval officers' transport. At least he had the copies of their *fichas* for Bernal, who would certainly want Naval Intelligence to do some checking.

Bernal had left his hotel at 7.45 a.m. in Lista's company, in order to visit Navarro in the ops room before his appointment with Rear Admiral Soto at San Fernando. He had time to listen to the cassette-recording sent in by Ángel Gallardo, but understood even less of it than his youngest inspector. A full translation was urgently called for.

At the Captaincy General at San Fernando, the rear admiral received him with his usual bonhomie, and filled him in on the night's events.

'No light signals this time, Superintendent, but some mysterious movements were spotted on the radar screens between Cape Trafalgar and Sancti Petri island, which couldn't be accounted for. I sent out two fast patrol vessels, but they saw nothing. Later we intercepted the radio message, the one I read out to you on the phone.'

'Was there any response to that message?' asked Bernal.

'No, that's the strange thing. The Melkart message was repeated twice, then there was silence. It's possible that the

107

recipients replied on a different frequency, which our radio officers were unable to pick up in time, though they searched for it.'

'What does "Erythrea" mean to you, Admiral?'

'Nothing at all, nor does "Melkart".'

'Well, at least I've found a reference to Erythrea in Adolfo de Castro's history of Cadiz. I've brought a photocopy of page thirteen for you to see. You'll see I didn't get far in that hefty tome, but I've left it with Navarro so that my inspectors can plough through it to see if "Melkart" occurs.'

'And what does Erythrea mean, Superintendent?'

'As you'll see, it was thought to be an ancient name for the island on which the old city of Cadiz stands.'

'Do you think that these codenames have been chosen from Antiquity, then?'

'It's possible, though pretty careless of them, I think, because if you crack one of them you may get all the others. It's a foolish system, completely out of use. You saw the date given in the message was the tenth, next Saturday. Now my female agent in Cadiz has come across an operation planned to take place that same evening, at the military fort of Santa Catalina. I've brought you a copy of her report. I should also inform you that I've passed it on to the JUJEM in Madrid who are taking certain steps in the matter.' The rear admiral perused Elena's report and looked grave. 'Our problem is this, Admiral,' Bernal went on, 'is there any connection between the Santa Catalina conspiracy and the Melkart business? The latter certainly ties in with the dead frogman and the murdered Marine sergeant.'

'On the face of it, it seems unlikely,' said the rear admiral. 'The Melkart affair has been entirely naval until now, whereas this other business—' he waved Elena's report— 'seems to have to do with the army, perhaps with some dissident officers who are still fighting old battles.'

'We must talk to the Americans again and make them come clean,' said Bernal with some firmness. 'I've just picked up this report from the Cadiz Comisaría sent in by my agent at Rota, who followed your Moroccan visitors to the Casino at El Puerto, where they met three US naval officers in a *salle privée*. My chief interest is in a cassette-recording of their private conversation which we've listened to, but can't understand. Have you an interpreter of English here who can make us a transcription and translation of it?'

'Yes, I'll arrange it at once.'

'Good. We won't tell the American commander about it yet, but I've got photocopies of the US naval officers' documentation. Perhaps we'll ask Weintraub about their duties at the Rota base. At least it will give us a bargaining counter.'

The weather improved as they set out from the Captaincy-General at San Fernando on the N-VI for Rota; the Levante had dropped and the sun shone warmly. As they left El Puerto de Santa María on the local road Bernal was astonished to see the wealth of wild flowers that had sprung up as though by magic on the stony edges of the fields and vineyards. The Super Mirafiori glided to a stop at the entrance to the naval base and their passes were inspected by the guards of both Navies. The car purred on and reached the security building.

Commander Weintraub met them in proper uniform on this occasion, and he was flanked by two aides and the same interpreter as before. Rear Admiral Soto let Bernal do the talking, and he decided to go at once on to the offensive.

'I don't think you were entirely frank with us on our last visit, Commander, and we've had to find out things the hard way. The information we required was not then available, perhaps. But events have moved on: we have had another death to investigate, a Marine sergeant at Sancti Petri, whose murder we have kept from the newspapers for the moment.'

The Commander looked serious as he heard this translated and condescended to take the wet cigar out of his mouth to say how much the death was regretted, but how could the US Navy help the Superintendent?

'It would be helpful if you would let us inspect the secret anti-personnel weapons you have, especially the type that involves a laser beam.'

When this had been translated, the Commander looked at his aides in some dismay. 'Well, Superintendent, it may be that such weapons exist, but what makes you think we have them here?'

'My pathologist's report on the dead frogman,' replied Bernal. 'There is really no doubt about it, and our Navy has no such weapons.'

'I'm not denying that anti-personnel weapons of this type have been issued to our men for training purposes, but they have not been deployed in action, Superintendent.'

Bernal listened gravely to the interpreter's version of the Commander's answer. 'One has been used on the unidentified sub-aqua diver and caused his death,' said Bernal firmly, 'and I'm sure your commanding officer must have a record of the incident, which occurred almost a fortnight ago.'

'I have no authority to discuss this matter with you, Superintendent,' replied Commander Weintraub, more uncertainly, Bernal thought, and he resolved to press his adversary harder.

'If you have not, then I shall ask Madrid to take up the affair at a much higher level than this.'

The Commander blanched when he heard the reply. 'Now hold your horses, Superintendent, hold your horses. First, we don't admit that there was any incident involving the deployment of the new laser anti-personnel weapon.' When he heard this translated, Bernal got up as if to leave, but the Commander waved him back to his chair. 'However,' he went on, 'there may have been an accident during a secret training exercise on the night of the twenty-fifth of March, as a result of which an unknown third party may have been badly injured. I stress that the exercise was a mock Red Alert for training purposes, with a simulated attack on the harbour defences. None of our men was injured nor is any missing. Neither the US Navy nor the Government of the United States admits any legal responsibility in this matter.'

Bernal noticed that the Commander had read the last part from a prepared statement.

'May we have a copy of that statement, Commander?' he asked. 'Just for the record, you understand.'

Commander Weintraub looked at his aides. 'OK, Superintendent. We have a Spanish translation made for you.'

Bernal exchanged looks with Soto: so the Americans had assumed it would come to this. At least Bernal would have something to send to Madrid in respect of the dead frogman.

The Commander rose, lit a fresh cigar, and motioned to a tray of bourbon and soda, as though he supposed the formal meeting at an end.

'Just one thing more,' said Bernal in a mild tone. 'We want information on a new type of midget submarine seen in the Bay. Our Navy has no record of being informed by the US Navy that such vessels have entered service here.'

The Commander slumped back into his chair and chewed savagely on his cigar. 'No such craft have been commissioned, Superintendent. The only submarines in use here are the ones already notified to your Government.'

Bernal noticed Soto's surprise at the question and the Commander's quick glance at his aides.

'Very well, Commander, I take your word for it. Should you have any information about such vessels, doubtless belonging to some foreign power, entering the Bay, I should appreciate your imparting it to Rear Admiral Soto immediately.'

When Soto and Bernal politely declined the offer of drinks and indicated they were pressed for time, Bernal turned back and handed the American security chief a list.

'I should also be obliged if you could send us some account of the duties of these US naval officers who are assigned to your base, Commander.'

Commander Weintraub read through the list with a puzzled expression. 'OK, Superintendent, I'll look into it. What have these guys been up to?'

'Nothing as yet, but we like to keep abreast of events, Commander,' was Bernal's parting shot across the American's bows.

As they drove out of Rota base, Soto asked Bernal what he thought the three US naval officers were involved in.

'I don't know, but they can stand some investigation. By the way, do you think you could arrange for your chief political liaison officer to join us, either for dinner tonight or for lunch tomorrow? It will be on me this time. Shall we try El Anteojo in the Alameda de Apodaca?'

'I'll organize it, Comisario. But we *gaditanos* won't let visitors do the paying.'

Bernal sighed. 'I hope I'm not going to have the same battles with you as I have with my colleagues in Madrid. I also think it's time for a boat-trip, especially since it's such a warm day. Do you think you could conjure up one of your patrol vessels for us?'

'Naturally. Our facilities are at your disposal. Where do you want to go?'

'Just along the coast as far as Cape Trafalgar and back. Shall we say four-thirty p.m.?'

Elena Fernández was finding the religious life extremely trying. She had attempted to break the monotony by helping Sister Encarnación in the kitchen for much of the morning; this enabled her to talk to the kindly old nun and learn a great deal from her chat, as well as to keep an eye on Father Sanandrés's office door through the side window that gave on to the southern walk.

After they had helped the cook prepare three dozen *herreras* or codling in baking trays dressed with coarse sea-salt in typical Cadiz style, Elena heard the old-fashioned doorbell clanging and saw Sister Serena, the portress, going to open it. The visitors were the same colonel and captain whom she had overheard on the previous day and her pulse raced with excitement.

Telling Sister Encarnación that she was going to meditate before Sext, she slipped up to her cell for her prayer book. She took the opportunity of opening the secret compartment in her suitcase to remove the miniature Rolleiflex camera and hastened back to the cloister. She was disappointed to see it was empty, so she sat on her usual marble seat in the north walk and pretended to be engrossed in her devotions.

After a while Elena heard the door of the prior's room

opening and saw him emerge in the company of the two army officers. Making sure that the cloister was otherwise deserted, Elena took out the tiny camera and trained it between the two large flower-pots on the sill of the cloister-arch, in the hope that the trio would stroll within range. But she was frustrated when the three men departed along the southern walk in the direction of the chapel. She wondered whether she should take the risk of following them: after all, it would not look too suspicious if she went there to pray.

With sudden resolution Elena tucked the camera into the side pocket of her habit and walked boldly to the chapel door. She paused on the threshold at the holy water stoup and reconnoitred. The chapel appeared to be completely empty. Where could they have gone? Probably the prior had taken them to the vestry. She advanced down the aisle and stopped at a shrine of Our Lady of the Palm to the right of the main altar. There she lit a candle and knelt as though in prayer, while listening for voices, but she could hear nothing. Then she thought to look through the glass panel at the base of the altar and could see some artificial light coming from the natural cave where the miraculous spring issued forth, coinciding, she had begun to assume, with the times of high water in the Bay, to judge by the daily variation in the timing of that curious ceremony of the Diurnal Adoration.

Craning her neck between the large vases of lilies and gladioli on each side of the high altar, she could just make out the tops of the caps of the army officers and the bald pate of Father Sanandrés. What could they be up to? She looked round for a hiding-place and spotted the confessional box of polished oak on the right side of the church. Making sure she was unobserved, she slipped into the confessor's side of the box where there was better cover, and shut the door, asking herself whether she was committing sacrilege. Through the wooden lattice she had a good view of the altar and of the door leading to the vestry and the cavern below. Varga the technician had assured her that the camera would work in quite poor light conditions, especially since he had loaded it with a very fast black-and-white film. She tried it

113

for size through one of the diamond-shaped holes in the lattice, and found that she could see a wide section of the wall opposite through the tiny viewfinder. She adjusted the zoom lens and sat down to wait.

In the gloom of the confessional, Elena looked at her watch in some desperation. What could Father Sanandrés and the two army officers be doing all this time in the cave below the high altar? If they didn't come up soon, it would be time for Sext and she would look a fool if she were discovered sitting in the priest's seat in the confessional, and she'd be in real trouble if Sister Serena noticed her absence from the noon office.

It was nearly ten to twelve, and soon the bell would ring and the religious brothers and sisters assemble not far from where she was crouching. Her hopes were raised when she heard a door opening, and she trained her camera on the vestry opposite, but no one emerged. She squinted through the fretwork of the lattice down the aisle and was appalled to see that Señora de Bernal had entered the chapel and was making for the image of Our Lady of the Palm, where she now lit a candle and knelt to pray.

Then Elena heard muted masculine voices and the vestry door opened suddenly. She started taking pictures, in the hope that some of the shots would be usable, and through the viewfinder she could see the colonel and the captain coming out. She continued rapidly taking shots, hoping that the very faint noise made by the wind-on lever wouldn't be noticed. The prior and the officers abruptly stopped talking when they saw Eugenia Bernal praying at the side-altar, and the officers looked inquiringly at Father Sanandrés, who gave a reassuring nod. He bowed to Eugenia as they passed. As soon as they left, with Señora de Bernal's back still turned to her, Elena summoned up the courage to open the confessional door as slowly and quietly as she could. Just when she thought she had succeeded in slipping out of it unheard, there was an awfully loud creak as the door swung back too far, and Eugenia turned her head sharply and rose to her feet.

'Oh my dear, you won't be able to make confession until this evening. There's an hour set aside for it; didn't the sisters tell you?'

She gave no sign of considering it odd that Elena had emerged from the priest's side of the confessional.

'Thank you so much for telling me,' said Elena. 'I must have misread the booklet.'

'Not at all, my dear. Will you pray with me here before Sext?'

'Of course, señora.'

'Perhaps this evening you will help us to decorate the *paso* for tomorrow's procession?'

'I'd be honoured.'

Elena wondered what Bernal would have made of the scene if he had chanced upon her kneeling next to his over-pious wife in front of the heavily decorated statue of Our Lady of the Palm, whose robes contained gold and silver threads that glistened in the warm candlelight. Neither of the genuflecting figures noticed the stern and suspicious gaze of Sister Serena that bore down on them from the latticed gallery above the main door of the church.

After their visit to the Rota base, Bernal dropped Rear Admiral Soto off at San Carlos en route to his ops room in Cadiz. There Paco Navarro greeted him with a number of reports that had come in.

'Ángel has rung from Jerez to say that the four Moroccans have departed in a light aircraft, the destination notified to the airport authorities being Rabat.'

'You'd better pull Ángel in now, Paco. I want him to offer back-up to Elena at the convent. I'm unhappy about the risk she's running at the hands of the army plotters should they discover her mission.'

'How will we get Ángel in there? What pretext can we use, *jefe*?'

'For the moment get him into a house opposite the convent, from which he can keep watch on the comings and goings and try to get photographs of the colonel and captain who are plotting with the prior. We must find out who they are, and keep discreet surveillance on them.'

'OK, chief. He's going to phone me from Rota shortly for further orders. The other piece of news is that Miranda and Lista have found a reference to "Melkart" in that old history of Cadiz. Unfortunately, the book has no index, so they've had to plough through the whole text. Then Lista went to the Faculty Library up in the old city to check in the Espasa-Calpe Encyclopædia.'

'Send them in, Paco. I can't wait to know the explanation.'

'I've a feeling it won't help us a lot, chief.'

Miranda, who was usually a shy, bookish man, now entered carrying a sheaf of notes, while Lista brought the two copies they had managed to obtain of Castro's history.

'Here's what we've found out so far, *jefe*,' said Miranda. 'Melqart was a Syrian god, worshipped by the people of Tyre in the seventh century BC, and the name is thought to have meant "king of the city". Later he was identified with the Greek Herakles, and the Carthaginians set up temples to the Tyrian Hercules, one of them being here at Cadiz, where legend has it that both Alexander the Great and Julius Cæsar came to pay their respects.'

'And is it known where the temple dedicated to Melqart was situated, Miranda?'

'On Sancti Petri island, which was known as Heracleum in Roman times. Erythrea, or Eurytheia, is identified with the island or promontory on which the old city of Cadiz stands today. It was also known to the Greeks as Aphrodisia, and had a temple dedicated to Venus. Under the Roman Empire there was a temple in honour of Juno.'

'I don't see where all this gets us,' commented Navarro. 'It could be that "Melkart" is an acronym and has nothing to do with the Tyrian Hercules.'

'There's too much of a coincidence, Paco,' objected Bernal, 'especially with the other reference in the radio intercept to "Erythrea". Get me Inspector Ibáñez in Central Records in Madrid, if you can.'

While he waited for the call to be put through, Bernal pondered further over Miranda's and Lista's notes. Miranda asked him for new orders. 'Go round to that Arabist at the

116

Faculty, the man who's the great-grandson of Adolfo de Castro who wrote the history of the city. It's time he came up with something.'

When Navarro had got Ibáñez on the line, Bernal asked him first why he was working during Semana Santa.

'I hope to get a few days off from Thursday, Luis, but these new computer programmes are driving us crazy. When we've ironed out the kinks it'll be a great system.'

'Would you do me a favour, Esteban? Would you look up the name "Melkart" on your VDU?' Bernal spelled the word out for him. 'It may be spelled with a *k* or a *q*. I've no idea if it's an acronym or a call-sign in a cypher. But I've a feeling it's North African in origin, probably Moroccan. It could be an organization along the lines of the Polisario Front. Also the word "Erythrea", or "Eurytheia", was picked up in the radio intercept. Will you see what you've got in the International Section? Many thanks.' Bernal gave him the ops room number in Cadiz.

'If you feel like a sea trip this afternoon, Paco,' Bernal said, 'you could come out in a naval cutter with Soto and me.'

'No, thanks, chief, I'm a poor sailor. But Lista's free to go along.'

'I hope he's good at spotting whales,' said Bernal enigmatically.

At least the sea looked calm and the sun was out, thought Bernal, as he and Lista boarded the naval cutter that Rear Admiral Soto had provided. Soto introduced the Superintendent to the lieutenant in charge of the vessel, and they cast off at once from the small quay at the Navy's base at Torre Gorda. It was just on the turn of afternoon high water, and Bernal wondered whether the holy emission had occurred at the Convent of the Palm on time. He resolved to ask the local experts about that strange phenomenon.

In the cockpit of the launch, the rear admiral had ordered powerful binoculars to be fixed to a tripod for Bernal to be able to survey the coast. There was also a detailed chart of the shoals and currents, together with the Instituto Geográfico y Catastral's maps of the coast, from Chipiona at the mouth of the Guadalquivir to the north-west as far as the Rock of Gibraltar to the south-east.

'On the way south, Admiral, I'd like to pass between the island of Sancti Petri and the mouth of the channel.'

'I'll give instructions to the lieutenant. Let me know when you want to slow down or stop for a closer look at the shore.'

'Can this launch go up the Sancti Petri channel or has it too much draught?'

'It can go all the way to San Fernando and La Carraca, if you wish.'

'Let's go up a little way, as far as the old *almadraba* or tunny fishery, say. I just want to get an impression of the approach from the sea.'

The cutter, which was capable of almost forty knots, sped alongside the low dunes that stretched south-eastward from Torre Gorda to Sancti Petri without their seeing anything of interest until they reached the northern tip of Sancti Petri island, when Bernal requested that they reduce speed. He inspected the island through the fixed binoculars, while Lista and the rear admiral raked the rocky shore with hand-held glasses. They could make out the ruins of the castle and the unmanned lighthouse beyond.

They soon reached the entrance to the channel that curved away north-westward towards San Fernando, and the launch approached the narrow entrance with caution. To their right they could see the deserted army barracks and the wooden landing-stage under which the body of the Marine sergeant had been found hanged. They waved to the two civil guards on duty there and entered the channel.

Bernal noticed at once how the scene changed in the salt-pans, and gave an impression of abandonment and menace. The stretches of grey mud were broken only by the occasional clumps of reeds where sea-birds nested, calling to their mates and giving raucous and resentful cries as the passage of the launch disturbed them. Within 350 metres they could see the bulk of the deserted *almadraba* where for centuries caught tunny had been prepared. Beyond it, where the channel narrowed, Bernal spotted a building on a rise to the north.

He pointed and asked: 'What's up there, Soto?'

'It's the Ermita del Cerro, the hermitage on the ridge, though it's not much of a rise, I admit. No one goes there these days.'

By now they had left to starboard La Isleta, an eyot of firm land amid the sterile salt-marshes, and they could see the houses of San Fernando ahead.

'I think that's far enough, Admiral, if your men can put about here. I'd like to go down the coast for a while.'

When they had re-passed the wooden jetty and left the Sancti Petri channel for the open sea once more, Bernal noticed the slight swell and pitching caused by the current as they turned southwards. On the nearby beach he could see a number of holiday-makers, drawn there no doubt by the sunny day, and even two or three brave souls swimming in the water. Behind them stretched a row of *chiringuitos* or beach cafés where drinks and fried food were served during the season. Now they appeared to be still shuttered from the winter.

'That's La Barrosa, a beach very popular with the people from Chiclana and San Fernando,' commented Soto, 'but the beach shelves very sharply, making bathing hazardous.'

As they proceeded down the coast, Bernal, Lista and the rear admiral inspected the littoral carefully; here it rose steadily into quite substantial cliffs of a mixture of red sandstone and shell-limestone, which had fallen down in large chunks at various points on to the beaches and into the sea itself. They passed another watch-tower, the Torre del Puerco, before the headland at Cabo Roche, beyond which the tiny River Roche emerged through a cleft into the sea.

'Have you spotted anything worthy of the name Whale Bay, Admiral?' asked Bernal.

'I know of nothing along this coast that could give rise to such a name.'

Beyond the handsome town of Conil, where the white-washed houses gleamed in the strong sunlight, the cliffs continued as far as the Torre Nueva, when they began to get lower, until the coastline became quite swampy and wooded west of Zahora. Ahead of them they could see Trafalgar light on a low spit of sand running out from the coast.

'What one would give to have been a spectator here on 21 October 1805, Admiral, and have seen the battle between the English ships and the combined French and Spanish fleet.'

'I'm rather glad I wasn't, Comisario; I might have had to command one of those old ships of the line.' But as Bernal turned away from the binoculars, he went on: 'I'd like us to go a little further for you to see Los Caños de Meca just beyond the cape. They consist of an incredible series of caverns, apparently natural, though old wives' tales claim that they are the remains of an ancient city fallen into the sea. The local fishermen sometimes bring up Greek and Carthaginian coins, just as they do at Cadiz.'

'Ah, that explains how Trafalgar got its name, Admiral. One of the more recondite bits of information I acquired from reading Adolfo de Castro's history was that it comes from the Arabic words *Taraf al-Agar*, "Promontory of the Caves".'

'We can't go in too close, Superintendent, because the underwater rocks are very dangerous, but you'll have a good view.'

Bernal swept the rocky caverns with the powerful glasses and saw how much they resembled fantastic oriental palaces eroded by the ferocious seas which even on such a calm day dashed against them.

Finally the launch described a large arc towards the open waters where the Atlantic joined the Strait. Here the swell was much more noticeable, causing Bernal's stomach to lurch unhappily. He managed to turn the binoculars to the north-east and glimpsed a very large grey bulk in the limpid western light.

'That's Gibraltar, I assume?'

'Yes, it is,' said the admiral, 'and if you turn your glasses to the south-east, you may just spot the other Pillar of Hercules, Ceuta.'

When they had turned back north-westwards, Bernal went to the door of the cabin and lit a Kaiser in the lee of the wind.

They were now re-passing Conil de la Frontera and Bernal went back on deck to survey the coastline, which was now more visible with the ebbing tide; the bright rays of the early evening sun cast deep shadows between the rugged cliffs. Lista was continuously scanning the beaches, and suddenly he called Bernal to his side.

'There's something that looks like a small black craft in front of that inlet, *jefe*.'

Bernal went to the fixed binoculars and scanned the beach in the direction Lista was indicating, just beyond Cape Roche.

'Could we go in closer, Admiral? We might as well take a look at it, whatever it is.'

As the launch approached the small cove, they could see that it was accessible by land only by a very steep cliff path, at the top of which was a small lookout post. At the north-west end of the tiny bay, there appeared to be a black boat shaped like a submarine in difficulties in the thick foaming surf. When they were within two hundred metres, Lista shouted: 'It looks just like a black whale!'

All on board but the helmsman were now lining the starboard rail and peering at the strange vessel.

'Watch out that you don't beach us,' the lieutenant warned the helmsman.

'It's all right, sir, I know this beach,' he called out. 'It shelves very steeply, but there are some underwater rocks at the northern end. I won't go in too far.'

'Oh lord, sorry, *jefe*,' cried Lista, 'it's only an oddly shaped rock! I could have sworn it was a craft of some kind, moving in the breakers.'

'It's still of interest, Lista,' remarked Bernal. 'Why didn't we see that rock on the way out?'

'Because the tide has ebbed,' said the rear admiral. 'It's remarkably like a small whale or a dolphin, isn't it?'

The elongated black rock stood out like a piece of statuary on a natural pedestal of milk-coloured shell-limestone, and appeared the more striking because of the colour-contrast with its base and with the red cliffs beyond. The tail-end was quite lifelike, much more so than the snout, but the breakers that constantly washed over it and through a hole at the fore-end, which resembled a cetaceous eye, gave it life and movement.

'I'm sorry, *jefe*,' said Lista miserably, 'I've wasted your time.'

'On the contrary,' said Bernal, 'don't apologize. I think you've found the Bay of the Whale. Let's go into the cabin and look at the charts.'

Bernal looked at the IGC map carefully. 'This would be a perfect place to make a clandestine landing or to have a secret rendezvous. There's a minor road connecting the spot with the N 340 at Barrio Nuevo, ten kilometres south-east of Chiclana.'

'It's the place I'd choose myself,' admitted Soto.

'We'll have the Marine Section of the Civil Guard keep it under surveillance,' said Bernal. 'Would it be possible to land on Sancti Petri island on the way back?'

'I think we might manage a brief visit before low water. There's a small landing-stage on the south-east side.'

When the launch approached the strange island, the nesting birds rose from the low rocks in a shrieking protest and swirled overhead. The stone quay had large rusted iron rings for small boats to moor, and seaweed-covered steps led up to the ruined castle.

'I'm sure I've seen this place in dreams, before actually visiting it,' said Bernal. 'It's as though I've always known it.'

'One of the last people to stay in these ruins was the composer Manuel de Falla, when he was composing his great cantata *La Atlántida,* which he never finished. He said that the rhythms of the crashing waves and the sheer antiquity of the site entered into his music and took hold of him.'

'I'm not surprised,' said Bernal. 'If this was really Herakleion, the site of the Temple of Melkart, the Tyrian Hercules, and was visited by so many Greeks, Carthaginians and

Romans who expressed astonishment at the enormous height of the tides—something quite unfamiliar to them in the Mediterranean—then one can understand how they must have felt they were on the dangerous western edge of their world on this spot.'

The chill breeze of evening now sprang up, and Bernal shivered as though visited by the spectres of participants in ancient and unspeakable rites.

'Let's just make a rapid inspection, Admiral, and then we'll head for Cadiz.'

They saw no sign of human occupation in the ruined, roofless castle, so long battered by the Atlantic gales and defaced by thick deposits of guano. The desolation of the scene seemed to affect them all.

At the western edge of the low cliff, they could feel a rumbling beneath where they stood.

'Is there a cavern underneath this rock, Soto?'

'Yes, it's a sort of blow-hole, where the tide rushes in and the spray shoots up through a chimney beyond the castle walls.'

'I've seen something similar at Cascais, west of Lisbon,' commented Bernal, 'at a spot called *A Boca do Inferno*—the Mouth of Hell.'

He walked to the point indicated by the rear admiral and looked down into a deep chasm, where he could just glimpse the sea-water ebb and flow on the sandy bottom. There he was surprised to see two deep parallel grooves in the shingle and an obviously new rope-ladder leading less than half-way up from the base of the shaft.

Back in her cell after the Lenten lunch of baked fish and green salad which had followed the celebration of Sext, Elena Fernández rewound the film in her miniature camera. After extracting it with care, she sealed the tiny reel in a black plastic cartouche. She wrote a brief report and enclosed it with the exposed film in a stout envelope addressed to Comisario Bernal. All would now be ready for the afternoon visit of the lay women attending the Diurnal Adoration.

She rested on her narrow truckle-bed and wondered what else Bernal might expect of her. Clearly she must inspect the vestry and the holy cave as soon as the opportunity presented itself. She must try to find out what Father Sanandrés and the army officers had been doing down there. Meanwhile all she could usefully do was to observe them during their visits to the convent, which seemed to occur only in the mornings.

The afternoon was pleasantly warm, so she decided to go down and sit in the sunny cloister. There she met Sister Encarnación, who suggested they they help Señora de Bernal in the rear yard. The float for Maundy Thursday would represent the Garden of Gethsemane, and Eugenia was engaged in cutting off the heads of hundreds of blue and white Dutch irises and threading them into a net stretched across the floor of the *paso*.

'Those boxes of flowers must have cost an awful lot of money,' Elena commented.

'The brethren of the Cofradía have collected all through the year and they've organized many social events to raise sufficient for this,' said the kindly old nun. 'They do splendid work. These flowers for Thursday have cost over one hundred thousand pesetas.'

'And it's going to take us the best part of two days to thread them into this net,' said Eugenia Bernal.

They worked on until it was nearly time for Nones, when Señora de Bernal made her way to the church. Sister Encarnación pulled Elena back and said in an urgent whisper: 'Could I have a private word with you, Señorita? I know your father is an important man and he might be able to intervene. I'm very worried about the army officers who come here each day. I fear they are a bad influence on poor Father Sanandrés. He will let his enthusiasm run away with him at times. I've seen it often among those of us who lead the contemplative life: when an opportunity for action occurs, we tend to overdo things. And Sister Serena, who's a right-wing fanatic, has a hold over him. She's a very dangerous woman.' The old nun crossed herself.

'I'd be glad to help in any way, Sister,' said Elena, trying to conceal her eagerness. 'You also promised to show me the holy cave.'

'So I did,' exclaimed the old nun. 'I'm getting forgetful. Now it can't be this afternoon, because the tide won't have ebbed enough. Let's meet there tomorrow morning after Prime. Of course, these old bones won't permit me to descend to the bottom with you, but I'll show you its secret. Then we'll have a chance for a private chat at the same time.'

They heard the main doorbell ringing, and then the large bell was rung for the Diurnal Adoration. Elena felt in the pocket of her rough habit to reassure herself that the envelope containing the film was still there. She was relieved to see that the tall Catalan woman had arrived with the others as usual, and that she didn't try to attract Elena's attention.

When the office ended with the ceremony of the miraculous water, Elena slipped out and waited in the south walk. Soon the Catalan woman emerged and said: '*Hola, señorita*' as she passed. Elena gave her the envelope and smiled in gratitude. She turned back to encounter Sister Serena on the threshold of the church, who looked at her with deep suspicion.

'Weren't you at the ceremony, señorita?'

'Yes, yes, I was, but I thought it was just finishing. I was waiting for Señora de Bernal to help her with the decoration of the float.'

'That's most obliging of you, señorita,' said the tight-lipped nun coldly. 'I hope your days of retreat here will be of spiritual benefit to you.'

Had she seen her pass the envelope? Elena asked herself worriedly. Sister Serena always seemed to be on the watch and tended to pop up wherever one went, as though she was Father Sanandrés's eyes and ears throughout the convent.

Elena spent the rest of the evening helping Eugenia Bernal with the flowers, under the stern direction of Sister Serena. Of kindly Sister Encarnación there was no sign. Perhaps she had been banished to the kitchen.

★

Bernal asked the lieutenant to fetch two coils of rope from the launch for Lista to descend into the shaft and inspect the rope-ladder and the strange marks faintly visible in the sand at the bottom.

'We mustn't linger too long, Comisario,' warned the rear admiral, 'or we'll be trapped by the low water which will prevent us from sailing. And it will soon be dusk.'

'How long have we got?' asked Bernal.

'About an hour,' said Soto, looking at his watch. 'Why don't we get one of the crew to go down with your inspector?'

'The fewer people who trample on those marks the better. Lista is trained for the job.'

Slowly the thin inspector was lowered by the two crewmen until he was within reach of the rope-ladder, which was attached to a stanchion driven into the rock-face. He tested it for strength, and then was able to climb down with greater ease, using a small torch to inspect the walls of the chimney as he descended.

'Is the shaft natural?' Bernal asked the rear admiral.

'I think so. The sea erodes the limestone at its weakest points, and we find these blow-holes in various places along the coast. There are some under Cadiz itself.'

Lista reached the bottom and began to inspect the wide parallel grooves on the shingly floor.

'It widens out into a large cavern, chief,' he shouted up, 'which lies under the castle. This passage leads out to the sea.'

Lista disappeared from view for a time, then returned.

'What are those markings, Lista?' shouted Bernal, his voice re-echoing down the shaft.

'They've been made by a vessel of some kind and run out to a small beach outside the cave. They stop just in front of the large cavern. If you pass down the camera with the flash-gun, I'll take some shots of them.'

The apparatus was brought from the cutter and passed down to Lista on another rope. Soon the job was done, and Bernal called him to climb back up.

'What sort of vessel would leave parallel tracks like that, Admiral?'

126

'That's what's puzzling me, Comisario. It couldn't have been any ordinary boat. A catamaran, perhaps?'

'Once Lista's up, we'll make a quick search of the castle ruins.'

'Don't leave it too long; the tide's ebbing fast.'

Bernal and Lista made a rapid inspection of the roofless stone structure, passing from room to room in the failing light without seeing any sign of human occupancy, though various sea-birds flew up at them with angry shrieks.

'We haven't got time to do a thorough job, Lista. You'll have to return with Varga tomorrow morning, as soon as the tide permits.'

As they were returning to the quay, Lista bent down and shone his torch on a small object. Taking a pair of tweezers from his pocket, he picked up a cigarette-butt.

'Here's something, chief. None of us have dropped it, have we?'

'It looks fairly recent, Lista. Can you see what brand it is?'

Lista turned it round carefully. 'Gauloise, I think.' He put it in a small plastic bag to take back to the forensic lab.

'That's interesting,' remarked Bernal. 'A French make. That still fits in with my tentative theory, at any rate.'

Early in the morning of Maundy Thursday, Ángel Gallardo looked out of the window of his sparse room in the small *hostal* and surveyed the Calle de la Concepción. He had asked for the second floor, which gave him a good view of the street and of the main gate of the Convent of the Palm opposite. He had taken the precaution of walking round the entire block and had seen no other way into the convent.

He gazed up at the small barred windows of the grim building and wondered whether the window of Elena's cell overlooked the street, which was so narrow they could have come close to shaking hands across it. But he had seen no signs of life, apart from dim lights in some of the cells the previous night. So far no one had entered or left by the main gate.

He ate the meagre breakfast of lukewarm, weak milky coffee and a hunk of dry bread which the rough-looking proprietress of the *hostal* had brought up to him, grumbling at having to climb two flights of stairs, which she proclaimed she would do for no other client.

Ángel had a zoom-lens Pentax ready for action on the window-sill, and he watched the street slowly coming to life in the early morning sunshine.

At 7.30, the wicket-gate set in the large double door of the convent was opened, and a grim-faced nun emerged carrying an empty basket. He took a shot of her as she turned up the street. Nothing else happened until she returned ten minutes later with the basket now filled with *pistolas* of fresh bread. Ángel sighed and settled down for a long wait.

At roughly the same time on the same morning, Bernal assembled his team at the main Comisaría in the newer part of Cadiz, the only exceptions being Elena and Ángel who were on duty at the Convent of the Palm. The briefing meeting was also attended by Fragela, the local inspector, Dr Peláez, the pathologist, and Varga, the technician.

'I thought it would be useful if we reviewed the case so far,' Bernal began, 'for I think we are dealing with one main conspiracy, plus a subsidiary but unconnected plot.' He took up a blue-covered file. 'First, the unidentified frogman whose body was taken from the sea last Friday evening was a North African, probably Moroccan, member of an organization we shall call "Melkart". He may very well have been a serviceman on special operations, to judge by his physique. I'm hoping for some information about this clandestine organization this morning from Inspector Ibáñez in Central Records.' Bernal now opened the file. 'Let's consider what probably occurred. The frogman seems to have been attempting to penetrate the defences of the Rota base from the sea. This is likely to have meant that he was brought into Cadiz Bay in a submarine, possibly a new type of midget submarine. Such a vessel was spotted at night some weeks ago by fishermen from Rota, when their fishing-boat was nearly overturned by it. The type of vessel is unknown, but Rear Admiral Soto is trying to find out about it.'

'Could such a vessel have crossed over from the Moroccan coast?' asked Navarro.

'The Navy thinks it highly unlikely it could have carried sufficient fuel for that,' replied Bernal. 'They consider it more probable that it was launched from a larger ship somewhere in the Strait. Now our first problem is to decide when that intrusion occurred. The American head of security at Rota, Commander Weintraub, has given me a written statement about a so-called "incident" on the night of the twenty-fifth of March, when a third party may have been gravely injured. This incident involved the use of a new laser-beam anti-personnel weapon.'

'I'm very glad to hear that confirmed, Bernal,' commented Dr Peláez. 'As you know, it's what I concluded at the second post mortem on the deceased frogman. It's a completely new method of homicide, unknown to the textbooks.'

'It was extremely clever of you to spot it, Peláez, and your discovery dismayed the Americans, I can tell you. The problem about the date of the incident is that the local pathologists and yourself estimated that the frogman had been dead for eleven or twelve days, whereas the Americans' statement would suggest only eight days had elapsed. How can that discrepancy be resolved?'

'It could help to explain a number of factors that have worried me all along, Bernal. I was puzzled by the hypostatic staining or lividity on the back of the deceased frogman, which would suggest that he had floated on his back after death, whereas it is more common for a body to float face down. Mind you, the local doctors were correct in their estimate of eleven or twelve days from the extent of the internal putrefaction.'

'So what is the solution?' asked Bernal.

Peláez took off his thick pebble-lens glasses and polished them carefully as he spoke. 'If the body was at first kept in air, before being pushed back into the sea, it would have seriously affected the rate of putrefaction.' He replaced his spectacles and beamed at his captive audience. 'Let's suppose that the midget submarine deposited the frogman at the mouth of Rota harbour on the night of the twenty-fifth of March. He succeeds in penetrating the defences but is soon detected, and is then fired on from one of the laser-guns while he is still in the water. There he quickly dies, and is lifted out on to dry land and placed flat on his back.'

'That would have been the moment when they would have stripped him of his technical equipment and certain other things, which they wanted to examine in order to ascertain his purpose and origin,' said Bernal. 'They also removed his false teeth to prevent identification.'

'And all this time the cadaver is in a recumbent position, allowing the hypostasis to form beneath his body as the blood drained from the uppermost vessels by gravitational force,' commented Peláez. 'He must have been kept in that position for forty-eight hours or more, during which time internal putrefaction would begin to develop at least twice as fast in air as it would have done in cold salt water.'

'Perhaps during that period,' said Bernal, 'urgent official consultations were taking place about how to dispose of him. It's even possible the cadaver was examined clinically by a surgeon, who may have advised that the cause of death could not easily be determined. Then they may have decided to pass it off as a scuba-diving accident, and took him out at night and dumped him in the Bay.'

'It's then that the putrefaction rate would have been slowed down by the sea-water,' said Peláez, 'although the marine creatures were able to take a nibble at the head and limbs, which made it impossible for us to identify him.'

'That means that all the calculations the rear admiral did for us on the possible movements of the body in the tides and currents of the Bay were a waste of time,' remarked Bernal wryly.

'Not necessarily,' said Peláez. 'At least you happened to work out that the cadaver probably set out from Rota, and the Americans, no doubt, just sent it out a sea-mile or so in a patrol boat, from which it was dropped into the water two or three days later than you thought, thus helping it on its way to where it was fished out. In any case, the analysis of the diatoms in the water trapped in the windpipe of the deceased confirms that his body had entered the water in that corner of the Bay.'

'We'll probably never know for certain what occurred that night,' Bernal concluded, 'but we can report it to Madrid as a military incident. Now the next question is: why should a Moroccan organization send in a frogman to the joint American–Spanish base at Rot ? After all, the Moroccans are now allies of the USA, just as we are. It seems unlikely on the face of it that the intruder was planning to sabotage vessels in the harbour, though we cannot rule it out.'

'The irritating thing is, *jefe*,' commented Navarro, 'that the Americans must know what he was up to from the equipment found on the body, but they may still not know who he was or where he came from.'

'And we're in the opposite case,' replied Bernal. 'It's ironic, isn't it?'

'Isn't there the possibility of doing a deal with them by exchanging the information?' asked Miranda.

'It's not our task to consider that,' said Bernal, 'and we have no authority for it, but I'll put it to Madrid.'

'What about the midget submarine?' asked Navarro. 'Do the Americans know about that?'

'I asked them, but they claimed they didn't,' said Bernal, 'so we can't be sure. Apropos of that, Varga will put on the screen the photos Lista took last evening at Sancti Petri island. They show very deep grooves in the shingle at the bottom of a shaft or blow-hole just outside the ruined castle there. As you can see, the markings indicate that a strange kind of craft has been there very recently. The grooves you are looking at are almost a metre wide. The Navy is trying to find out what kind of craft would leave such marks. Soto's initial suggestion was a small catamaran.'

'Could they be using Sancti Petri island as a temporary base?' asked Lista.

'That's entirely possible,' replied Bernal. 'That's why I want you to go back there shortly with Varga to make a thorough search. The tide will be right for landing by ten-thirty, Soto says.' Bernal now took up another blue file. 'That brings us to the second death, that of Sergeant Pedro Ramos at Sancti Petri village at the entrance to the channel that leads up to our naval dockyards at La Carraca and Bazán. You'll recall that he reported on Sunday night a light signal from the sea and took down a partial Morse message which he radioed in to his base at Chiclana. It mentioned the code-word "Melkart" which was also deciphered from the frogman's tattoo. The next morning Ramos was found hanged under the wooden jetty, but it turns out to have been a simulated hanging. He had been throttled first with a fine cord, which itself is a suggestive method: it is common in Arab and Eastern countries. My initial supposition is that his radio message was intercepted by the intruders at Sancti Petri island or near it, who came upon him unawares and put him to death, which they then tried to pass off as suicide.'

'Why should the intruders have been at the island, chief?' asked Navarro.

'Because it was off that island that an unidentified vessel had twice disappeared off the Navy radar screens at San Fernando.'

'And what about Whale Bay mentioned in the intercepted radio message?' asked Miranda.

'Lista has solved that for us, I think,' said Bernal. 'It's probably a small cove near Cape Roche, where a rendezvous is planned for Saturday night at eleven-thirty p.m. Lista spotted that there is a black rock shaped like a whale in that lonely bay. My greatest worry is this: what is being planned by these Moroccans that involves our coast virtually from Cape Trafalgar to Rota? I first thought that they might be planning a landing, but that seems to be an incredible notion. Soto tells me that their Navy is very small, and mainly consists of fishery protection vessels. They have recently acquired more naval craft and arms from their deal with the Americans, but their chief gain is in foodstuffs and finance, while the USA has obtained a third line of defence beyond NATO and beyond their bilateral treaty with us.'

'Are the goings-on at the convent connected with this affair in any way?' asked Fragela.

'I still regard that as a separate and minor internal matter,' said Bernal. 'Some dissident and extremist officers in our army are planning to release two prisoners from the Santa Catalina fort on Saturday evening, under cover of the Easter celebrations in the town. I agree that the time is a coincidence, but no more than that. Elena has smuggled out a film which is being developed for us and should provide photos of the colonel and captain concerned. Once we have those pictures we should be able to identify the plotters easily. Perhaps you and Fragela would see to that this morning, Paco.'

'Of course, Comisario,' said Fragela.

'I've notified the Ministry of Defence in Madrid, and the JUJEM is taking certain measures. I think it sufficient for the moment to keep Elena Fernández and Gallardo at the convent, observing the movements of the conspirators. They will inform us if they need any back-up. Now,' Bernal went on, opening a third blue file, 'to return to the Melkart affair: I've racked my brains about what else the Moroccans could be up to. There is a possible clue in the conversation Ángel Gallardo recorded at the Casino at El Puerto. It was conducted in English, but we've now received a full transcript and an official translation from the Navy at San Fernando. It's clear from this that three of the Moroccan visitors were not traders or merchants as their passports stated, but naval officers, who had been flown over to Jerez airport in a private plane piloted by an air force officer. It seems that they were sounding out the three US Navy officers about imminent shipping movements at Rota, and about the defences of the harbour, having apparently offered them bribes to pay off their huge gambling debts. Soto and I are consulting our Defence Ministry about what to do: the Minister may well decide to inform the American Government about this grave danger to security at the joint base.'

'What about the placenames Ángel heard mentioned in that conversation?' asked Navarro.

'Our enclaves in Morocco were mentioned *en passant*, in

the context of their being an affront to Moroccan pride. There was also mention of the Melkart Organization, but there is no explanation of what it stands for.' Bernal took a sip of water from a small beaker. 'My conclusion from all this is that Melkart intends to attack or neutralize our ships that are currently in the Bay and the American submarines at Rota. I'm seeing Rear Admiral Soto later this morning for a conference with his admiral and his political liaison officer. I personally feel that we should take immediate precautions, and put all our naval units on Red Alert and recommend that the Americans do the same.'

'But why should the Moroccans want to do this?' asked Miranda.

'My guess is that they're planning something in Morocco and want to forestall any interference from this side of the Strait. I take it you've all seen on television or read in the press about what is going on in the Falklands between Britain and Argentina. The British authorities at Gibraltar are heavily engaged in provisioning additional ships to supplement the task force they have dispatched to the South Atlantic. As a result, NATO's naval strength is much depleted, and there's no chance whatsoever of the British intervening in anything that might happen in North Africa, even assuming they would want to be involved.'

'What do you suggest we do now, *jefe*?' asked Navarro.

'Concentrate on Sancti Petri island today. This evening we'll have a further conference after I've seen Soto and his colleagues.'

After Prime, Elena Fernández sat in the cloister until the members of the Order had left the chapel and gone about their various tasks. She had been surprised not to see Sister Encarnación in her usual place, but concluded that she had been allotted some kitchen chore, despite the fact that it would be most unusual for one of the nuns to miss any of the canonical hours.

When all seemed peaceful, Elena re-entered the chapel and ensured that it was empty. She walked up the aisle and opened the vestry door. Seeing no one inside, she tried the steel door on the right, which she assumed led to the cave beneath. She was disappointed to find it locked. She glanced at her watch and saw it was past 8.0 a.m. What could have happened to the kindly old sister? She vacillated, wondering how safe it was to wait there. Perhaps Sister Encarnación would soon arrive with the keys to show her the holy grotto.

Elena became more nervous as the time passed: five minutes, ten minutes; then, just as she resolved to leave and go and ask the cook whether she had seen the old nun that day, she heard masculine voices in the church. Oh God, what should she do if they came into the vestry? She looked desperately about, and saw the long row of chasubles and albs hanging in a half-open cupboard, and with sudden resolve she hid herself behind them as best she could.

At that moment Father Sanandrés entered, accompanied by the same colonel and captain as on the two previous days. Elena held her breath and hoped no part of herself or her clothing was visible. In her right pocket she had the miniature Japanese cassette-recorder, and sliding it slowly out she switched it on and pointed its powerful directional microphone towards the newcomers.

'But you must help, Father,' the colonel was saying, 'it's your duty to Spain and to God, as well as to the memory of the late Caudillo.'

'What about the extreme danger to my sisters and brethren of the Order if you are discovered?' objected the prior in a whinging tone. 'I'm not thinking about myself, of course.'

'There will be no risk, none at all,' said the younger captain firmly. 'You know the admiral has agreed to get them away within twenty-four hours.'

'Are you sure it will work?' asked the prior nervously.

'Of course it will. You've shown us how.'

'But there may be spies among us, among the lay visitors, who will spot what's going on. Not to mention one of the sisters, who may be a weak link.'

'That's why we go tomorrow night,' said the colonel gruffly, 'one day early, under cover of the Procession of the Silence at midnight. It's the perfect opportunity. Either your people will be in bed or out on the street, so that we'll be able to slip into the convent with our men when the city is in darkness. No one will see us.'

'And you don't have to be involved at all, Father,' wheedled the young captain. 'Just give us the keys to the padlock on the iron gate and to this door, that's all we ask.'

'You'd best go out in the midnight procession yourself, Father,' ordered the colonel, 'exactly as arranged. That way you've got a complete alibi.'

The prior was obviously hesitating.

'Come on now,' said the colonel, 'just show us how to operate the trick mechanism in the cave. That's all you have to do.'

'Very well,' said the prior at last, with great reluctance, 'but God help me.'

'God will help us all, Father. This is God's work,' the colonel reminded him.

There was a metallic scraping noise as Father Sanandrés unlocked the steel door, and the three of them descended to the cavern below, shutting the heavy door behind them.

In high excitement at what she had overheard, Elena crept out from her hiding-place and gently tried the steel door. It was locked from the other side. She decided that her first priority must be to pass this new information on to Bernal, and that she should do nothing further that might jeopardize that aim. She peeped round the outer door of the vestry and could see no one in the church. She left quietly, failing to observe Sister Serena's narrowed eyes watching her from the latticed gallery.

In the lodging-house opposite the convent, Ángel watched the two army officers arriving soon after 8.0 a.m., and photographed them as they waited for the door to be opened by the portress. He knew that Bernal had arranged to send a message in to Elena via the Catalan woman that afternoon to inform her that he was keeping observation on the religious house, and to tell her to make a signal with a white handkerchief from a window if she wanted assistance.

After half an hour the two officers emerged once more,

and Ángel got better full-face shots of them. No other activity occurred until nine o'clock, when a small dark-haired woman dressed in black came out, carrying empty shopping-bags on her arm. Ángel guessed she might be the cook on her way to market, but he took a photograph of her in case.

The rest of the morning was uneventful, apart from the return of the supposed cook, loaded with vegetables and fruit. Ángel looked forward to being relieved by one of Fragela's men at 1.0 p.m., so that he could take the film to the lab to be developed.

Lista, Miranda and Varga landed at the island of Sancti Petri in a coastguard cutter at 10.45 a.m., accompanied by three men of the Guardia Civil. The fine weather had continued, and the sun was quite hot on their heads as they climbed the stone steps to the ruined castle.

'The tide's too high for us to make the descent to the cavern, Carlos,' said Lista, showing his colleague the natural shaft, from the bottom of which came the roar of waves.

'Let's start by making a thorough search of the castle,' suggested Varga, 'while the Civil Guards comb the rest of the island.'

They spent a tiring and fruitless morning poking among the fallen masonry inside the shell of the seventeenth-century building, where they were frequently surprised by alarmed sea-birds as they came upon their hidden nests, and at one moment Miranda was attacked by a very angry gannet.

At one o'clock the Civil Guard sergeant returned to report that he and his men had found nothing of interest, except for assorted flotsam and jetsam trapped in the low rocks. None of this appeared to be connected with the clandestine Melkart organization. Lista looked down the shaft and at last could see some natural light coming in from the sea below the castle. Varga rigged up a powerful arc lamp and shone it into the blow-hole.

'I can see sand at the bottom now,' he said. 'Soon we'll be able to go down. You can still see those parallel grooves on the shingle. The tide hasn't altogether obliterated them.'

Miranda leaned over to take a look. 'If they were very pronounced yesterday, as on the photographs you took, Juan, doesn't that mean they had been made very recently?'

'Yes, you're right. Probably yesterday morning after high tide.'

'Then we'd better be careful and go armed when we descend.'

'Let's have lunch now,' said Lista, 'to give the tide more time to recede.'

When they returned to the blow-hole Lista said: 'There's no need for all three of us to go. Varga and I can do the job while you control the operation from up here, Carlos.'

Miranda, not being very athletic or having much of a head for heights, agreed readily.

The Civil Guards rigged up ropes for Varga and Lista to be lowered. They could see that the rope-ladder was still in position in the shaft, but unaccountably reached only just under half way up.

'I'll go first,' offered Lista, 'since I've been down before.'

After five minutes had passed, he reached the bottom and waited for Varga to join him. He took rather longer, being stockier and more uncertain of the location. In the morning light streaming into the rocky passage from the sea, the inspector and the technician could see that the grooves in the sandy bottom were still some fifteen centimetres deep and led through a high-roofed passage for about 150 metres to the water's edge at the western side of the island. There they found a small beach of shingle, edged with sharp rocks.

'It's a very dangerous place to bring a boat in, isn't it?' commented Varga.

'Especially at night,' said Lista. 'It would have to be a small craft and you'd need a good light on it.'

They saw that the two parallel grooves ran down into the sand at the edge of the breakers. As they turned to explore the inner end of the rocky passage, Varga looked up at the steep sides of the cliff, which were covered with guano.

'You certainly couldn't get up those rocks without climbing equipment,' he remarked. 'But look: there's a mark painted above the cave entrance.'

138

Amid the grey and white guano on the rock face, they could see some squiggles placed there in dull greenish-white paint.

'It's in Arabic characters, I think,' said Lista. 'They aren't easy to spot at first. Take a photo of it, will you?'

After this had been done, Varga asked Lista to assist him to climb up to the painted sign, and they slung a rope round a high boulder to make the ascent easier. Once up, Varga took a small scraping of the paint with a penknife and put it carefully into a clear plastic envelope.

'I'm pretty sure this is luminous paint,' he commented as he clambered down again. 'We'll soon be able to tell when we go inside.'

As they returned slowly along the rocky passage, they examined every centimetre of the walls and roof, which were composed of large fossilized oyster-shells interspersed with small pieces of limestone. At the base of the blow-hole, they shouted up to Miranda that they were going to inspect the inner part of the cave.

'Turn the light out,' said Varga. 'Let's test this paint for luminosity.'

In the darkness of the inner cave, they saw that the scraping of paint glowed pale green.

'So when they come at night, they look out for the luminous sign,' said Lista. 'But they'd have to have pretty sharp eyed to spot it.'

'They probably know this island like the back of their hand,' said Varga, switching on the powerful lamp again. 'It's just an additional check for them, I expect.'

'Let's take a look at the inner cavern,' said Lista. 'When I was here yesterday the torch I had wasn't powerful enough to light it up. If they've got anything stored, it'll probably be back here above the waterline.'

The passage, which was some three metres wide at this point, continued for about fifty metres. Then it suddenly opened into a large cavern, which had an uneven rock-strewn floor and a high roof with long stalactites festooned from it.

'It's dry up there at any rate,' said Varga, shining the

139

lamp across the roof. As he lowered it, they were astonished to see a number of figures leaning at drunken angles among the rocks.

'My God, it's like a pagan temple,' exclaimed Lista, whistling gently.

They went up to the nearest figure and examined it closely. It was obviously manmade and carved from white marble, but the action of the sea over many centuries had worn away the features and pitted the surface so that it presented a curiously effaced appearance.

Varga ran his hand over the head of the figure.

'I think we're looking at the remains of the Temple of Melkart,' said Lista in an awed voice. 'What a pity these figures have been eroded by the sea. They would have been a national monument if they'd been decently preserved.'

Varga shone the light into the back of the cavern, where they spotted a sudden movement on one of the larger statues, and Lista took out his service pistol and cocked it. They advanced cautiously towards the figure, which gave the impression of having a headful of blue-black hair, on which something seemed to beckon at them.

Varga laughed suddenly. 'It's only a starfish waving his legs at us.'

'But what's that that looks like hair?' asked Lista in an appalled voice.

Varga went up to the statue and inspected the head. 'It's encrusted with mussels and the starfish is feeding on them. There's no one here.'

The grotesquely encrusted head filled Lista with horrified fascination, and he said, 'What if under those mussels is the head of Melkart himself, the Tyrian Hercules?'

'Could be,' said Varga. 'Let's leave that to the archæologists. They'll come swarming down here if they get to hear of this.'

They made a thorough search of the large cavern, but found nothing of military interest.

'Now if you were using this place as a temporary base, where would you keep your supplies and equipment?' Lista asked.

Varga considered. 'Well above sea-level. And the only possibility here is the roof, but you can see that there's nothing up there.'

'The rope-ladder,' said Lista with a sudden flash of understanding. 'It stops almost half way up the shaft. Let's find out why.'

After taking flash photographs of the inner chamber and close-ups of the sea-eroded statues, they returned to the base of the blow-hole. Varga went up the ladder first, examining the sides of the natural chimney with extra care.

'Here's the high-tide mark,' he shouted down to Lista, while Miranda observed them from above. 'It's about twelve metres up. If there's anything hidden it must be above this point.'

He was nearly at the top of the rope-ladder when he called out: 'There's a wide fissure here.'

'Is it wide enough to enter?' asked Lista.

'I don't think so, but I can get my arm in.' He shone the lamp into the cavity in the rock. 'There are some boxes here.'

'Hold on, I'm coming up,' shouted Lista.

Gradually, with the assistance of a rope and basket lowered by Miranda and the civil guards, Lista and Varga emptied the cache and brought its contents up to the top of the shaft. The hoard consisted of eight boxes of munitions, with markings in French. They found there were two dozen underwater grenades, ten small limpet mines, a quantity of plastic explosive and two harpoon-guns.

'Shall I send a radio message from the launch to the Comandancia de la Marina and ask for instructions?' asked the Civil Guard sergeant.

'No, don't do that,' said Miranda. 'The message might get intercepted. We'll have to work out what Superintendent Bernal would want us to do.'

Lista said, 'I think we ought to remove this stuff and disarm the enemy.'

'I agree,' replied Miranda. 'Obviously they'll realize someone has been here, but better that than that they should use those munitions to destroy our ships in harbour.'

'In any case they may not return until the time scheduled for the operation,' said Lista, 'and then it would be too late for them to obtain replacement supplies.'

'Let's load it on to the patrol boat,' said Varga, 'and make sure we haven't left any trace of our visit.'

Before he left for the security meeting, Bernal took a call from Inspector Ibáñez from Central Records in Madrid.

'I've found a brief file on Melkart for you, Luis. It's a group of Muslim fundamentalist officers in Morocco and Algeria pledged to reunite the whole Maghreb under strict Kuranic law. They've apparently been plotting to usurp the throne in Rabat and oust Hassan II, and their network extends throughout the Moroccan armed forces.'

'That's very valuable information, Esteban. Could you send me down the contents of the file? I want to cross-check some names.'

'I'll send it down by the next plane out of Barajas.'

Bernal asked Inspector Fragela to accompany him to the formal security meeting at the Captaincy-General of the Navy. He had earlier telephoned the Defence Ministry to obtain top-grade security clearance for the local inspector, considering him indispensable for the investigation.

Rear Admiral Soto met them in the entrance hall and took them to his office.

'I'd better explain the set-up, Comisario. The admiral of the fleet, who is the Captain-General of the Armada, will preside at the meeting, and three vice-admirals will also be present. They are responsible for fleet movements, personnel and supplies, respectively. We shall also have the benefit of the advice of the commodore in charge of political liaison. In addition, the military governor of Cadiz province and the chief of the Civil Guard have been invited.'

'What form will the meeting take, Admiral?'

'The captain-general will make the introductions, and then ask you to give a résumé of the cases of the deceased frogman and the murder of Sergeant Ramos. Next there will be a pooling of information, followed by the taking of decisions about what counter-measures to adopt.'

'Very well. We've brought the up-to-date files with us.'

As they ascended the elegant marble staircase to the conference chamber of the Captaincy, Bernal saw a group of admirals waiting on the landing. Suddenly he stopped and pulled the rear admiral back.

'Who's that admiral on the left, Soto?' he asked urgently.

'Why, that's the vice-admiral in charge of supplies.'

'I'm sure he's the one I saw in the Convent of the Palm last Saturday talking to Father Sanandrés.' Bernal looked at Soto and Fragela, thinking hard. 'I suggest we make no mention at all of the events at the convent or of the plot to free the two army officers from the fort of Santa Catalina. This vice-admiral may well be implicated in that business. Do you know whether he has extremist views, Soto?'

'Most of us do, Comisario,' said Soto laconically. 'It's in-built from our training. But that fellow is more extremist than most.'

'You'll have to decide what to do about him after the meeting's over,' said Bernal. 'Remember that the JUJEM have decided to allow the army plot to come to fruition, under discreet surveillance, so as to obtain firm evidence against the conspirators that will stand up at a court-martial.'

'I agree it's best to say nothing,' said Soto gravely.

'Very well. Let's go into the lions' den.'

The captain-general received them all with gruff courtesy and asked each participant to identify himself to the others. He then asked Bernal to give a brief outline of the incidents that had occurred in the Bay. The others listened to his succinct account with keen interest, especially to the part that concerned the meeting with the American security chief at Rota. When he had finished, the captain-general asked Bernal whether anything had been found on Sancti Petri island.

'As we meet, my men, together with a detachment of the Civil Guard, are making a thorough search. I've asked them to send me urgent word if they discover anything.'

'I have some news that may be of interest,' said the chief of the Civil Guard. 'Some of my men arrested two

Argentinian officers who were posing as tourists in a boarding-house at Algeciras this morning. These agents entered the country at Madrid-Barajas a week ago, and were continuously shadowed by our Intelligence men from the CESID. They carried large sums in US dollars, and purchased munitions from two different arms dealers in the capital. Then they hired a station wagon and drove down to Algeciras, where they bought a rubber dinghy with an outboard motor. They made a dummy run last night across the bay to Gibraltar under cover of darkness and partially penetrated the British defences. While they were out, my men searched their room and found a quantity of limpet-mines, plastic explosive, and two sub-machine-guns. It's clear that they were planning an attack on the British installations, but the head of the CESID decided that such an action would have put our citizens in great danger, as well as the *llanitos* at Gibraltar. After consultation with the President of the Government, it was decided to order their arrest and deportation to Buenos Aires.' There was a murmur around the room, which Bernal interpreted as one of disapprobation. 'The President,' the Civil Guard chief went on, 'resolved also to have the British ambassador informed. The Government take the view that it would be an embarrassment to become involved in the Malvinas-Falklands dispute.'

'I think it's an outrage,' expostulated the vice-admiral whom Bernal had recognized from his visit to the convent. 'The Argentinians should have been allowed to go ahead and blow the British base up. Then we could have taken the Rock, or what was left of it.' He looked round at the others as though for confirmation of his views.

'If our late Caudillo never judged the moment right for such a move during forty years,' commented the captain-general with exquisite irony, 'then it would have seemed foolhardy for the present Government, with such a short lifespan, to grasp that particular nettle.'

The vice-admiral glowered, and chewed on his cheroot of Canary tobacco. 'But we've never had a chance like this before,' he spluttered.

'May I remind you, Vice-Admiral, that there were a number of chances during the Second World War,' said the captain-general, 'but the time was never considered ripe.'

The political liaison officer now intervened. 'The British are clearly not ungrateful to us. I've just been sent a signal by my British counterpart at Gibraltar, who informs us of secret troop movements north of Tetuan, west of Axdir and north of Nador. They have also noted small-scale naval movements south of the island of Alborán, which belongs to us, as you all know.'

'How did they come by this secret information?' asked the captain-general.

'The troop movements were spotted by routine satellite pictures, while the naval activity was picked up by British radar.'

They all looked at the large wall map of the Strait.

'You will observe that the troop movements are close to our possessions at Ceuta, Al Hoceima, the Peñón de Alhucemas and Melilla,' the commodore pointed out. 'I have passed this information to Madrid and to the military governor of our African territories.'

'What puzzles me is this,' commented the captain-general. 'What are the Moroccans really up to on this side of the Strait? What does the Melkart organization aim to do?'

Bernal waited to see if any of the others would volunteer anything, but none did. After a pause he said quietly: 'I have received some information from Central Records this morning. Melkart appears to be the name of an élitist group of officers who are pledged to reunite the Maghreb and reimpose strict Muslim law. They may well intend to carry out simultaneous coups d'état in Rabat and Algiers, and may also be planning with their counterparts in Tunis to bring Bourguiba's long rule to an end. It certainly shouldn't surprise us if their aim is to take back Ceuta, Melilla and our other enclaves in their territory.'

'Take back?' snorted the extremist vice-admiral. 'Those territories have never belonged to them! Do you realize how much Spanish blood has been spilled over the centuries to

145

defend our possessions in North Africa? Morocco and Algeria are just tin-pot countries carved out of the desert after the Second World War by the former belligerents. De Gaulle did his best to hang on to the French possessions, but he was betrayed in the end, just like our late Generalísimo— may he rest in eternal peace—when we gave up the Spanish Sahara to Hassan.'

'I wasn't suggesting that we should give our enclaves up to them, Vice-Admiral,' said Bernal. 'I'm simply guessing at the motives of this clandestine organization.'

'You think it's certain they're planning an attack on our territories there, Comisario?' inquired the captain-general.

'I'm sure of it. Their activities in the Bay of Cadiz are probably intended to neutralize our fleet, and they must be anxious for the Americans not to intervene.'

'Our fleet is already on Yellow Alert, Comisario,' said the captain-general. 'Do you consider that we should go on to Red Alert?'

'I most certainly do, sir, and that's what I have recommended to my superiors in Madrid this morning,' said Bernal firmly.

'But do you realize what that would mean in terms of manpower and cost?' asked the vice-admiral in charge of personnel. 'We'll have to recall all the officers and crews from shore leave and embark them.'

'So I should expect,' said Bernal. 'More than that, I'm inclined to propose that you should sail the fleet.'

'Sail the fleet?' queried the third vice-admiral in astonishment. 'I should point out that a number of our vessels are undergoing repairs and refits; it would take days to get them ready.'

'It must be done by Saturday evening,' replied Bernal, 'if you don't want to risk losing them in harbour by sabotage, as well as losing our Moroccan possessions.' He pointed to the wall map. 'I propose that all the fleet sail, from Cadiz and Cartagena, with reinforcements brought down from El Ferrol. The southern flotillas should proceed for Ceuta, Alhucemas and Melilla, with troops aboard to strengthen the garrisons there.'

A wave of excited chatter broke out, and the captain-general called the meeting to order. 'Gentlemen, gentlemen. I suggest we keep calm. The Superintendent's views must be given weighty consideration.'

At that moment of drama, a naval lieutenant entered the room and handed a message to the captain-general, who read it immediately.

'You are required urgently on the telephone, Comisario,' he said to Bernal. 'You can take the call in the next room. The lieutenant will show you the way.'

As he left, Bernal felt as if he had lifted the lid of Pandora's box and was being overwhelmed by what was released from it.

Paco Navarro was calling him from Cadiz. 'Lista has just phoned in from Torre Gorda, *jefe*. He and Varga have found an arms cache in the shaft at Sancti Petri island, above an extraordinary cavern under the castle which could be the ruins of the Temple of Melkart.'

'Have they removed all the arms and brought them ashore?'

'Yes, chief. They thought you'd want to disarm the enemy.'

'Very good. But they may have another cache somewhere else. What did the hoard consist of?'

Navarro read out the list to him and Bernal jotted it down on a notepad.

'And the markings on the boxes were in French?'

'Yes, chief, but there was no manufacturer's mark. Varga is studying the munitions now with the naval armourer at Torre Gorda.'

'They're probably of Belgian manufacture, commonly available from the international arms dealers.'

'How's the meeting going, chief?'

'Stormy at the moment, but I think they'll see sense sooner or later.'

Bernal returned to the conference room and the gathering fell silent as he took his seat once more. Fragela gave him a wry glance; at least he was an ally who would give him a full account of what had transpired during his absence. The captain-general looked at Bernal expectantly.

'Well, Comisario? Any news?'

'A considerable arms cache has been discovered at the island of Sancti Petri.' He read out the list of limpet-mines, plastic explosive, underwater grenades and machine-guns. 'All this matériel is now at your naval base at Torre Gorda, so we've managed to draw some of Melkart's teeth.' Bernal lit a Kaiser and drew on it. 'I think we must conclude, Admiral, that they intend to attack your ships, and it seems to me that they would be much safer at sea than scattered round the Bay.'

'But now there's much less danger,' said the vice-admiral in charge of naval operations. 'And our electronic devices should spot the intruders before they reach the ships.'

'May I point out that you appear to have no such devices at the mouth of the Sancti Petri channel that leads directly to La Carraca and Bazán? That must be where they are planning to penetrate.'

'Nothing can sail up there,' said the vice-admiral dismissively. 'There isn't sufficient draught for a submarine, and any surface launch would be spotted and stopped long before it could reach our ships.'

'You are forgetting the mysterious midget submarine,' said Bernal quietly. 'You still haven't found out what sort of vessel it might be, have you?'

They admitted they didn't have any information as yet.

'Then why take such an enormous risk with two capital ships and three destroyers? Get them out to sea and doing something important, such as reinforcing the garrisons at Ceuta and Melilla. What ships do you have on station there at present?'

The operations vice-admiral looked uncomfortable: 'A frigate at Melilla and two at Ceuta,' he admitted.

'And the military strength?' Bernal inquired of the provincial governor.

'I'm not certain, Comisario, but there should be two and a half thousand troops at Ceuta and half that number at Melilla, though many may be on leave for Holy Week.'

'Could they withstand an overland attack purposefully launched?'

'It would depend on its size, obviously. If the whole Moroccan army were to be deployed . . .'

'Then what have you to lose by strengthening the garrisons there?'

'It would weaken our defences here,' the captain-general pointed out calmly.

'How long would it take to bring support ships from the northern fleet?' asked Bernal.

'At least forty-eight hours.'

'Well then, there is still time. We have two days. And I assume that troop reinforcements could be brought down from Jerez and Seville to guard the installations here. We mustn't forget that Melkart has helpers on shore, here and now, and we have no idea where they are.'

'How can you be so sure?' asked the captain-general.

'Because they were signalling to the shore, but we don't know to whom. We have an opportunity, though, to capture them at the rendezvous near Cape Roche on Saturday night, if we plan it carefully.'

Further intense discussion followed, with Soto, the political liaison officer and the military governor supporting Bernal's views about what action should be taken, while the three vice-admirals opposed them. Bernal gained the clear impression that the captain-general leaned to his view.

'I don't think we can get much further this morning, gentlemen,' he said, 'except to put our fleet on Red Alert forthwith. This will involve calling all officers and men back from shore leave, and hastening all repairs to enable the ships to sail, if necessary. I shall put Comisario Bernal's further proposals to reinforce the North African enclaves to the head of the JUJEM after this meeting. In the meantime, I expect you to cooperate with the Comisario and his colleagues in planning detailed counter-measures, especially with a view to capturing the members of the Melkart organization both on our shores and in our territorial waters. Vigilance, secrecy and decisive action: let those be our watchwords, gentlemen.'

Elena Fernández spent Thursday morning in a fever of excitement. She wrote out a report for Superintendent Bernal explaining the circumstances in which she had made the cassette-recording of the conversation between the prior and the army plotters. She also mentioned her determination to explore the holy cave when the opportunity presented itself. She included a brief account of Sister Encarnación's request for a private meeting, and the old nun's failure to turn up at the appointed time.

She sealed the report, together with the cassette, in a manila envelope addressed to Bernal, which she concealed in the deep pocket of her habit, and set out for the kitchen. There she offered to assist the cook to prepare the simple lunch of lentil stew accompanied by a salad of Swiss chard. At least there was a good selection of fruit for dessert. Elena supposed that the food would get ever more meagre as Good Friday approached.

The cook was a sullen, taciturn creature, who usually did little more than grunt, so that Elena had wondered if she was educationally subnormal. Still she would make an effort to get something out of her.

'Have you seen Sister Encarnación today?'

'Naw,' muttered the dark-haired woman, squeezing a hot lentil between forefinger and thumb to judge if it was softening satisfactorily.

'Hasn't she eaten anything? I didn't see her at breakfast.'

'Sister Serena took her breakfast up.'

'Is she ill, then?'

'Suppose so.'

At least this would explain the old nun's failure to turn up at the vestry after Prime. Seeing there was little else to be done, Elena went to the rear yard where she found Señora de Bernal and Sister Serena still threading flowers into the net on the float of the Garden of Gethsemane.

'Will you be walking in the procession with us tomorrow night, señorita?' asked Eugenia. 'It's the most solemn one of the week, you know.'

'I suppose I should,' said Elena doubtfully, 'but I'm not sure if I'll have the strength to walk all that way.'

'It's only three kilometres,' said Eugenia, 'but it's the slow pace that is the real penance.'

'There are plenty of pauses,' said Sister Serena sharply, 'and you're a very healthy young girl. It'll be good for your soul.'

Elena saw that her professional duty would be to remain in the convent and watch for the arrival of the army plotters with the prisoners, assuming that the operations to free them was successful. She would have to make an excuse for not going at the last moment.

Bernal had left the meeting at the Captaincy-General with Fragela, and they returned to Cadiz in their Super Mirafiori 124 after arranging to meet Rear Admiral Soto and his political liaison officer for lunch in El Anteojo Restaurant. As they sped along the Vía Augusta Julia, Bernal asked Fragela what had been said during his temporary absence from the meeting.

'It was mainly a tussle between the three vice-admirals and the military governor of the province, who took your side throughout, Superintendent. The others muttered a good deal about a Comisario from the DSE in Madrid come to teach them their business, about how expensive and difficult it would be to sail the fleet at short notice, and about the dangers of over-reaction.'

'It's time they saw some real action,' remarked Bernal grimly. 'They're just a bunch of desk-admirals, who've never been in an action at sea. It upsets their tidy minds actually to perform the task they're paid to do.'

'The political liaison officer was also sympathetic to your point of view, Comisario, but warned that sailing the fleet mustn't be made to look like a threat to the British at Gibraltar. He proposed that they be informed in secret of the reason for the naval movements. He thought the

Americans should also be informed, in accordance with the bilateral agreement.'

'He's right, of course, but the CIA and British Intelligence will find out even before we tell them. Can the commodore be trusted in the other matter of the army officers' plot, do you think?'

'I'm sure he can, since the rear admiral says he's been fully cleared by his Segunda Bis intelligence officers.'

The car at last pulled up outside the modern, plate-glassed restaurant on the Alameda Apodaca, and Bernal looked at his watch.

'We said two p.m., didn't we, Fragela?' The inspector nodded. 'Then we've got time for a stroll. Let's take advantage of the sunshine and walk up through the *mirador* as far as the Candelaria Battery.'

The wide walk overlooking the Bay was filled with strollers: sailors wearing their *lepantos* with the name of their ship embroidered across the front and their billowing collars which were white for Holy Week rather than the usual blue; elegantly dressed ladies with black mantillas draped over jewel-encrusted combs stuck firmly into their high-piled coiffures; and a number of young women pushing prams.

Bernal looked up at the buildings facing the sea and saw a number of foreign flags. 'I see the consulates are still maintained here.'

'Not as many as there used to be, Comisario, since the commercial port has declined.'

'I suppose they chose their houses for the coolness and the excellent view?'

'Mainly as an observation post, to watch the shipping entering and leaving the Bay. That's the reason for all the towers on the merchants' houses throughout the city.'

By now they had reached the battlements at the Candelaria Battery which afforded a wider view as far as the open sea.

'Those are the two groups of rocks between which the body of the frogman was found, are they?' asked Bernal, pointing to the north.

'Yes, they're uncovered at low water.' Fragela looked out

152

to the west. 'There are three warships sailing out to the Atlantic, Comisario. A destroyer and two frigates.'

Bernal gazed at the battle-grey ships steaming purposefully westwards. 'They must be British warships out of Gibraltar sailing for the South Atlantic.'

They strolled back down the *alameda* and sat at a table at the terrace bar owned by El Anteojo, and ordered two *gin-tónics*. When the rear admiral's official car drew up alongside them, Soto leapt out and said to them excitedly: 'Did you see? That was HMS *Glamorgan* with two frigates, armed to the teeth and sailing at full speed.'

'Your fleet should be sent out of port too, Admiral,' said Bernal, 'if it doesn't want to get blown to smithereens.'

Inspector Miranda went to call on Dr de Castro at the Faculty of Letters as Bernal had requested. He found the good doctor engrossed in his scholarly books at the edge of his work-desk, which was piled higgledy-piggledy with letters and papers to a height of almost half a metre.

Miranda's tidy nature was shocked at the sight of such disorder, and he speculated on how many of the letters were unanswered.

'I'm sure I've got a note for you on Melkart somewhere,' de Castro announced. 'You know of course that he was the Tyrian Hercules, whose temple was at Herakleion, which some authorities identify with Sancti Petri island.'

'I think we've got that far,' said Miranda, 'and later we may be able to give you news of an archæological find there.'

'Excellent. It's all grist to the mill.' Dr de Castro surveyed the incredible pile of papers speculatively. 'Now let's see. Yes, it was about six months ago.' He put his hand approximately a fifth of the way down the pile. 'I had another inquiry about Melkart. Ah, this could be it.'

As though by magic he extracted the letter he wanted from the many hundreds stacked on the desk. 'Yes, it was from the manager of an hotel near Chiclana. Here it is, the Salineta Hotel. He had received a strange request from Rabat, written in French, asking whether he would rent out his hotel to a Moroccan business organization called

Melkart during the winter months, when the premises are normally shut. He wrote to me to ask if I knew anything about it, but I didn't.'

'And did he rent it to them?'

'Ah, that I don't know. I didn't reply to him, since I couldn't help.'

'May I keep this letter, Doctor?'

'Of course. There are plenty more of them here, as you can see. I don't read them all.'

Paco Navarro looked at the letter Miranda had brought in and wondered whether he should wait for Bernal to return from his lunch with the rear admiral. But what if the Melkart accomplices on shore were really holed up at the Salineta Hotel? It was urgent to find out. He decided to ring Captain Barba of the Civil Guard at Chiclana, who had been so helpful in the investigation of Sergeant Ramos's death.

When he got through to him, Barba was anxious to assist. 'I know the hotel, Inspector. It was popular as a spa before the Civil War since there are natural sulphurous springs there. It has recently been modernized, with an open-air swimming pool and a tennis-court built in the grounds. It is patronized in the summer months mainly by older professional families, but not by foreign tourists.'

'Could you find out from the locals whether it is open for Holy Week?'

'I'm sure it isn't, Inspector. The season doesn't start down here until the end of May, and the hotel is usually shut up for the winter months, but I've heard talk of its being let out to a business organization.'

'Don't go there or ring them up, Barba, but find out what you can otherwise. If possible, we'd like to know the whereabouts of the manager or the owners of the hotel, so that we could contact them. Superintendent Bernal will be in touch with you when he returns.'

Elena noticed that Sister Encarnación was still missing at lunch, and determined to ask Sister Serena about her.

'Our dear sister is *in clausura*, señorita, until Good Friday,' she replied coldly. 'She's undertaking the strictest of penances. Perhaps you should consider doing likewise.'

Waiting in the cloister for the ceremony of the Diurnal Adoration, Elena watched Sister Serena's comings and goings, but there was no sign of Father Sanandrés and no further visit by the army officers.

At 5.45 p.m. the main doorbell clanged and Elena waited with keen interest to see if the Catalan woman had arrived so that she could pass to her the vital message for Superintendent Bernal. At that moment Eugenia Bernal came up to her and suggested that they pray in the church before Vespers. Elena reluctantly followed her and they knelt together before the statue of Our Lady of the Palm until the angelus was rung.

Elena and Eugenia took their place behind the religious members of the house as usual, and Father Sanandrés, looking worried, Elena thought, emerged from the vestry attired in purple vestments. As the office began, Elena glanced round at the group of lay women behind her, but failed to spot her contact.

When Father Sanandrés had delivered the final blessing, he advanced to the foot of the altar and looked down through the glass panel into the holy cave. There he stood for some time with outstretched arms, and as the minutes went by, Elena could sense that the lay women were pressing forward in considerable anxiety, and soon there were some muttered exclamations of disappointment.

'It's failed today!' 'The sacred water won't come up!'

Finally Father Sanandrés turned to face the congregation and raised his right hand: 'On these final days of Lent, when we should do the strictest penance, it seems that the miraculous water will not flow.' There was a prolonged wail from the lay women. 'Tomorrow there will be no ceremony of the Diurnal Adoration, for it will be Holy Friday. I hope you will all come to walk with us in the Procession of the Silence and accompany our own *paso* of the Descent from the Cross.''

Elena turned to look at the gaggle of grumbling, disappointed women, but still could not see her contact. She

155

slipped out of her pew, seized with the urgency of sending the message to Bernal, and waited in the doorway of the church. She was immediately joined by Sister Serena.

'Perhaps you'll go and help Señora de Bernal with the float, señorita, while I see these women out.'

'Of course. I'll wait for her here.'

Elena desperately surveyed the faces of all the lay women as they passed, under Sister Serena's stern gaze, but the tall Catalan woman clearly hadn't come. There was no chance of sending the envelope out with one of the others while the tight-lipped nun stayed so close. She furiously debated with herself what she could do. There was no chance of getting to the only telephone in Father Sanandrés's office, which was always locked; she had tried the door several times. She herself could go out, of course, and 'phone the message to Navarro, but such a request to break her retreat would give rise to great suspicion, and it was essential for her to remain under cover until the officers' plot came to fruition.

After the portress has escorted all the women to the main door and sent them packing, Elena went miserably to the rear yard, where Eugenia Bernal was already at work. There was her last resort: Señora de Bernal could be confided in and asked to contact her husband.

Before supper, Elena went up to her cell and looked forlornly out of the barred window. Was there any other way she could get the message out?

A few metres from where she was standing, Ángel Gallardo was puzzling over the scene he had witnessed outside the convent almost an hour earlier. The group of women had assembled clutching empty glass bottles, and the wicket-gate had been opened by the severe-looking nun. When the tall chestnut-haired woman reached the narrow entrance, the portress had barred her way and a lively altercation had ensued, most of it inaudible to Ángel. After all the other women had been admitted, the tall woman had stalked off in high dudgeon down the street.

Ángel knew that Navarro had intended to send an urgent message in to Elena Fernández, informing her that he was

156

on hand in the *hostal* opposite to provide back-up whenever she signalled to him. The trouble was that he did not know what the contact looked like. He began to suspect that she might be the tall woman he'd seen being refused admission to the convent, and that could only mean that Elena's cover had been blown, perhaps without her realizing it. He decided to phone Navarro at once,

Bernal and Fragela arrived at their ops room exhausted from nearly three hours spent planning the detailed counter-measures to the Melkart operation. They had agreed an encirclement by land and sea of Whale Bay near Cape Roche ready for the secret rendezvous at 2330 hours on Saturday, 10 April, and they had resolved to ask for an anti-submarine net with passive sonar devices to be placed across the mouth of the Sancti Petri channel, reinforced by a detachment of civil guards hidden in the old barracks near the wooden landing-stage there. The Navy had already increased its vigilance on its bases, and the officers and men were even now returning to duty.

Navarro gave Bernal the most urgent news first. 'I've got a possible lead on the whereabouts of the Melkart accomplices ashore, *jefe*. Captain Barba is making inquiries at Chiclana for us.'

Bernal listened to the report of Miranda's visit to Dr de Castro and examined the letter from the manager of the Salineta Hotel. 'We must inform Soto, and arrange to stake out this hotel as soon as Barba confirms that the Arabs are there. They must be followed wherever they go. My guess is that they will lie low until Saturday night. The danger is that they may have smuggled ashore a supply of arms and munitions which they are holding in the hotel ready for the operation.'

'There's also a report from Ángel, chief. The Catalan woman was refused entry to the convent this afternoon, so there has been no contact with Elena. He fears her cover has been blown.'

Bernal looked grave and considered what action to take. 'She may be in danger, Paco, if they suspect her. But if we go in prematurely, we'll cause the officers' plot to be aborted, against the orders of the JUJEM which wants it to be allowed to proceed under our surveillance. Let me think about what to do.'

'Elena is very resourceful, *jefe*, as she's already shown on a number of cases. She'll come out herself if she has to.'

'Even so, I'm reluctant to leave her for two more days without back-up. Get Lista to talk to the Catalan woman and find out what went wrong, then ring me at my hotel.'

In the Hotel Francia y París, Bernal found a message waiting for him.

'A lady telephoned you twice from Las Palmas, Comisario,' said the girl receptionist. 'She's left a number for you to call.'

'I'll make the call from my room,' said Bernal.

Up in his comfortable room overlooking the small square filled with golden orange-trees, he took off his shoes, sat on the bed and lit a Kaiser. Soon he was talking to Consuelo.

'Luchi? Where've you been? I've been calling you in Madrid for three days, and now they've told me you were back in Cadiz,' she said accusingly.

'I'm sorry, *querida*, I've never left Cadiz, but I had no number to call you at. How was the journey?'

'Slow,' she replied, 'but restful. The villa is delightful, on the hill above Las Palmas with wonderful views of the town and the sea. I've had the telephone connected, as you can see, and there's a pleasant garden to sit in. The maid I've contracted to live in is very willing. Above all, it only takes ten minutes to drive down to work at the bank. It'll be a lovely place to wait for our child.'

'I hope to come out and visit you soon, but this case is very complex and may take time to resolve.'

'It's not the dead frogman!' she exclaimed. 'I thought as much.'

'I can't tell you more over the phone, but you might like to know that all my team has come down from Madrid.'

'Has Eugenia relented about the legal separation?'

'She's much too involved in decorating religious floats for the processions. I'll try to talk to her again before I leave.'

Good Friday had dawned warm and bright, with only a gentle breeze from the west. Bernal called a meeting of his team at 8.0 a.m., including Ángel, who had been temporarily relieved by one of Fragela's men.

'The first piece of news,' began Bernal, 'is that the inquiries made by Captain Barba of the Civil Guard at Chiclana have confirmed that the Salineta Hotel has indeed been let to a group of Arabs for the past month. I want you, Miranda and Lista, to help Barba organize the stake-out. Be careful you aren't spotted, but try to see what activity there is and how many men are there. Remember they are probably trained soldiers.'

Bernal now turned to Navarro. 'Has there been any contact with Elena?'

'None, chief.'

'I'm concerned about her. We've got to get in there somehow. I myself could go in, perhaps without raising suspicion, on the pretext of visiting my wife. The thing is, she thinks I returned to Madrid on Monday, so she'd be pretty surprised if I turned up; that might put Father Sanandrés on his guard. Has there been any activity there, Ángel?'

'None at all, since the lay women left yesterday evening.'

Lista now spoke. 'I visited the Catalan woman at her home and she claims that Sister Serena, the portress, told her she was too sinful and needed to undertake a severe penance before she could be readmitted to the Diurnal Adoration, whatever that is.'

'It's when they get given the special water from the well under the chapel,' said Bernal. 'I understand that it's the only source of fresh water in the whole city, all the normal supply being brought from El Puerto. The well is supposed to be the ancient Fuente de la Jara, which had some connection with the Roman Temple of Venus Marina. We'll have to ask Peláez to test its properties and see if it's the elixir of life.'

'The most vital factor is that we've identified the colonel and the captain involved in the plot to free the prisoners,' said Fragela. 'My men followed them last night and they went to dine with the vice-admiral in charge of supplies at San Fernando. They couldn't get close enough to hear any of their conversation.'

'I take it the Segunda Bis of the army is collaborating with you and your men, Fragela, as the CESID ordered?'

'Yes, they are. They have been watching these officers for some time.'

'I'm off to see Soto now,' said Bernal, 'but please inform me at once if there's any movement at the convent.'

Elena Fernández had slept little during Thursday night, and before she was called to Matins early on Good Friday she had made her decision: she would speak to Señora de Bernal and ask her to take the envelope out to her husband. Father Sanandrés and Sister Serena obviously trusted the Superintendent's wife, who in their eyes was probably above suspicion. Then Elena would be free to explore what she could in the holy cave and try to discover its secret or 'trick', as she'd overhead the army colonel call it.

After the meagre breakfast of stale bread fried in strong-tasting olive oil washed down by weak milky coffee—again kindly Sister Encarnación was missing from the meal—Elena made her way to the rear yard where she found Eugenia Bernal sprinkling the flowers on the float from a watering-can. At first Sister Serena kept hovering around, making it impossible for her to talk privately to her chief's wife, but finally the nun was called away by the prior. Elena decided to seize her chance.

'Señora, can I talk to you in utmost confidence?'

'Of course, my dear.'

'I don't think you know that I'm one of your husband's inspectors from Madrid.'

'I was sure of it, my dear. I recognized your voice when

160

you first arrived. We've talked on the telephone on one occasion, haven't we?'

Elena was alarmed to hear this. 'I hope you haven't told the prior and the others that I'm in the police,' she said anxiously.

'I certainly haven't said anything,' replied Eugenia.

Elena now felt she might as well be hanged for a sheep as a lamb. 'I also ought to tell you, señora, that I'm really here on special duty on your husband's orders, and he told me to confide in you if I was in difficulties.'

'And are you, my dear?'

'Yes, I am. I must get a message out to him and I hoped you would help.'

'Naturally I will, but he's back in Madrid now.'

'No, he isn't, señora. The Government ordered him to stay put in Cadiz and lead an important investigation.'

Eugenia was clearly astounded to learn of this, but agreed to do as Elena wanted.

'I should like you to deliver this envelope to him, but without anyone else in the convent knowing about it.'

'I'll see what I can do,' said Eugenia, 'but it would look odd if I went out before the procession leaves at nine p.m.'

'Could you think of some excuse?' asked Elena desperately. 'He really must get it as soon as possible. Couldn't you say that you were going to get more flowers for the float or something?'

'But we have more than enough as it is, dear. Leave the envelope with me and I'll see what can be done. Where will I find my husband?'

'You could leave it at the Hotel Francia y París up the road from here and ask the receptionist to ring him urgently. Please, on no account let anyone else here know about it,' said Elena pleadingly, slipping her the envelope containing the recorded cassette and her report. 'I really mean no one at all.'

Ángel resumed his watch on the convent at 8.45 a.m., thus missing seeing the cook on her way to and from the market, but Fragela's man had logged it in the book, with the exact times. Soon after nine o'clock, Ángel spotted a movement in one of the cell windows opposite, and saw a pale hand appear at the bars of the grille. It protruded as far as it could and dropped a piece of paper into the street. It might be Elena sending out a note, Ángel thought, and showed his head out of the *hostal* window-frame, so that she could see him. But the hand was quickly withdrawn and the window closed.

Ángel ran down to the street and went to retrieve the folded piece of paper, which had come to rest in the gutter. He returned to the hall of the boarding-house and opened the note. It contained just one word, SOCORRO, followed by a cross drawn in a shaky hand. Would Elena have written HELP like that, and above all would she have drawn a cross under it? He decided to ring Navarro at once.

Bernal went up to Soto's office and found the rear admiral waiting for him.

'Everything is being done to prepare the ships for sailing, Superintendent. The only problem is with the assault-ship *Velasco*, which is in the middle of a refit at La Carraca. The artisans are working flat out to finish the job by tomorrow morning.'

'That ship might be crucial for carrying troops,' said Bernal. 'They must finish it on time.'

'The final decision on whether to send the fleet to North Africa will be taken by the JUJEM and the Government on Saturday morning. In the meantime they have ordered ships from El Ferrol to sail south to reinforce Cadiz, and other vessels from Majorca and Minorca to Cartagena. They weighed anchor this morning.'

'That's good news,' said Bernal.

'The JUJEM has also ordered troops from Seville down to San Fernando, but has put a squad of GEOs at our disposal.'

'Those special operations lads might come in handy at the Salineta Hotel,' commented Bernal, and gave the rear admiral the latest information on the Moroccans holed up at Chiclana.

162

'I've got some information for you, Bernal. Look at this confidential catalogue the vice-admiral in charge of supplies and procurement deigned to pass to me this morning.'

The pamphlet bore the name of a British firm and was addressed to naval procurement services worldwide. It advertised a revolutionary type of high-speed boat which had the additional capacity of diving below the waves and parking on the sea-bed, or of creeping up to a target undetected. It measured only 5 metres long, 1.5 metres wide and 1.25 metres high, and could carry four divers for 100 sea-miles before exhausting its fuel supply. Its top surface speed was 30 knots, but on diving its two electric motors could take it six sea-miles under water. Its size enabled it to escape most radar detection and sonar sensors. The craft was available to foreign navies and could prove to be a vital weapon against piracy, smuggling or terrorism. Bernal thought it might also be used for those purposes if it fell into the wrong hands.

'I see they claim that a number of these craft have already been ordered by foreign navies, Soto. It could well be one of these that the fishermen spotted in the Bay. I suppose you've noted that its side-walls are deflated by a pump when it dives and are pressed to the sides of its fibre-glass hull. That could account for the parallel grooves we saw in the sand at Sancti Petri island.'

'I agree, Comisario. This could be what they are using.'

'Could you find out if any have been supplied to Morocco?'

'I'll certainly try.'

Elena felt a great weight had been lifted from her mind when Eugenia Bernal agreed to get the message out to her husband. Now she decided to get into the cave below the altar if she could, and she entered the church, which seemed to be empty. She approached the statue of Our Lady of the Palm, which had today been draped in black, and lit a candle, while looking carefully around. There was no sound apart from the guttering of the candle flames. She tried the door of the vestry and found it unlocked. Once inside, she touched the handle of the steel door, and was astonished to find that it turned. She went in as quietly as possible and listened as low voices floated up to her from the holy cave.

Elena recognized Sister Serena's harsh voice and Father Sanandrés's whining tones, but she couldn't make out what they were saying, except that they were having an argument. They were out of sight in a small room below the vestry, with the door half-closed. Elena climbed down the stone steps and approached the holy well, which had a stone surround above the natural limestone rock. She decided to conceal herself behind it and eavesdrop on what she could.

Soon Father Sanandrés and the sister emerged, and they went up to the vestry without turning round, leaving the small lower door unlocked. When they were out of sight, Elena peered down the well shaft but could see nothing. Then she slipped through the small door and found herself in a kind of changing-room, where a wet-suit hung from a hook on the wall. She examined the outfit, and saw that it had just been used in water. She touched it and brought a drop of water to her lips: it was salt water, unlike the fresh water that the women took from the well each day. Here was a mystery she thought it important to solve. The flippers of the wet-suit had left a trail on the stone floor which she now followed up to a blank wall. She touched the brickwork carefully, and tapped it gently with her knuckles. The central layers of bricks gave out a hollow ring, clearly suggesting a false door.

Elena looked around carefully, but saw nothing but a small statue of Our Lady of the Palm on the side wall, with a posy of flowers in a holder below it. She examined the statue closely, and touched its whole surface, but none of it appeared to act as a lever or switch as she suspected. Then she touched the palm held in the Virgin's hand, and the hidden door suddenly swung open beside her and a rush of cold air emerged from the dark passage beyond. She got out her small torch from the pocket of her habit and switched it on. As the entered the tunnel, the door swung shut behind her. Following the passageway for some twenty metres, she found herself in a natural cavern, at least as large as the holy cave, and in the centre was the mouth of a wide chimney in the rock, with an aluminium ladder leading downwards.

Looking over the edge, Elena could hear the sea far below her at the bottom of the shaft. With sudden resolution she hitched up her brown habit and started to descend. The climb was long and difficult, and she counted the steps to get an idea of the depth. Now and then she stopped to shine her torch on the walls. Soon she could hear the sea much more loudly, and wondered if she should have donned the wet-suit before setting out, but it was too late now. Perhaps it would be low tide soon, so that she could inspect the bottom of the shaft and find out the secret of the holy cave.

After counting 135 steps in the ladder, Elena felt dizzy, and stopped for a while. Now there was a dim light at the bottom, which she hoped was daylight. As she started down again, her rope-soled sandals slipped on a piece of seaweed, and she missed a couple of rungs. In order not to fall, she clutched at the rocky side of the shaft and cut her hand on a razor-sharp fossilized oyster-shell. Elena steadied herself to tie her handkerchief around her fingers, and resumed her descent. Now the noise of the sea was very loud and the breeze snatched at her hair. At last her foot touched sand, though her leg went calf-deep into the sea-water that now surged more sluggishly, with longer pauses between the waves.

Glad to be off the ladder, she waded through the water and found a large cavern beyond the base of the shaft where there was some hydraulic machinery that spluttered gently. So this was why Father Sanandrés descended so often into the cave. She observed how the pipes from the machine ran upwards into the roof. They looked ancient and must be connected with the fresh-water well, she judged. Perhaps that explained why the water welled up in such a surge in the holy cave below the high altar. It was a 'trick' after all, but one that appeared to date from the last century by the look of the machinery.

She sat on a rock and saw that the wound on her hand still bled profusely and had saturated her handkerchief. She tore off a strip of her petticoat and made a thicker bandage. From where she sat, she couldn't see the whole of the cavern in the light of her small torch, but saw enough to realize that most or all of it must get submerged at high water, judging by the abundance of mussels and starfish. After a while, she went to inspect the long, steeply sloping passage that led to the sea. The waves had receded considerably, and she proceeded cautiously, examining the walls as she went. Finally she reached a point where she could look out into a small bay, which had a long breakwater to the right.

The exit was blocked by a rusty iron gate, the bars of which left no space for her to crawl through. A new rust-proof padlock and chain were firmly secured to the latch. She looked through the bars and saw a fort above the breakwater, which had walls built in the shape of three points of a star. Surely that was the castle of Santa Catalina which she had seen on her first evening in Cadiz, before entering the convent? Then this cave must come out at La Caleta, under the ruined bathing establishment.

In a sudden flash she saw how she had misunderstood the conversation she had recorded between the prior and the army plotters. The escapees from the castle were to be brought in through this passage and up the aluminium ladder to the convent, where they would have a safe refuge until the admiral could get them away by sea via this exit. She must inform Bernal at once, since he would doubtless order a watch to be kept on the main door of the convent, which would tell him nothing.

Elena hurried back to the base of the shaft, forgetting the effort the climb would require of her in her eagerness to return. Just as she reached the top and placed her tired hands on the edge of the stone floor, she received a savage blow on the head, and immediately lost consciousness.

Bernal returned to the Cadiz Comisaría well satisfied. Everything on the Melkart front appeared to be going well. Any diplomatic approaches would have to be left to the Foreign Ministry in Madrid; they might consider the possibility of high-level discussions with King Hassan and President Chadli Benjedid, who might be unaware of what was afoot.

Paco Navarro greeted him with the urgent report from

Ángel about the note appealing for help which had been thrown out of the convent window and which was not in Elena's handwriting.

'Order the car back, Paco. I'm going in there now to see what's up. Fragela can accompany me, but I'll go in alone, as though it's a social call.'

Fragela parked the car in the Calle de Jesús Nazareno below the convent, and watched as Bernal approached the large door. Ángel was also observing him from the *hostal* window opposite.

Bernal took hold of the old-fashioned bell-pull and heard the clanging within, but no one came. He tried again after a minute or two, and finally the small judas-window was opened in the wicket and a man's face appeared: 'There's no ceremony today and the procession won't be leaving until nine p.m.'

'I'm Comisario Bernal, and I want to see my wife who's in retreat here this week.'

'Oh, Comisario, I'm Bishop Nicasio. I remember you from your last visit.' The cleric opened the gate. 'Please come this way and I'll look for the señora. I think she's still seeing to the float.'

'Just take me to her. I don't want to disturb her labours for long.'

In the rear yard he found Eugenia spraying the flowers with water.

'You've saved me a journey, Luis. I was just coming to look for you.'

Bernal looked around and asked: 'Where can we talk in complete privacy, Geñita?'

'We can go to the parlour if you like.'

'No, not the parlour,' said Luis. 'Let's go to the large cloister.'

They sat on the marble bench in the north walk, where Eugenia handed him the envelope. 'That's from your Señorita Fernández. I recognized her by her voice at once.'

'I hope you didn't say anything about it to the prior or anyone else.'

'No, of course not. I knew you were up to something,' she

167

said, looking at him accusingly. 'What's it all about?'

'Let me read this note first, then I'll tell you.' Bernal read rapidly through Elena's report and glanced at the tiny recorded cassette also contained in the envelope. At last he turned to Eugenia and looked at her gravely. 'Those two army officers who come here are trying to persuade Father Sanandrés to do something illegal, and I intend to stop them. On no account must you get involved, Geñita, and it would be best if you moved out of the convent to my hotel.'

'But I can't leave now, Luis, before the Procession of the Silence in which I'm to be a penitent.'

'What time does the procession take place?'

'The *costaleros* and the members of the Brotherhood of the Palm will start assembling at eight-thirty, and the *paso* will depart at nine p.m. We won't be returning until one in the morning.'

'That helps me in a way, Geñita. I suggest you come to my hotel room when the procession ends. You can collect your things from your room here sometime tomorrow. You'd better take my room card from the hotel. I'll warn them at Reception that you'll be arriving soon after one a.m. Now you can take me to see the holy cave.'

'But you've seen it already, Luis. Sister Serena took you there. She told me so.'

'I want to go there again. Make it look as though you are showing me round as you would a lay visitor.'

Eugenia led him to the church, which was empty, and up the aisle to the high altar. Bernal looked through the glass panel beneath, but could see nothing other than the empty mouth of the well.

'I doubt if the door to the cave will be open, Luis. I'll call Sister Serena, if you like.'

'You mustn't do that, Eugenia,' he said sharply. 'On no account must you mention this affair to anyone here. Keep out of it, you hear?'

They entered the vestry and Bernal tried the handle of the steel door, which was unlocked. He climbed down the steps, as Eugenia hovered uncertainly in the doorway, and looked around the cave. Then he saw that the small door at one end below the vestry was ajar, and went in. He searched the dressing-room, but there was no wet-suit hanging there as on his previous visit. Bernal examined the floor and gained the impression that it had recently been mopped down.

He climbed back up the steps to where Eugenia unhappily waited. 'When did you last see Elena Fernández?' he asked his wife.

'She was at lunch with me, Luis, but then she said she was going to have a rest in her cell.'

'And Father Sanandrés and Sister Serena?'

'Yes, they were at lunch too.'

'Is anyone missing as far as you know?'

'No, Luis, no one. Mind, I haven't seen Sister Encarnación for two days. The portress says she's doing a strict penance in her cell until tomorrow.'

'Does her cell overlook the street?'

'I don't know, Luis. The nuns' quarters are in *clausura* and I don't go there. My cell is on the inner side.'

Bernal realized that it was essential for him to listen to the cassette Elena had recorded as soon as possible. 'Eugenia, I have to get away at once. Remember what I have said about coming to the hotel straight after the procession is over. Don't return here. But you must do one thing for me: if you don't see Elena Fernández at Vespers, bring word to me at the Hotel de Francia y París, will you?'

'Yes, of course. She said she'll be coming in the procession with the rest of us.'

'I'll be watching out when you leave, Geñita. I'll talk to you again then. You won't be wearing one of those *capirotes* over your head so that I can't recognize you, will you?'

'Only the members of the Cofradía wear those. We'll be in these habits and barefoot.'

Bernal reflected that her feet would get cut to ribbons on the cobbled streets.

Inspectors Lista and Miranda were crouching at Captain Barba's side in a clump of holm-oaks watching the Salineta Hotel through binoculars.

'They've done a bit of shooting practice before you arrived,' Barba told Bernal's inspectors. 'They used the deserted quarry below the hotel.'

'And now they're playing tennis,' commented Miranda. 'How many of them are there?'

'They all look alike to me, but I think I've counted fifteen Moroccans so far. They seem to be in tiptop physical condition.'

'I expect the chief is right about their being army officers,' said Lista.

As he spoke a large Cadillac came into sight along the winding road from Chiclana.

'Hullo, they've got visitors,' said Barba.

The policemen concealed themselves in the thicket as the gleaming car swept past them.

'It's got an Arabic number-plate,' observed Miranda.

The car entered the palm-filled yard in front of the hotel and drew up in front of the main steps. Two burnoused Arabs alighted and were immediately admitted.

'I'll get my men to check that registration number and find out if they entered the country at Algeciras, and when,' said Barba.

'Don't use your radio, will you?' cautioned Miranda. 'They're probably listening in to all the Civil Guard and police radio traffic.'

Elena Fernández slowly recovered consciousness, and thought she was awakening from a dream in which she was trapped in a dark cave with dripping walls and the roar of the sea beneath her. She put a tentative hand to the wound on her head and felt it gently for signs of bleeding, but it had already congealed and dried. Her head spun, and when she shut her eyes she could see blue and white stars. She sat up very cautiously, feeling her limbs to see if she had broken any bones.

Realizing she was near the rim of a shaft, she edged slowly away, but stopped again as her head began spinning. I must be concussed, she thought. Suddenly she remembered where she was and recalled that she had some urgent task to do.

To get to Bernal, that was it. Hadn't she had a torch? She felt around for some time until she touched the cold metal and tried to switch it on, but the glass was smashed. Shivering from the cold, she started to drag herself along the passage away from the shaft. The sea sounded very loud in her ears, or was it the pain in her head? She tried to see the time on her watch, which had a luminous dial, but her eyes wouldn't focus properly. She continued to crawl for some time, until her hands touched the base of a door that was firmly closed.

Elena thought she could hear voices from the other side of it and tried to call for help, but found she couldn't produce any sound other than a low grunt. She decided to rest until she felt stronger, but her muscles began to convulse with shock. She opened her eyes and looked up, thinking she could see a statue of Our Lady. Was she in a church, then? She stretched out her arm to the small statue, clawing her way up the wall until her hand nearly reached it. With a supreme effort she managed to clutch the palm in the statue's right hand, and suddenly the door swung open, tumbling her into the lighted room on the other side. The light smote her eyes most painfully, and she relapsed into unconsciousness once more as the door clanged shut behind her.

As soon as he left the convent, Bernal entered the *hostal* opposite to confer with Ángel Gallardo.

'I haven't been able to see Elena,' he said, 'but my wife says she went to her cell at three-thirty to rest and should be down for Vespers at six. I couldn't insist on being taken to see her without raising Sister Serena's or Father Sanandrés's suspicions. The kindly old nun, Sister Encarnación, hasn't been seen for two days; she is allegedly doing strict penance in her cell, but I strongly suspect that it was she who threw the note asking for help out of the window of her cell.'

Bernal showed Ángel Elena's report and pointed to the mention of the holy cave. 'I got my wife to take me down there, but I found nothing. I noticed that the lower changing room had recently been mopped down. I want you to watch carefully for any comings or goings, especially of the army officers, and ring me immediately if you spot anything.'

'OK, *jefe*. I wonder what Elena got on that cassette.'

'I'm going to find out now.'

Back at the ops room, Bernal, Navarro and Fragela listened to the cassette Elena had recorded. When they came to the passage concerning the operation to free the officers from Santa Catalina fort being brought forward, Bernal said: 'We shall have to take immediate steps to stake out the convent and the castle itself. We must be ready for them when they bring out the escapees.'

'Is there any way we can get some men into the convent, *jefe*?' asked Navarro.

'There's one way,' said Fragela. 'At eight-thirty p.m. the *costaleros* and the members of the Cofradía of the Palm will go to the convent to bring out the float to join the Procession of the Silence. That would give us a chance to smuggle in some agents. I happen to know the head of the Brotherhood and I'm sure he'll cooperate by providing some extra robes and hoods as a disguise.'

'That's an excellent plan,' commented Bernal. 'I suggest you ask him for the loan of five outfits for yourself, Ángel Gallardo and three of your men. I take it you'll be able to conceal arms beneath the cloaks—service pistols at least?'

'Yes, Comisario. The members of this particular Cofradía wear a long purple soutane with a white cloak over it, and a tall scarlet *capirote* with slits for the eyes.'

'Please organize it at once, so that when the *cofrades* arrive at the convent, you and Ángel and your men will be with them, suitably attired. Once inside the building, you'll have to conceal yourselves until after the float has left by the main gate. Then you can await the arrival of the army plotters and arrest them all. Navarro, you can stay here to coordinate the operation, and I shall be in continuous contact from an unmarked police car up the hill from the convent.'

'I take it we can use portable radio transmitters to keep in contact?' asked Fragela.

'I think so. Unlike the Moroccan business, I doubt

172

whether these army conspirators will listen in to all our broadcasts. It's a small-time affair, so far as one can judge. Let's use a code in any case.'

'I suggest a religious code, chief,' said Navarro. 'If there is any interception, it will then appear that the messages are connected with the timing and movement of the various processions.'

'Very good,' said Bernal. 'Work something out with Fragela, will you?'

Elena Fernández shivered violently as she opened her eyes in the dimly lit cave. She tried to remember where she was and how long she had been there. It was like emerging from a nightmare in which she had been obliged to keep climbing an apparently endless vertical ladder while angry waves lapped at her feet. She managed to raise herself on one elbow and screwed her eyes to focus on her watch. 7.45? But was it morning or evening? She forced her memory to work, and became aware of something that she had urgently to do.

Beneath where she lay, she felt a vibration, as though of machinery, and she listened intently. In the middle of the cave stood a large rock with a stone-edged well set in it. A whooshing noise seemed to come from it, getting ever louder. Suddenly a large jet of water rose from its centre and began to overflow on to the rock and the floor. Oh God, she would be drowned! She saw the flight of stone steps two metres away from where she was lying and crawled desperately towards them, clawing at the ground as she went. At last she reached the first step and forced herself on to it, as the water began to lap at her feet. She looked back at the well, where the noise of the jet suddenly changed, sounding as if it were temporarily clogged: emerging from the well was a pair of human legs wearing black stockings and flat-heeled shoes, with a large brown flowing garment spread from them around the stone surround of the well. The legs bobbed obscenely, as though their possessor were engaged in sexual activity with an unseen partner.

Then the force of the water-spout lifted one leg over the

ledge and part of the torso became visible. A white garment was now released which was washed out on to the rocky pedestal. Elena recognized it to be a wimple. Dear God, in front of her was the body of a nun, held upside down in the narrow mouth of the well, sustained in that grotesquely undulating posture by the force of the water-jet. She scrambled up the steps in terror, and attempted to reach for the door-handle. Poor Sister Encarnación, she sobbed. What a ghastly way they had disposed of her. Elena shuddered as she sank into unconsciousness once more.

At 8.15 p.m. Bernal sat in the front passenger seat of an unmarked Renault 18 parked in the wide street of Jesús Nazareno below the convent, and watched as the twenty-eight members of the Cofradía de la Palma made their way up the slope to the main door. They included Fragela with three of his agents and Ángel Gallardo, all attired exactly like the regular *cofrades*, except that they had pistols and small walkie-talkies hidden under their wide capes.

The scene was eerie, almost menacing, as the brethren advanced up the Calle de la Concepción. When they had been admitted, Bernal ordered the police driver to take him to the Plaza de Calvo Sotelo, where they parked under the orange-trees outside the hotel. Bernal studied a printed plan marking the route that the Procession of the Silence would take, and saw that it would arrive at that point within twenty minutes of setting out from the convent. He spoke into the car radio to Paco Navarro at the ops room. 'Can you hear me, Brother Francisco? The brethren and *costaleros* have arrived on time. The *paso* will be departing shortly. Over.'

'Message received, Prior. I expect to make contact with our *cofrades* in a few minutes. Over and out.'

Bernal sat in the car smoking incessantly as he watched the crowds gathering on the pavements of the square and whole families leaning out of the balconies of the houses to watch the most solemn of the Holy Week processions, which would be conducted in complete silence.

174

At 8.45 all the street-lights were suddenly extinguished. 'Is it a power failure?' Bernal asked the police driver.

'No, Comisario. This happens every year. All the lights will be out in the old city until midnight during the Procession of the Silence.'

'I hadn't counted on that,' said Bernal worriedly, realizing that the army plotters had almost certainly decided to carry out their plan during this annual black-out. The only light in the square came from the brightly lit hotel and from the windows of the houses. 'It must be an ideal time for pickpockets. Don't you get a lot of trouble when this happens?'

'Oh yes, and we receive a number of complaints about indecent assaults as well. It's a free-for-all out there, especially with the drunks coming out of the bars.'

After a while a dull clanking could be heard, and the people in the small square fell silent. A warm glow of undulating yellow light was approaching, and the float of the Descent from the Cross was carried swaying slowly into the square, preceded by two dozen hooded *cofrades* in purple, white and scarlet. As they came up to the church of San Francisco, their leader, Father Sanandrés, dressed in the vestments of a bishop, beat a large crook on the ground, signalling to the *costaleros* to lower their heavy burden temporarily to the ground. Behind the float were a dozen women penitents, bareheaded and dressed in brown sackcloth, with light chains around their naked ankles, each of them bearing a lighted candle in one hand and a small scourge in the other with which they lashed their shoulder-blades gently from time to time.

Good Lord, thought Bernal, Eugenia must be among them.

He got out of the car and went up to the double row of women, who stood with bowed heads. Towards the back he spotted Eugenia looking anxiously at the façade of the hotel.

'Oh, thank God, Luis. There you are. Your Inspectora didn't turn up at Vespers at six, and I'm worried about her after what you told me. I couldn't come out earlier to tell you, because Father Sanandrés asked me to help arrange the penitents in their chains.'

'I'm going down to the convent now, Geñita. Remember what I said. Don't go back to your cell. Come straight here to the hotel and ask to be taken to my room.'

As soon as they had been admitted to the convent, Fragela and his three men and Ángel Gallardo, their features hidden by the tall pointed *capirotes*, made their way with the float-bearers to the dimly lit main cloister. When the bearers withdrew to the rear yard to manœuvre the heavy silver-framed *paso* through to the main gate, the policemen slipped into the north walk and hid behind the palm-trees in the shadows.

Once the procession had formed and departed, Fragela radioed the information to Navarro.

'You'd best stay concealed here with your men,' Ángel whispered to Fragela, 'and wait for the army officers to arrive with the escaped prisoners. Then you can arrest them as soon as they enter the gate. I'm going to search for Elena Fernández.'

The convent had fallen completely silent after the departure of the procession, and Ángel wondered who had remained to man the gate. He wasn't familiar with the geography of the building, but he recalled the sketch Bernal had drawn on the blackboard in the ops room. He reached the door of the church without seeing anyone, and entered the darkened aisle. The only light came from the cluster of candles burning low under the statue of Our Lady of the Palm. Ángel thought he could hear water gurgling in the distance, and remembered that the vestry door should be to the left of the high altar; he had to bend his head to prevent his *capirote* from catching on the lintel. The light was on inside, and Ángel spotted a steel door to the right, whence came a whooshing sound. He opened it a few centimetres and peeped through the slits in his hood.

This must be the holy cave, he thought, which was flooded now to a depth of more than a metre, but his gaze became fixed on an inverted corpse, of which he could see only the legs covered in black stockings, bobbing grotesquely up and down in a jet of water emerging from the well. He felt something clutch at his foot and looked down.

After talking to his wife, Bernal went back to the Renault and spoke to the police driver. 'Have any messages come in?'

'Yes, Comisario. Inspector Navarro wants you to call him back urgently.'

'Brother Francisco, come in. This is the Prior. What's up? Over.'

'Two of the penitents have broken loose, Prior, as soon as the street-lights were extinguished. We're trying to locate them. Over.'

'How did they manage to stray from the flock, Brother? Over.'

'By the sea wall. Over.'

'I'm on my way to round them up. Over and out.'

'The two prisoners have been sprung from the castle of Santa Catalina,' Bernal told the driver. 'Do you think you can get me down to the Calle de Concepción at once?'

'It will be difficult with these processions, Comisario, but I'll try.'

Elena Fernández had managed to drag herself to the top step in the holy cave, just above the water-level. Suddenly she felt a rush of air above her head as the steel door was opened, and she looked up in fright at the robed penitent whose eyes looked down at her through the narrow slits in his tall scarlet hood.

'Help me,' she gasped.

The figure tore off his tall hood and her heart lifted as she saw Ángel's familiar cheeky grin, tempered by concern for her condition.

'Are you all right, Elena?' he asked anxiously, lifting her into the vestry.

'I'm a bit concussed, that's all. Something hit me on the head back there in the rock tunnel.'

'Is that the missing nun down there?'

177

'I'm afraid so. She was a kindly old thing. You must catch them, Ángel.' She tried to summon up more strength.

'Don't worry. Rest now. Fragela and his men are covering the gate to arrest them when they enter.'

'But that's not it, Ángel. That's what I've found out! They're going to bring the prisoners up the ladder from a cavern under La Caleta and then through a passageway into this cave.'

'Let me get you to safety first. Then I'll get Fragela, and call the boss.'

The police driver took almost ten minutes to get Bernal to Jesús Nazareno, from where he could see the entrance to the convent.

'I'm reluctant to go in at this moment and spoil the operation,' Bernal said. 'Let's wait and watch.'

Soon the radio crackled into life and Navarro's voice came over.

'Urgent to Prior. Change of plan. The penitents' route has been changed. They'll be coming under the float, understood? Under the float. Over.'

'Message received, but not fully understood. Over.'

'The Prior should enter now to receive them. Over.'

Bernal realized that Navarro was telling him that the escapees were being brought to the convent by a different route, from *underneath*. Then he recalled the earlier message about how they had escaped by the sea wall. Could there be an underground passage that led into the building?

'Drive up to the main gate at once,' he ordered the driver, with sudden resolution. As he jumped out of the car, the wicket-gate was opened by a hooden penitent.

'Thank heavens you're here, Superintendent,' said Fragela. 'We've found Inspectora Fernández and a dead nun in the holy cave.'

'Is Elena badly hurt?' Bernal demanded.

'She's got a bump on her head and some concussion. I've called an ambulance.'

Ángel and one of Fragela's men now came along the south walk supporting Elena, who caught sight of Bernal.

178

'Chief,' she gasped, 'you must stop them. They're going to bring the two prisoners up through a shaft that leads from La Caleta into the cave. I was down there this afternoon and saw some hydraulic machinery, which seems to operate the well. I think they've drowned Sister Encarnación. Her body's down there. I've failed you, chief,' she wailed.

'Now don't worry, Elena. Go and get that wound attended to while we sort all this out. Of course you haven't failed. You've done brilliantly,' he assured her, and headed for the church with Inspector Fragela.

'The cave's half full of water, Comisario. I don't see how they'll get up through there.'

'With sub-aqua equipment they can. We'll have to be ready for them. You'd better radio through to Navarro to send more men down to La Caleta to cut off a possible retreat. Elena says there's a cavern with an entrance under the old bathing establishment. And he could send us more men here.'

'What about the body of the nun, Superintendent? Shouldn't we recover it?'

'Get your men to lift it on to the floor by the side of the well. Once we've captured the conspirators, we'll call Peláez and Varga in. Perhaps it would be best to post your three men in the vestry, and you and I can watch the cave through the glass panel under the altar.'

'I don't think the cave will fill with water,' said Fragela. 'It appears to drain away through the rocky floor.'

'Have you searched the rest of the convent?'

'We haven't found anyone yet. As soon as my reinforcements arrive, we'll go through it all room by room.'

After half an hour had passed, the two detectives crouching by the high altar saw the water-level in the cave suddenly fall as the steel door from the underground passage was forced open, and two frogmen in black wet-suits appeared.

Fragela gave a signal to his men waiting in the vestry, who pulled out their pistols. Now two more frogmen emerged into the cave and pulled off their helmets. Their voices floated up through the half-open door.

'I can't understand where all this water came from. It's long past high water and yet the place is half flooded.'

Bernal could see that the speaker was the young army captain he had seen on a previous visit.

The other speaker was the colonel. 'At least we've got these good fellows out of gaol. Let's get them changed and take them up to their cells before the procession returns.'

'This water is fresh, not salt,' said one of the escapees.

The colonel also tasted it. 'It's that mad prior. He must have set that old machinery in motion to get his so-called miracle to perform on time. Don't drink too much of it, or it may have a peculiar effect on you,' he laughed.

They began to climb the stone steps leading up to the vestry, without noticing the body of the nun lying beyond the well. As they entered the small room, Bernal and Fragela went in with drawn pistols and joined the agents waiting there: 'This is the Judicial Police!' shouted Bernal. 'You are all under arrest!'

The Cadiz policemen quickly handcuffed the four army officers, who were still blinking in surprise. The colonel was the first to recover his composure.

'Who are you and by whose authority do you dare to arrest me?' he demanded.

Bernal showed him the heavily embossed gold star of his Comisario de primera's badge and declared: 'By order of the JUJEM and the Ministries of Defence and the Interior. You will be taken to the Comisaría of the Judicial Police for questioning.'

'We've committed to crime,' said the young captain boldly. 'We're loyal to our country, which is more than can be said of you.'

'You will be interrogated first about the death of a religious sister of this convent whose body is lying in the holy cave from which you have just emerged,' said Bernal firmly.

The four men looked at one another in astonishment, but they kept silent.

After they had been taken away in a brown police van with wire-covered windows, Bernal awaited the arrival of his pathologist and his scene-of-crime technician.

'We'll have to arrest Father Sanandrés as well,' he said to Fragela.

'How will we be able to catch the vice-admiral who was planning to get the escapees away by sea, Comisario?'

'I think we'll leave him to Rear Admiral Soto. I'd rather the Navy had the chance to clean out its own Augean stables. They've been extremely helpful to us and it's the least we can do for them.'

Dr Peláez arrived out of breath, his short-sighted eyes gleaming.

'You only just caught me, Bernal. I was going to take the last plane back to Barajas tonight. I should have known you'd produce another *fiambre* for me. Where is it?'

'We've got a dead nun for you to examine, Peláez. Elena says she popped out of the well on a jet of water upside down.'

'How extraordinary. You always bring me such interesting cases. Let's go down and take a look.'

'The water-level has subsided considerably,' said Bernal, 'but we'll have to get hold of the prior to find out how to turn that hydraulic machinery off.'

'It seems to work in conjunction with the sea-level below at La Caleta,' commented Fragela.

When Bernal looked closely at the corpse of the dead nun for the first time, he exclaimed in surprise: 'But that's not Sister Encarnación, as Elena supposed! She was the old nun who laced my drink here last Saturday. This is Sister Serena, the portress. You'd better get your men to search the cells at once, Fragela.'

Bernal left Peláez and Varga to get on with their job while he sat in the church and pondered on who had attacked Elena Fernández and caused the death of Sister Serena. He debated first whether it had been the two army officers on their way to free the prisoners; yet they had not entered by the convent gate, because Ángel had been keeping observation on it all the time. It seemed unlikely that they had entered the shaft from below, climbed up to attack Elena and then gone back down to free the prisoners at 8.30 p.m. There was no sense in it. Had it been Father Sanandrés before he left with the procession? Perish the thought! Although he may have wanted Elena out of action, what possible motive could he have had to kill his loyal nun? Bernal realized that he could get no further until Peláez was able to tell him both the cause and the approximate time of death of Sister Serena. He would also need to debrief Elena fully, if her concussion allowed, and interrogate the four army officers. Like the pathologist and technician, he was going to have a busy night.

After informing Madrid of the arrests, Bernal and Navarro had questioned the officers individually until 5.30 a.m. without obtaining any information about the death of the nun. They now turned to Father Sanandrés, who looked haggard from his lengthy penitential walk followed by a sleepless wait in the police cell he had exchanged for his monastic one. He was extremely nervous and ready to talk. He explained that the old hydraulic machinery was normally started and stopped by the rising and falling of the tide in the cavern below, but occasionally it jammed and on these occasions he put on a wet-suit and went down to free a sticking valve. He appeared quite unabashed at perpetrating this pious fraud, and maintained that the water from the well really did possess miraculous properties.

'When was the last time you saw Sister Serena?' asked Bernal. 'She didn't go in the procession with you, did she?'

'No. She was to stay behind to look after Sister Encarnación, who was unwell from overdoing her Lenten fast.'

'So when did you last see her?'

'At Vespers, at six o'clock.'

'And where did she go after that?'

'To the kitchen to make some broth for Sister Encarnación. I was surprised when she didn't come down to see the *paso* leave after all the work she put into decorating it. But Señora Bernal helped me sort out the penitents.'

I bet she did, thought Bernal. 'Now tell us about the army colonel and captain.'

The prior at first affected innocence about the officers'

182

plot, pretending to be shocked at hearing about the escaped prisoners secretly entering his convent.

'Can you explain how they obtained the keys to the padlock on the iron gate at La Caleta and to the steel door that leads into the vestry?' Bernal pressed him.

The prior shook his head, and Bernal signalled to Navarro, who switched on the recording Elena had made of the prior's conversation with the army plotters. Father Sanandrés hung his head, and soon decided to make a full confession, with which Bernal intended to confront the two officers.

At dawn Peláez came in looking tired but triumphant. He handed Bernal his report on the autopsy. 'Here it is, Bernal. The nun drowned. She'd been dead between three and three and a half hours when I first examined her.'

'Any signs of violence?' asked Bernal.

'Some laceration on the side of the head and on the knuckles, probably occasioned at the time of death.'

'Was she murdered?'

'I don't think so. It could have been an accidental fall into the well. She definitely drowned in fresh water. The heel of her shoe had come off. Varga found it in the rocks by the side of the well, and the hem of her habit was unstitched. He's found some threads from it caught in the broken heel. She could have leant over to look down the shaft, caught her heel on the hem of her habit and toppled in.'

'She was a very inquisitive type,' said Bernal. 'But I still want to know who knocked Elena out.'

'I'm going to the Residencia Sanitaria to look at her now, but I don't suppose she'll welcome Varga's going over her with a magnifying glass.'

Bernal managed to get two and a half hours' sleep in his hotel room on the Saturday morning, waking up to find Eugenia seated on the other bed, soaking her bleeding feet in a bowl of mustard and hot water while reciting her rosary. When he groaned and sat up, she stopped praying and looked at him.

'Do you want some coffee, Luis?'

'Yes, please. Ring down for some, will you?'

He sat on the edge of the bed and lit a Kaiser, loosening his shirt collar.

'What happened, Luis? What did you do with Father Sanandrés?'

'We arrested him and took him to the Comisaría. He's made a full confession of his involvement in the officers' plot.'

'And Sister Serena?'

'She's dead. We found her drowned in the holy well.'

Eugenia looked horror-stricken and crossed herself a number of times, rattling the rosary beads. After a while she asked about Sister Encarnación.

'Fragela's men found her locked in her cell, with only a small piece of dry bread and a carafe of water. She's been taken to the Residencia Sanitaria where she's in the same ward as Elena Fernández.'

'What happened to your Inspectora?'

'She got a crack on the head and I can't find out who did it.'

'Don't you think it may have been Sister Serena, although it's uncharitable to speak ill of the dead?' suggested Eugenia, crossing herself once more. 'She was a very fanatical and curious person, always following Señorita Fernández about in the convent. I think she suspected that she was a spy.'

'You may well be right, Geñita. But what did she hit her with? That's what puzzles me.'

Bernal dragged himself back to the ops room at 10.0 a.m., and asked a bleary-eyed Inspector Navarro if there was any news.

'Madrid has ordered the four army officers to be sent there under armed guard. The CESID will take over the interrogation.'

'And Father Sanandrés?'

'We are to hold him here, *jefe*.'

'Any news from Chiclana?'

'Lista and Miranda have reported in this morning. Since

184

the two Arabs arrived in the Cadillac yesterday, there's been no activity.'

'I wonder if it's safe to let them get to the rendezvous this evening at Cape Roche, Paco. I'm inclined to propose that we nip them in the bud where they are. I'll have to go and consult with Soto at San Fernando.'

When the police driver took Bernal along the Vía Augusta Julia towards San Fernando he glanced towards the inner Bay and pointed out a frigate steaming slowly towards the new bridge.

'That bridge swings open to let ships pass, does it?' Bernal asked him.

'It lifts up in two arms in the middle, Comisario.'

Does it now, mused Bernal.

The streets of San Fernando were crowded with sailors returning to duty, and Soto received them in the Captaincy-General building which had a wartime atmosphere.

'You'll be glad to learn that the JUJEM has agreed, Bernal. The fleet will sail from here after dark this evening for Ceuta, while our ships at Cartagena will sail for Melilla and Alhucemas. Replacement vessels will arrive here from El Ferrol tomorrow morning.'

'I'd like to see a strong guard put on the new bridge across the Bay, Soto.'

'On the José León de Carranza? Why?'

'The large ships can't get in and out without its being raised, correct?' The rear admiral nodded. 'Then it's a weak point. You must put a guard on its control towers and its approaches. I suggest that all the bridges around San Fernando also be heavily guarded. Is the anti-submarine net in position at the mouth of the Sancti Petri channel?'

'Yes, but it's in the lowered position at the moment.'

'That's fine, if the sonar detectors are properly installed and sensitive enough to pick out one of those midget subs.'

'They put in the latest type, but just in case we're raising the net at every high tide.'

'What about our troop movements?'

'The army reinforcements will arrive from Jerez and

185

Seville tonight. The special squad of GEOs are at our disposal at Chiclana.'

'Good. We may need them. What's happening on the diplomatic front?'

'I gather that the Foreign Minister has asked to see the Moroccan and Algerian ambassadors separately tomorrow morning. The British and the Americans have been informed that we intend to reinforce our North African garrisons. They are passing us information obtained by satellite about further troop deployment in northern Morocco.' The rear admiral pointed to a copy of the *Diario de Cádiz*. 'I expect you've read about the student riots in a number of Moroccan towns.'

'I haven't had time to look at the papers yet, but I'll see *El País* when it arrives at lunch-time. Those riots could be an organized diversion, Soto.'

'I think the JUJEM realizes that.'

Late on Saturday morning, Varga showed Bernal the heel of the dead nun's shoe. 'It's definitely got threads caught in it from the loose hem of her brown merino wool habit, chief. That seems to indicate that it was an accidental tripping-up that caused her to topple into the well-shaft.'

'What about the blunt instrument that was used on Elena?'

'I've found minute traces of black leather around the wound on Elena's head.'

'A cosh of some kind?'

'Dr Peláez thinks it was a flat object with quite a sharp edge, judging by the shape of the injury. I'm going back to the well at low tide. It'll be a devil of a job to drag it, because of its narrowness and depth. I'm also investigating how that machinery works. It's a complex nineteenth-century piece of engineering manufactured in France.'

'Probably installed by some earlier perpetrator of pious fraud.'

'By the way, *jefe*, the lab has sent up the report on the water samples taken from the dead nun's lungs. The comparison test with the fresh water from the well matches exactly. She definitely drowned there. There's one very curious feature: the water contains minute traces of natural œstrogen.'

'You don't mean the water can really cure barren women and help them conceive?'

'He says it's not impossible in cases of functional sterility, if the women began to drink it five days after menstruation.'

'And does he really think this hormonic property is derived from the *ostiones*—the large Cadiz oysters growing at the base of the well?'

'He says to tell you that the Greeks and the Romans may have been right after all.'

On Easter Saturday afternoon, Bernal decided to move his ops room nearer to the scene of the action; Captain Barba had agreed to accommodate him and his team in the Civil Guard barracks at Chiclana, where there was a permanent land-line to Rear Admiral Soto in the Captaincy-General at San Fernando.

On his way there, Bernal had been cheered by the sight of two destroyers and four frigates arriving from El Ferrol. The *Diario de Cádiz* had put out the Ministry of Defence's cover story: there was to be a 'Spring Exercise' in the Strait, which would be joined by naval units from El Ferrol and the Balearic stations. The Army would also send down special detachments to take part in land exercises, and the Air Force would try out its new Mirage III jet fighters. Bernal wondered if the Foreign Ministry had calculated that this show of strength would dissuade any official Government involvement in an attack on the Spanish enclaves in Morocco. In any case, the international news was entirely dominated by the Anglo-Argentine war in the South Atlantic and General Haig's flying visits between London and Buenos Aires. Perhaps that was the diversion the North African plotters were counting on.

At midday, Miranda and Lista reported from the Salineta Hotel that the Arabs there had brought out four Land-

Rovers from the garage and were loading boxes into them. Bernal decided to consult the rear admiral at San Fernando.

'I'm concerned that these Moroccans should reach the rendezvous with such a large quantity of arms and munitions, Soto. Shouldn't we call in the GEOs and attack them where they are? It could be done immediately they show signs of moving out, preferably after dark, of course.'

'I'll consult Madrid, Superintendent.'

By 2.0 p.m. the JUJEM had agreed to Bernal's plan. Road-blocks were to be set up around the Salineta Hotel and the GEOs were to infiltrate into the grounds. At the first sign of a break-out they were to move in.

When the brilliant sunset light streamed into Cadiz Bay, the fleet began to get steam up in the boilers, and as the western edge of Europe was plunged into night, the new bridge was opened and the ships slipped quietly out into the outer Bay and thence to the open sea. Their movements were plotted on the radar screens and marked on a large operations map at San Fernando, while the radio officers intercepted all broadcasts to listen out for the North African intruders.

By command of the Foreign Ministry, the frontiers between the Spanish enclaves and Morocco were sealed and troops moved up to guard them; by the morning their harbours would be bristling with the guns of the southern Spanish fleet.

At 8.45 p.m. Lista sent a message that the Arabs at the Salineta Hotel were emerging in commando dress and revving up the Land-Rovers.

'I want to go up there, Navarro,' said Bernal on a sudden impulse. 'The GEOs will be going into action.'

His police driver negotiated the steep winding road out of Chiclana and when they got to the top of the rise, Bernal ordered him to switch off his headlights. They reached the first road-block, where Bernal showed his special pass and his DSE gold star, and were allowed through. Bernal ordered the car to be stopped on the hill above the hotel. Below them they could see the building lit up in the headlights of the four Land-Rovers which were slowly moving towards the exit. All at once there were brilliant flashes as the GEOs hurled stun-grenades at the Moroccans' vehicles, which came to an abrupt stop. Star-shells exploded overhead and lit up the scene in an eerie bluish-white light. They could hear the sound of sub-machine-gun fire from the sides of the Land-Rovers, and answering fire from the clumps of holm-oaks. Then two of the vehicles caught fire, exploding violently with pyrotechnic brilliance and an ear-shattering roar.

'I hope our lads are all right,' said Bernal anxiously.

Soon a car drove up the hill towards where they were parked, and Miranda got out.

'They've all been rounded up, *jefe*,' he said, 'apart from those that died in the two jeeps that blew up.'

'What about our men?'

'A couple of minor burns, that's all. You should have seen the GEOs operating at close quarters, chief. They're fantastic.'

At 11.25 p.m. light signals from the sea were reported by the Civil Guard who were keeping Cape Roche and Whale Bay under surveillance. Bernal had instructed the marine guards to return the signals with the letters M, L, K, T in Morse to see if they could draw the intruders' vessel into a trap on the beach. The Civil Guards telephoned to the ops room at Chiclana to report that the ruse appeared to have failed and by 11.45 the signalling had ceased.

Soto had reported from San Fernando that the radar operators were plotting a small blip on their screens emanating from off Cape Roche and moving north-westwards along the coast.

'Take me to Sancti Petri village,' said Bernal. 'I'm sure the Moroccan intruders will attempt an attack through the channel.'

The police driver took him and Ángel Gallardo along the narrow road that led across the salt-pans towards Sancti Petri.

'Drive on your side-lights only now,' Bernal warned him. 'Your headlights may be visible from the sea.'

They reached the darkened village and were halted by more Civil Guards, who inspected their passes, then saluted as they waved them through. Bernal ordered the car to be parked out of sight between the deserted barrack buildings, and sought out the officer-in-charge.

'Have you ordered the anti-submarine net to be raised?'

'Yes, Comisario, it's been up since high water at nine-fifteen.'

'How much draught is there at the moment at the mouth of the channel?'

'About two and a half metres, Comisario.'

'That's probably ample for them,' commented Bernal.

With Ángel Gallardo he sheltered in the lee of the barracks from the chill night breeze. 'The Levante is getting up,' he said with a shiver. 'It cuts through you like a knife.'

'Would you like a slug of *coñac*, chief?'

Bernal took the proffered hip-flask. Then, cupping his hands, he lit a Kaiser.

'Do you think they'll still come, *jefe*?'

'They'll come. They're desperate men. Anyway, I'm anxious to see one of these midget submarines. I think our Navy should invest in a few of them.'

At 12.25 a.m. the officer-in-charge came up to report. 'There's no sign of activity, Comisario, and San Fernando radar has informed us that the unidentified small craft disappeared from their screens ten minutes ago.'

'Now's the time to get your men to strain their eyes,' said Bernal. 'Get them to watch the island of Sancti Petri through their infra-red glasses. That disappearance means that they're in the Temple of Melkart looking for their munitions cache.'

The Civil Guard colonel looked at Bernal as though he had taken leave of his senses, but went to do his bidding.

After fifteen minutes had passed, Bernal and Ángel Gallardo could make out the noise of an outboard motor approaching. 'They're coming in anyway, Ángel, despite the loss of their reserve munitions. They must have a supply on board with them.'

Suddenly the chugging of the diesel engine stopped, and

there was the faint sound of air-pumps and then a loud bubbling. The whir of electric motors could be heard very faintly.

'They've submerged,' said Bernal. 'They're coming into the channel.'

The colonel of the Civil Guard came up to Bernal. 'My men have spotted a small black craft coming in from the island, but it's now disappeared.'

'It's submerged,' said Bernal. 'Be ready to fire on it when it hits the anti-submarine net.'

He hurried to the wooden jetty with Ángel.

There was a loud grinding noise, then a splashing, as the small vessel came to the surface, and the Civil Guards opened fire on the stricken midget submarine. Four frogmen jumped off it as it exploded with a bright orange flash. They tried to dive and escape towards the sea, but the Civil Guard marksmen picked them off one by one and soon the four bodies were laid out in a row on the wooden jetty. The burnt-out submarine was dragged to the small beach of grey sand.

'At least your men have been able to avenge their dead colleague, Sergeant Ramos,' Bernal told the colonel. 'These were probably the intruders who murdered him and hanged his body underneath the piers of this jetty.'

Inspector Fragela and Rear Admiral Soto accompanied Superintendent Bernal to Jerez Airport on Easter Sunday evening, after giving him a splendid lunch in El Faro. When it was announced that the Aviaco flight to Madrid would be delayed for up to an hour, he told his Cadiz colleagues not to wait.

He sat in the small lounge of the airport sipping a Larios *gin-tónic*. He had bought all the Madrid newspapers and read the accounts about the Melkart Operation which had fizzled out. The papers were agreed that there had been 'incidents' on the Moroccan border with the Spanish enclaves at Ceuta and Melilla, which had 'happened to co-incide' with the 'Spring Exercise' of the Spanish fleet then 'paying a routine visit' to the Spanish ports in North Africa.

It was clever of the Ministries of Defence and the Exterior to manipulate the news so as to avoid diplomatic repercussions. Soto had informed him that the Melkart plotters had been foiled, not only by the prompt actions taken at Cadiz, but also by the direct intervention of King Hassan and the Algerian President; a purge was now taking place in their armed services. The JUJEM was satisfied about the security of the Spanish enclaves for the moment, though the fleet would be kept at sea for a few more days to complete the 'Spring Exercise'.

Most of Bernal's team had left Cadiz, apart from Elena, who was to be kept in hospital for a while longer, and Ángel who had opted to keep her company. Eugenia had returned to Madrid by the night train and had promised to prepare a dinner of spider-crab *paella* (it was a good thing the plane was late, he thought). Dr Peláez had not been pleased to be proffered a row of Moroccan corpses to cut up, because the cause of death was clear in each case and they offered him no real challenge.

As Bernal was lighting another Kaiser, Varga came into the lounge searching for him. 'I found it, chief!' he said triumphantly.

'Found what, Varga?'

'The blunt instrument that was used on Elena Fernández in the underground passage at the convent. I told you that I'd found minute traces of black leather around the wound on her head?'

'Yes, I remember.'

'I've spent two days dragging the well in the holy cave and here's what I've found.'

He opened a plastic container and showed Bernal a very large, sodden black book.

'It's the lectern-bible from the convent church.'

'That clinches it, Varga. It was the nun who did it.'